PELICAN RISING

Other titles by Elizabeth North

The Least and Vilest Things
Everything in the Garden
Enough Blue Sky

PELICAN RISING

a novel

Elizabeth North

ACADEMY
CHICAGO
LIMITED

American Edition 1979
Published by Academy Chicago Limited
360 North Michigan Avenue, Chicago, Il. 60601
All rights reserved
Printed and bound in the United States of America

Library of Congress Cataloging in Publication Data

North, Elizabeth, 1932-
  Pelican rising.

  I. Title.
PZ4.N8573Pe 1979   823'.9'14   79-9884
ISBN 0-915864-94-0
ISBN 0-915864-93-2 pbk.

To Brian

An extract from a recent edition of *The Classified Nobility of the United Kingdom*

HAVERGAL (Dormant)

4th Baron Havergal of Havergal in the County of Norfolk, Henry St George Havergal (at whose christening in 1895 H.R.H. The Princess of Wales stood sponsor). Henry St George Havergal, D.L., J.P., T.D., educ. Eton & Balliol, served in 3rd Batt. East Suffolk Reg. 1914-1918, mentioned in despatches. Fellow of Royal Numismatic Society. 1920-1930 Hon. Assistant Curator Numismatist, British Museum. 1939-1940 served in B.E.F. wounded. 1940-45 controller meats dep. Min. of Food (Eastern area). Born 1895. Married 1st June 1932 Eleanor Mary (died 1968) 2nd dau. of Gen. Sir Bernard Mackenzie, G.C.V.O., C.B., C.S.I. (see Mackenzie of Pitlochry) and had issue:

1. Alberta Alexandra. b. 1933. Married 2nd July 1953 Richard Andrew Hartley Esq. eldest son of Andrew Richard Hartley (see Hartley of Hele) Lower Coombe Manor, Co. of Devon. Marriage diss. by div. 1968, and had issue of 4 daus. She married secondly Mr Bruce Sugden, only son of Mr & Mrs E. Sugden of 1435 Chestnut Avenue, Sidney, Australia. Address: Cliff Studios, St Ives, Cornwall.

2. Edwina Alexandra. b. 1936. Married April 3rd 1954 Meredith James Measures-Smith, only son of James Harold Measures-Smith L.D.I.C.S. of Newport in the County of Monmouth, and had issue of one son, one dau. Address: Hodsworth Hall, Yorkshire.

3. Davina Alexandra, b. 1938. Address: 136 Maryland Crescent, W.12.

On the death of his Lordship, Henry St George Havergal, on 9th September 1949, the Barony of Havergal fell into abeyance between his daughters: The Hon. Mrs Bruce Sugden, The Hon. Mrs Meredith Measures-Smith and The Hon. Miss Davina Havergal.

Creation 1840.

ARMS. PER PALE AZURE AND GULES A SUN IN SPLENDOUR BETWEEN THREE CHEVRONS OR.

CREST. A PELICAN RISING FROM A MOUNT VERT VULNING HERSELF PPR.

MOTTO. CADE SUPERBE.

Chapter 1

THE HON. EDWINA Measures-Smith drives herself home in her white Austin Mini on the morning of the first day of term. It is a clear day for late January, watery with high broken clouds, but when the sun comes out it strikes low into the eyes of the drivers so that sun-visors must be lowered whether in the high cabs of trucks and transporters or in saloons or in estate cars.

At home her engagement diary for today reads: "Tuesday: Ring man re. boiler flue. Ring Electrician. Ring Diana query this afternoon and evening. Bridge at Victoria's 2 p.m. Diana's Americans to dinner 7.45 approx. (Menu: Diana's game soup. Moussaka (query aubergines?) Veg. Query frozen peas or beans. Pudding chocolate mousse.)"

Diana always says her heart lifts when the children have gone back to school, however awfully much you miss them. But the thing, Diana says, is to plunge back into one's own activities.

The motorway is raised high above ploughed fields which stretch and roll as far as you can see on either side to east and west. Use the sun-visor of the Mini against the beams of the sun and dark glasses against the shine on the road, even when the sky darkens further south. Switch on the windscreen wiper when rain spots come, check the de-mister knob, flick the indicator arm to signal over-taking and sweep past three high trucks and one pantechnicon. Stay now in the outer lane; check speed at under seventy, but still check wing mirror for approaching police patrol.

To speed on the motorway means that you have been moving at more than seventy miles an hour, and you only do that on exceptional spring days when there is an exceptionally wide high view of arched sky coming at you from the south. And, if you are lucky enough to have clear reception on your car radio, you may drive accompanied by a whole ample burst of symphonic Brahms or Beethoven.

The ploughed fields stretching to the horizon on either side of the motorway are not a uniform brown, but many shades of it from pale to rich, sandy yellow to sepia, rust pink to peat; they are squares of lumpy fresh-turned earth or oblongs of dry raked soil divided by scattered winter trees, twiggy hedges and metal fences. Church towers jut up between them, and across them a double file of pylons on iron girder legs carry huge-hanging cables and march towards the road.

The engagement diary suggests just the active sort of day Diana would recommend before a dinner party. "The best hostess is a rushed hostess, I always say." Diana always says her best dinner parties have been those on the days when she's been to several meetings.

The motorway passes over villages, climbs between embankments and drops beyond flyovers, and then the country on either side becomes flatter and the view is again for miles in all directions. Six miles south the smoke from the power station can be seen rising towards the clouds and up through the spaces of blue between them.

When she gets home Edwina will pick up her engagement diary and confirm what is to be done this Tuesday. She will put her bag and coat on the oak hall chair, emblazoned on its back with the sun in splendour of the Havergals, and she will hang on the end of the banister rail the navy blue cap she wears on the back of her head this morning. She will consult the engagement diary and wash up the breakfast things before making the telephone calls.

Going south steadily there are minor roads below and above this major one, footbridges where villages are divided by it, and the double row of pylons coming from the left all the time towards the power station. Then there is the first pit-shaft and wheel and the first factory chimney to the right, and to the left thick evergreen woods and unploughed damp green fields. Here you must slow to make way for traffic coming in on the left over the canal; here visibility is confused with the pylon cables crossing, with a flyover and a railway bridge carrying blue diesel trains east and west. Great mounds of rich raw earth are being bulldozed for another motorway, so steady on the inside lane and read red notices about diversions and alternative routes. Above all this the twelve grouped funnels of the power station dwarf both the Mini and the lorries on the road.

At home the chocolate mousse is made already, and the moussaka will be cooked this morning. The queried aubergines should have been bought this morning, but were forgotten, and Diana will bring the game soup at lunchtime before afternoon Bridge at Victoria's.

The embankments after the power station are of pale grass shutting out land, buildings and woods, leaving only the sky in view. Here you climb in third gear until you reach the top of the ridge and see a long way down over houses and chimneys, woods and fields interrupted by great grey dunes of open-cast mining which end suddenly at trees and bushes.

Pick up speed and leave all this, through damp green grubby country with the smoke of cities on the right, and on the left flat land reaching to the coast, and ahead the way to the south. Although Diana would say this was too far south; she wanted to bring her children up in what she calls "real country" and "give them the rural experience, Edwina". To which Edwina always says, "The Rural experience is fine for driving through but not for living in, Diana".

On the home stretch of the motorway you edge into the inside lane and watch for the sign on stilts with green and white writing which says "Wakefield, Huddersfield, Leeds, Bradford, Alternative Route", and in small letters under-

neath "East Hodsworth, West Hodsworth". Slide down
under the underpass and into the road to the village which
runs west from the motorway. Pass the filling station and
head into the street of old houses, past the Church and the
school opposite, the post office, the pub, the grocer's and
the butcher's. East Hodsworth buildings are black and
sooty stone, although one or two houses have been sandblasted pale grey and their woodwork painted white, and
slatted shutters hung outside. It is not a true commuter
village yet. "Basically an old pit-village," Diana says, "but
what can one do when one's husband works just up the
road and can't cope with a long drive every day? Thank
goodness we all live well up on the hill." She often says
that the only thing to be said for East Hodsworth is that,
being one of the first in-comers there is simply everything
to do in the village and one can be on as many committees as one chooses. "Almost too many. One does rather
wish new comers-in would take an interest sometimes."

There are comers-in at No. 38 Main Street, opposite the
grocer's. No. 38 has not been sandblasted but the woodwork
has been painted white and a picture window with double
glazing has replaced the old casement. "Now I did think
the Douglases at No. 38 would contribute something,"
said Diana. "They may be sort of intellectuals and possibly
even Socialist, but they're young and have no children;
you'd have thought they'd be willing to be involved in
something."

"Perhaps they're shy."

"Perhaps we ought to have invited them socially to
something, had them to drinks perhaps."

"Perhaps village life is simply not their scene."

"You've talked to her, haven't you, Edwina, in the
shop?"

"No. I've only actually talked to him. In the shop and
once on the train."

No. 38 is where you turn your head in passing in the
morning to see if Stuart Douglas's yellow Ford is still
outside. The head-turning spot used to be the Church and

the vicarage to spot the vicar in his blowing black cloak going to read Matins to himself, but now the parish shares West Hodsworth's vicar and the vicarage is being pulled down.

"You could ask her to coffee. You're good with those sort of people on the whole, Edwina."

"She works though."

Tuesday is the day he leaves at about this time for University and sometimes waves as he gets into his car. He has mentioned in the shop where he only goes to get his cigarettes, that not everybody who drives through East Hodsworth, especially those who drive at about 9.30 in the morning, observes the thing about thirty miles an hour. He also mentioned this on the train, which doubly confirms that he notices the Mini in the morning. But today she must be late and his car is not outside No. 38.

"What did you talk about on the train?"

"Oh, this and that."

"Not about doing things in the village?"

"No. Not that."

"But you could still have his wife to coffee."

The houses stop, the village ends and the tall park gates appear on the left. The drive through the park for the first quarter of a mile is owned by the Parish Council and on one side is a football pitch and on the other a playground with slides and swings. Then comes the fence to the upper park and a cattle grid which must be bumped over into the pasture where sheep graze and trees are dotted evenly all the way up the hill. You turn to the east again here, back towards the motorway and climb dead straight between an avenue of beech trees with trunks flickering in the sun, twigs interlacing above the car against the sky. Diana's Robert owns all the land on either side, but the drive itself leads to Hodsworth Hall where Edwina lives. The top triangular section of its roof is first in view, but drive on and the triangle widens until you see the whole house on the far side of a low stone wall, gateless but with rounded gateposts with stone balls on top. Another cattle grid to rattle over with tubular tinkling under the car tyres and on to a circle of tarmac surrounding a ring of grass, and in the centre of the grass a stone plinth without a statue on it.

The wind may drop elsewhere, but never here. The tarmac circle is only sheltered by the house from the east and by a small shrubbery on the north. The south and west are wide open over the low stone wall. No one would try and plant flowers or make a border here, and the grass in the middle and at the edges of this open circle grows slowly. With no effort from the owners of the house the ground in front of it stays blank and neat, grass and tarmac.

The house itself could be a miniature Parthenon with too few pillars. It is at any rate a miniature of something Greek. Or it might be a miniature of something imitating Greek. Neo-classical, people say. "In actual fact," says Meredith, "it is very late neo-classical. Really very late indeed. William IV in fact ... late William IV, almost Victorian." The date of 1836 carved but rather faded in the centre of the pediment confirms all this. (The four pillars which support the pediment of Hodsworth Hall are neither fluted Doric with cushioned capitals nor convoluted graceful and ornate Ionic or Corinthian. These pillars are conical blocks of grey sandstone mortared one on top of the other, cemented and re-cemented throughout the years and furnished with square slabs of stone as capitals.)

It is not the sort of house to have people to morning coffee in, even if Christine Douglas was not a full-time teacher. With her high-piled hair and high heels she would still be dwarfed by the pillars in front of the front door and awed by the height of the rooms inside. There is no corner where you could sit with her and not feel patronising. It takes years to learn to run up the shallow steps with confidence and with the pediment above you, and to reach for the key and the morning letters from the mail box, and to swing back the two parts of the double front doors and hear your footsteps echo in the hall and up the curving staircase.

14

The hall, like all the rooms, is higher than it need be. Edwina throws letters which are not for her on the oak emblazoned chair and throws her bag beside them. Then she hangs her blue cap on the bottom of the banister rail and takes her own letters into the kitchen to read. She washes up the breakfast things, peels potatoes for the dinner party, fries the minced lamb and onions for the moussaka and in between times answers the telephone. Tonight will be easy; the Americans will smile against the coat of arms on the drawing-room mantelpiece, admire the family portraits and the gilt chairs, smile at the hole in the foot of Edwina's tights, the chip in the crested porcelain and at Meredith's rounded English vowels as he translates the Havergal motto on the Georgian silver as Fall Proudly.

Edwina spills the chocolate mousse into the Waterford glass dish and licks the bowl it came from. She carries coke to the kitchen boiler and gets grit and ashes in her hair. She opens the window to clear the fumes and hears the motorway she drove on still roaring below to south and north. Then she reads her letters:

Dear Mummy. Grotty as hell here as usual. Am in solitary confinement after weekend pub-crawl. No, seriously though, it is a cold. Missed Hist. Soc. expedition to Caernarvon Castle. Rumour has it that Miss R chatted up curator and was last seen disappearing into red sunset hand in hand. But—no such luck; she's back again. But the big count-down has begun. Forty days (in wilderness?) to end of term. O-levels four and three-quarter terms away and then it jolly well is going to be goodbye St Cecilias's and all who sail in her is it not? Nothing will become me like the leaving of it. Lots and Lots and Lots and Lots of love. How's Harry?
                                                        Alex.

The kitchen is on the north-east side of the house, with sash windows on the north and east walls. Its floor area is an exact square patterned with brown and white floor tiles.

Its walls are white gloss splashed in places with grease and scribbled on in felt pen by children, scribbles not quite washable off. The ceiling is way above; Diana said the only way to deal with high rooms was to paint the ceilings in dark colours right down as far as the picture rail, and Edwina painted it olive green. The table is white painted wood, tongue and groove boarding, and was part of the old Havergal garden furniture for long afternoons, wicker chairs and cucumber sandwiches. Collected from the terrace after Havergal was sold, the boards have warped and when orange squash, tea or coffee is spilt it can drop through the joins to the floor below.

Edwina opens her other letter:

Dear Mrs Measures-Smith. I think you must be as concerned about Alex as I am. I would add to this message of concern the agreement of the members of staff with whom she comes into contact. While I am not of a mind to take any drastic measures at this time, I would be enormously grateful if we could arrange to talk about it together at some time this term convenient to yourself. . . .

Without reading further Edwina goes into the long stone hall and out through the back door to tip potato peelings on to the compost heap. She carries a plastic bucket across the vegetable garden, walking on damp grass paths between undug borders.

This is the back of Hodsworth Hall, the chopped-off noisy side where the traffic echoes up against what was once an inside wall, into which windows were put when the old back servants' quarters were knocked down twenty or so years ago. The windows went in where windows were needed rather than best positioned for their proportional value, and they look out east over the motorway which shoots past and has been shooting past with more trucks and cars each winter and summer for ten years. It is a down-sloping field away from the vegetable garden. Hodsworth Hall is on a promontory above it.

The vegetable garden is as flat as places are when they were once built upon. The family who built the house knocked down the servants' quarters after the Second World War when they knew there would be no more servants. Then, when the motorway came, they sold out —the Hall to Meredith Measures-Smith, and the Dower House, the Home Farm and all the parkland to Robert Golding. The Baines-Robinsons of Hodsworth Hall moved to a castle in Ireland where there turned out to be plenty of servants and they are still, as Meredith says they have always been, extraordinarily wealthy.

In the vegetable garden in late January, the history of the place is irrelevant. The smell of diesel fumes and wet earth mix. There are horses in the field, Diana's children's ponies. The motorway curves away to the south, steel blue-grey, and when the sun comes out it glints on silver cylindrical trucks carrying milk, oil, or chemicals. Sometimes huge aeroplanes, V-Bombers with bat-like wings, come up over the motorway and over the house with widening smoke-trails.

"I'll pick you up at one," said Diana. Edwina goes in through the kitchen away from the noise and upstairs to get her Jaeger suit out of the cupboard on the wide landing. Then, when she is ready to go she stands in front of the tall mirror in the spareroom. On the lapel of her suit-jacket she wears a Havergal diamond brooch; on the third finger of her left hand she wears a Havergal emerald next to Meredith's engagement ring which has alternate diamonds and sapphires with one diamond missing.

The Jaeger suit when new three springs ago was six inches above her knees and she wore it with white tights and beige shoes to meetings of the Conservative Party at Constituency Level. In the Jaeger suit she had her hand shaken by the Member and was nearly co-opted on to the Ladies' Luncheon Club Committee—a short step, said

Diana, from membership of the Finance and General Purposes Committee and being asked to lunch at Westminster once a year. But, as she explained to Diana, the Luncheon Club did not seem to be what politics was about; nor was she even sure she had ever been a Conservative in any case.

The Jaeger suit is now let down as far as it will go to two inches above the knee and she still wears it sometimes with black tights and boots for playing Bridge in the afternoons, but not much otherwise. She stands by the long mirror in the spareroom and turns her head to the window, where between the two central pillars of the pediment the view extends down the middle of the avenue along the top of winter beech trees. Diana always says there is nothing quite like a Jaeger suit for long long wear and she buys one every year. And Diana needs them, continuing, as she does, to attend meetings at Constituency Level of the Finance and General Purposes Committee and to visit Westminister twice or three times a year. "And what a pity," she often says, "that you lost your political convictions, Edwina."

The Member of Parliament is likely to be a junior minister soon. He has expensively-cut thick grey hair which flops over one eye, and the day he shook Edwina's hand he wore a navy blue pin-stripe suit with wide lapels which did everything that could be done for the heavier man. His large warm signet-ringed hand is remembered by Edwina's small cool one, and sometimes on Saturday nights in bed with Meredith she is still seized by him brutally in a Westminster corridor's dark corner.

But this is Tuesday, and at one o'clock Diana's voice echoes along the hall and brings Edwina running down the wide staircase. Diana stands in the hall; her Jaeger suit is last autumn's heather-mixture check, midi-length, size 14. Edwina's is size 10, charcoal grey, nearly black, and she picks up her navy blue corduroy cap from the bottom of the banister rail and puts it on her head.

"I could lend you a proper hat, Edwina. One that would go with the suit."

"No thanks. I like this."

18

"Well, if you really think navy blue can be worn with black?"

"I've always thought this suit was charcoal grey."

"Have you really?"

She takes from Diana, not a hat, but the vacuum flask of game soup for the dinner party tonight and carries it into the kitchen. Diana's court shoes clatter on the floor behind: "Mrs Thwaite comes to you this afternoon, doesn't she, Edwina? Have you left her a note telling her what to do?"

"No."

"I must say I would if I were you. She'll just take it into her head to do whatever she thinks."

Edwina finds a large saucepan from a rack and pours into it the jelly-like consommé out of the vacuum flask.

"You don't like giving orders, do you, Edwina?"

"Not particularly."

"I find that very strange for someone with your background."

Edwina at the sink watches the sun slanting from the east window find the depths in the saucepan of golden soup.

"Coping with staff is such a problem these days," says Diana.

While Edwina stands swilling cold water into the silver inside of the vacuum flask and washing it into the stainless steel sink, Diana stands by the table and says how lovely it is, when all is said and done, now that the school holidays are over, to be going out together for a fun afternoon of Bridge. "You don't get out enough these days, Edwina. You should have come to the weekend school; I can understand anyone finding the fund-raising and lunch-party side of things a bit trivial, but I would have thought these discussions on what they call political dialectic were just up your street, whatever you pretend happened to your political convictions."

Edwina hands her the clean vacuum flask. They both walk through the hall and stop while Edwina, looking in the small mirror above the oak chair, fixes the navy blue cap more firmly on her head again and slings her leather bag on her shoulder.

"And the Young Wives' theological discussions, Edwina. You excelled at those."

They stand under the pediment and each puts up a hand to hold her hat on her head in a sudden gust of wind.

"I often think you are rather more spiritual than you let on, Edwina. I was saying to Robert only last night, what a pity it was for you that the vicar left."

The winter before the vicar left, the Jaeger suit was four inches above the knee, worn with maroon tights and shoes in his study on Tuesday afternoons. The vicar's dark hair grew from the centre of his head like a small boy's; he wore a narrow striped shirt showing only a few inches under his black frontage, and revealed gold cuff-links as he folded his arms, and black silk socks as he crossed his legs. Alternating with the Member of Parliament he haunted Saturday nights, being suddenly discovered at prayer in the vestry and having his black frontage ripped from the striped shirt and his gold cuff-links thrown into the chancel.

But there is still Contract Bridge for some Tuesdays and Diana says what a tragedy, as they leave the house, it would be if that went the way of politics and religion. "A woman with outside activities makes a much better wife and mother. And you do have such good cards."

The vicar left with Edwina a bright red book called *The Hypothetical Creator*. The fantasy, now fading, sometimes took place in the churchyard where the cuff-links chinked against gravestones and the socks hung over them.

Driving through the village Diana says, "The Douglases at No. 38, does Mrs Thwaite ever talk to you about them?"

"Among other things and people."

"From what she says I feel that they may not be very happily married."

"Fights in the night and so on, you mean?"

"Not that one attaches that much significance to what

Mrs Thwaite says. But one wonders what one could do to help."

Edwina turns her head at No. 38. "Does one?"

"I believe the Marriage Guidance Council is awfully good..."

"They haven't got any children have they?"

"The Douglases? No, but it is just as tragic for a childless marriage to break up as it is for any other, you know, Edwina. Children aren't everything." And they drive on past the Church.

On what remains of Edwina's share of the Havergal crested porcelain dinner service the gold-leaf pelican on the rim vulnes itself on the breast to let *rouge-de-feu* drops of blood fall into the open mouths of three gold leaf pelican chicks. Meredith in the dining-room dusts each plate before handing it through the serving hatch to Edwina in the kitchen where she will put them in the oven to warm through. "What did you do today?" asks Meredith from the dining-room.

"Nothing much," she replies, placing on the serving hatch the bowl of chocolate mousse. "Went out with Diana for a bit."

"I wonder," he says, voice fading as he carries the mousse from the hatch to the sideboard, "that you spend so much time with her still. You can't have much in common."

"The relationship," she calls, bending down to put the plates in the oven, "between Diana and myself has nothing to do with having things in common."

"I don't know what you are talking about." Meredith wipes the smaller Pelican pudding plates slowly with a clean dry cloth he keeps in the sideboard drawer.

Edwina at the kitchen table dices bread with a sharp knife to make croutons for the soup. "I mean that, without Diana, I should probably never do anything. And Diana, by encouraging me to do things, finds yet further purpose in her life. We are locked together, you might say, in some mutual, but possibly temporary, need."

21

Meredith says loudly through the hatch that since that time when she kept going to the Vicarage in the afternoons he has found it very difficult to understand anything she says. She is not the same person at all since then.

Edwina shouts back that she wonders who she should be the same person as.

"You could, for instance," Meredith calls, "try not to be the sort of person who lets us in for giving dinner parties we can't afford for people we don't know, just because Diana and Robert cannot think of any other way of entertaining their American business connections."

"You ought to be pleased that we are considered to represent an ideal English couple in an ideal English house. And, anyway, Diana has given me the soup and a bottle of wine."

Meredith lays the table while Edwina prepares the food. Inasmuch as they stay in separate rooms on either side of the serving hatch, they work efficiently. Meredith, tin of polish in hand, in shirtsleeves and braces, rubs the oval dining-room mahogany table in diminishing circles. Then he bends down, looks along the table to let the light reflect, and, where it does not reflect, he polishes, again, the dull neglected patches. "I wouldn't mind," he calls to Edwina, "if it was for someone we wanted to be friends with."

"For instance?"

'Well, say, the Rochdales. That would be a social occasion. This is business and not even a business with which I have any connection."

"Robert has put a lot of business in your way, hasn't he? What is wrong with Robert, apart from the fact that he is not a Rochdale and that his grandfather may have worn clogs?"

At Meredith's feet, Harry, rag in hand, polishes the brass claw feet which make the end of the fluted table legs. Meredith gave him the Brasso, the rag and the piece of newspaper which will protect the grey-green Wilton carpet. The carpet is the newest thing in the dining-room. Everything else came from Havergal, the Georgian table and sideboard with drop-brass handles, the curtains, the china, the Waterford glass, the knives with ivory handles and some of the silver.

Meredith and Harry polish in silence. The sound from the kitchen is of Edwina frying the croutons in butter. When the table is polished, Meredith will put on the heat-proof mats, cover these with white linen place settings which bear, embroidered in raised white stitching, the Havergal pelican. He will lay the silver spoons and forks on the mats, giving the guests he considers important the elegant Havergal silver, and the others the spoons and forks he has bought to match it as closely as possible. Edwina inherited only one third of the Havergal silver, her sisters having the rest. There may even be only Edwina's third left in the family, since, like Edwina, her sisters on the whole prefer cash and clothes and holidays abroad to heirlooms.

From under the table Harry stands up carefully so as not to bump his head. Meredith takes from him the Brasso and the rag, admires the claw table feet and gives them a final rub with his own polishing cloth. He pats Harry on the head and calls to the kitchen through the hatch: "Did you hear from Alex today?"

"Yes."

"Is she ... is she any more ... settled, would you say?"

Edwina, watching the croutons turn gold in butter in the frying pan, considering the problem of how to keep them crisp until the soup is served, calls through the hatch, "Well, if you can call grumbling about school as a crummy hole and a grotty dump being settled, well, yes, I suppose we could say Alex is settled."

Meredith opens the sideboard drawer which is lined with green baize, compartmented for knives, forks and spoons. At the same time, in raised voice, he reminds Edwina that Alex has agreed to stay the course until O-levels the the summer after next. "Alex is under contract," he says. "She has given her word."

"If you can call," Edwina tips the croutons into a pyrex

23

dish to keep warm in the oven until scattered on the soup, "if you can call the word of a fourteen-year-old, and she was fourteen when she gave it, a binding contract, then you have a case."

"Then I have a case." Meredith selects the Havergal spoons first from the green baize drawer.

"So a child's word is legally binding?"

"They should learn that it is."

"The essence of growing up is to be changing all the time."

"There must be consistency in some areas."

"People do change Meredith."

"You don't need to tell me that."

They both reach the hatch, Meredith holding Havergal table spoons, and Edwina the frying pan. Behind Meredith in the dining-room, Harry stands at the green baize drawer, turning over the Havergal forks, and the non-Havergal forks and looking on their backs for a silver hallmark of the head of a lion.

"It is Harry's bedtime," says Edwina.

At seven o'clock with the bathroom warm from Harry's bath steam, while talking to Harry, rather while letting Harry talk to her, Edwina dresses for dinner.

Harry talks about the new car Guy Rochdale's mother has, about the latest figures on the population of Tokyo and the speed of a V-Bomber. Harry can run the water the right temperature himself now, and remembers, as it is Tuesday, to fetch a clean towel from the airing cupboard. He has learnt to do that since he was seven, just as he learnt to brush his hair without being reminded and clean his shoes. When he is eight, other people will teach him to stand back and let his elders and betters go through doors first, raise his cap and call grown men "Sir". He will also learn not to mind having his shoulder length hair cut by school barbers and to wear grey shorts instead of needle-cord jeans with patches on the knees and badges on the pockets.

24

Harry talks about a programme he saw after the news on television about how the counties of England will soon be all mixed up and called something different in many cases. Rutlandshire, for instance, will not be Rutlandshire any more, but part of something else.

When he was five he was both washed and dried by his mother. When he was six he washed himself but she dried him. Now he is seven he does both. He says it is a pity about Rutland but the new counties would not work properly otherwise, and there is a good thing about Flintshire which used to be in two separate pieces in his atlas, but will now be joined together. It could not ever have worked very well in two pieces like it used to be.

"Why not, Harry? Everything in life can't be neat and tidy and in one piece, can it?"

"I don't know what you are talking about, Mummy."

Meredith, on his way to the bedroom to change from office suit to best suit, looks into the bathroom through the steam and is told about Rutlandshire and Flintshire. "That's right, Harry, yes, it would be a good idea. Yes, a very good idea to join the bits of Flintshire together. I expect they will do that, Harry. Well done. That's very interesting, Harry. And I expect, if you are very good tonight, you can come down and say how do you do to some people who are coming; they are Americans, Harry. From America, Harry. You know where America is, don't you, Harry? That will be useful when you go to a big boys' school."

Head and shoulders above the edge of the bath, un-puzzled face turned towards Meredith, golden hair growing like the vicar's from a centre point in the crown, Harry St George Havergal Measures-Smith appears through the steam. Meredith, being stirred by England and St George and gentlemen of England now abed, chose the names and wanted to add Monmouth for good measure. After all he, Meredith, was born in Monmouthshire and played Henry V in his last year at public school. Playing Henry, he often says, was the nicest thing that happened to him at school.

And being the father of Harry is, perhaps, the nicest thing that has happened to him since he left school. It was Edwina who brought about the rejection of the Monmouth in Harry's name; which may have been a good battle to win, especially if Monmouthshire like Rutlandshire should become a non-existent county in due course.

"Isn't he just lovely! Fancy that, the heir to all this. Edwina, I'm sure I may call you that, what a beautiful son you have. And Harry, I just love your yellow pyjamas. Would you loan them me, Harry? And will you be a lord? Will you be a lord, Harry?"

Harry explains, longwindedly, and with words to launch the evening briskly, that he cannot be a lord because his mother is not a lady. Then he fails to understand the laughter and adds that his mother is Honourable. The American lady cuddles him and he stands very still. (While his father explains that only daughters of dukes and earls bear the title of Lady and his mother is the daughter of a baron.)

"I should add," says Meredith, "that the title is in abeyance which means there is no clear single line of male descent. It is, therefore, in abeyance among all the descendants in the female line, of which there are, counting Edwina's sisters and the four daughters of one of Edwina's sisters, not to mention our own daughter, and of course Edwina herself, eight in all..."

"Really! Is that a fact?"

"You see some titles, certain titles, can be inherited through the female as well as in the normal primogeniturial manner..."

"It all sounds very very complex, Meredith, if I may call you Meredith..."

"And of course, not wishing for a minute for the death of Harry's cousins or his..."

"All those girls in the way of your title, Harry!"

"There is, however, a way of claiming a title in abeyance through the House of Lords ... that is of course our upper house, which could be compared to your Senate or your House of..."

"Is that a fact? But tell me, Meredith ... I mean isn't it so, that you in England worry less about being Earls and Dukes and Counts than you used to. I remember reading in your *Sunday Times* somewhere that there are people who actually give *up* being Earls and so on nowadays. You mean that you would actually *claim* a title for Harry ... go to all that trouble? My word, Harry! What a wonderful father you have. And I can see that you have a beautiful mother. What did you say her title was called? Honourable? She is an Honourable? I do like that. And look at that skin! I've been goggling all day at the English girls' skins, but Edwina is the real English rose!"

There are six gilt chairs arranged for the six adults in the room and Harry stands within the semi-circle handing plates of nuts and potato crisps. Behind him on the front of the stone fireplace is a coat of arms which, Meredith explains, is not, as it happens, that of the Havergals, but that of the Baines-Robinsons who owned Hodsworth, and happens to be not unlike the Havergal arms, except that the bird on top of the shield, the bird which forms the crest, is not actually a pelican but ...

The American lady says that is really so interesting and that she has been admiring ever since she came in these beautiful chairs. And Meredith explains that these chairs with their white and gold brocade upholstery are indeed also Havergal chairs and that, if one looks closely at the delicate gilt woodwork of the legs and the scrolls on the backs, traces of woodworm are barely extinct where he has treated the pests and retouched the damage with applied gold-leaf paint.

"You did all that Meredith! What a gifted person you are. And fancy finding a house like this in which to keep all Edwina's beautiful things and then finding a shield like the one on the fireplace which might have been Edwina's..."

27

"Yes," says Meredith, "and it was all just before Harry was born."

"Now isn't that strange and wonderful. You must have thought, Meredith, that moving into this house was kind of *meant*?"

Meredith leans back in his gilt chair, carefully, with a hand hardly touching the brocade of either arm. The American, Helen, perches on the edge of hers. The brocade, says Meredith, was first renewed, Havergal records reveal, although the chairs come from another female line, through Edwina's grandmother in fact, in the early nineteenth century, although the chairs themselves date from a much earlier...

At either end of the semi-circle of chairs is a round, single-stalk occasional table, a matching pair on single pedestals, slim, top-heavy, pink and copper grained rosewood, and by one of these stands Edwina pouring sherry into tall glasses with air-twist stems.

"Oh I just love it all," says Helen. She turns her head, still sitting carefully. "Could that be real Wedgwood—that vase where Edwina has arranged such lovely flowers?"

"No. Worcester actually," says Meredith.

Edwina holds the decanter in one hand and steadies each glass with the other as she pours. She stands back from the table so that her long velvet purple skirt cannot brush the pedestal.

"And that really beautiful portrait there?"

"Augustus John," says Meredith.

"My mother," says Edwina.

When Harry shakes hands and says goodnight to everyone, he is kissed by Helen and shuts his eyes. "Say, did you see that? He shuts his eyes, just like in the movies. Did you see that, Meredith? What marvellous children there are in this country today!"

From across the room Diana explains that England is now, like America, a land of opportunity. All children are healthy and beautiful now and not just her own and

Edwina's. "The Health Service you see, and State education, equal opportunity..."

"Is that a fact?" says Helen's husband from the far end of the semi-circle of chairs.

"You should see our new local comprehensive school," says Diana. "It has six football pitches, an indoor swimming pool, a trampoline and a concert hall."

"Your kids are in luck then."

"Oh yes..."

Edwina puts the decanter of sherry down on the exact centre of the rosewood pedestal table and says, "Yes, but we don't send ours to schools like that."

Over the game soup Lawrence, the American, asks why.

"Because of the choice," says Diana. "Because somewhere like West Hodsworth High is excellent in every way if used properly, but somewhere like Eton, *ensures* excellence you see. You feel you have *chosen* it for your child instead of just taking what is there."

"But it means sending your children away from home," says Helen.

"Alas *yes*," says Diana. "It's heartbreaking."

"Then why do it?" asks Lawrence.

"If only we didn't *have* to. If only we *all* sent them to State schools and improved the standard of pupils of those schools with our own children. If one of us did it, others might follow..."

The seating arrangement at the oval table gave Edwina Lawrence on her right and Robert on her left. Robert, as Diana always says, hates anything controversial at dinner parties. He bends over his soup silently while Diana talks to Lawrence about education and Meredith talks to Helen about the Havergals. Edwina, thus, must turn to Robert.

Now in his fifties, he bends painfully over his soup and stretches his right leg out straight under the table to ease his arthritic hip. He should, Diana says, have another operation, but last time he was six months off work, and

29

when a business depends so utterly on one man, that again would be disastrous. Robert, at summer dinner parties, used to talk about fly-fishing, but cannot fish any more. In the winter you could ask him about shooting, but his last pheasant is in the present soup. Once Robert bought a yacht, but it was no fun when you had to let the crew do it all for you. He still works a full office day, but no one talks about business at business dinner parties.

Down the table Diana tells Lawrence how boys' preparatory schools where they go at eight are getting more and more like home these days. They can stick posters on the dormitory walls and use the telephone when they want more sweets from home.

Robert could never lift his children up from the floor before they went away to school. The gardener carries their trunks to the car and Diana drives them there. Robert can drive himself to the office in his Daimler and round the Home Farm in the Range Rover. He prunes the roses in the garden and watches the children ride ponies in the holidays. He attends evening meetings of the Parish Council, but, otherwise, while Diana is out on Committees in Diocese and Constituency, he listens to the stereo gramophone she gave him. She found he likes Wagner as much as anything and she bought him books to read about The Ring. They go to Wagner when it's done in Leeds, but often have to leave before the interval when his hip becomes uncomfortable.

Down the table Meredith tells Helen that Edwina's great grandmother was painted by Winterhalter, but her sister has that portrait now.

Robert's grandfather started making trousers when he stopped off on his way from Russia to America in the early 1900's. Now the Company is public and Robert the chairman and chief shareholder, the third generation from its founder and the first son of the family to be sent to public school. Robert would have gone to University, Diana says, if he had not had to step into his father's shoes almost immediately after leaving Eton. Now he bends with difficulty over his soup. He and Diana go on holiday abroad every year, in the autumn after the children have gone back to school.

But only as a last resort do you ask, at dinner parties, where your neighbour is going on holiday this year, and, in any case, the soup is finished and it is time for Edwina to move to the kitchen, not having talked to Robert, and for Meredith to move to the hatch. While Diana tells everyone who is left at the table that having children at boarding school is to have, coming home at the end of each term, civilised young guests, charming people whom you appreciate and welcome.

In the centre of the dining-table is a three-branched silver candelabra. There used to be four of these, but the set was divided, one to Alberta, one to Edwina, one to Davina and one sold to reduce the family Death Duties debt to the Inland Revenue. Now this one, when the overhead lights are flicked off by Meredith when he has poured the wine, shines on the forks and spoons and the gold-leaf Pelicans. Its flames reflect six times over in glasses of dark red wine.

Down the table Diana is telling Helen how each holidays her eldest daughter is more loveable, more appreciative of home, more considerate of her parents. Edwina listens to Lawrence on her right telling her that she cannot have been much more than a school girl when she married. Does she really have a daughter all of fifteen years old? He finds that hard to believe.

It is hard to listen to Americans without wanting to dull the empty o's of your accent and stifle the stuttering buts and in facts, and let your voice flow like Helen's in the darkened dining-room where a strip of electric light shafts from the serving hatch on to the carpet in the corner. Helen tells Diana that her youngest son who is fifteen and just crazy about football has a dune-buggy down in Florida where they live and her eldest is going into Real Estate soon, but she just hates to think of them ever leaving

31

home. And Diana says that term-time, with the children away, gives the parents freedom not only to pursue their interests and commitments to public life, but draws them closer together, tightens the bond which knits the whole family together.

Edwina watches the flame reflected in the wine and on the beaded edge of the silver entrée dish and hears Lawrence say that, talking about commitments outside the home, back home it is the experience of many women that they find being wives and mothers these days an inadequate role in life, and perhaps that happens that way in England, but he can see that here it is not the case; Diana has been telling him of all the things she and Edwina do together, of the interest they take in the world around them, of the positive contribution they make to the world as they want it to be. He can see that they do not sit back and say "well I guess that's how it is", but they go out there trying to make it better. "I can see you are a woman who says yes to life, Edwina."

"Who says yes to what?"

"To life. It's what I tell my sons, my boys. I want them to say yes to life."

Down the table Helen says she just does not know what Donny gets up to with his friends and his dune-buggy but she knows it is a whole lot of fun for them at home. And Diana puts the case that children away from home in England free women to be full partners not only in the home but in the nation. And Helen says that she doesn't know about that, but she feels like a real full partner.

Lawrence says, "Do you feel that you say yes to life, Edwina?"

'You mean doing lots of things, belonging and joining?"

"I mean, Edwina, never saying no."

Diana says women are partners in the nation by supporting charities which help those the Welfare State cannot provide for, and also they are full partners in the nation by contributing to politics, and by becoming through the experience gained in these activities more aware of the world, whole citizens fit to advise their husbands and advance them in their careers.

Lawrence says, "If you live you burn, Edwina. I read that somewhere not so long ago."

Diana explains to Helen in the shadow of the candelabra flames that perhaps English women who live this life are specially what they call these days advantaged. And Helen says Donny works really hard in school and plays hard too. He's really into the music scene as well; Diana would just adore him. He brings his friends and their guitars to the barbecues they have in their yard in the fall. "I could never tell that kid goodbye," says Helen. "I feel such great love for him I just could not send him away from home until he wants to go." And Robert says he went to Florida once at Christmas time.

Edwina says, "Yes I suppose I sometimes burn I think." She lifts her glass and her rings flash as she moves her hand, and Lawrence says: "I find you very positive, Edwina."

When Meredith has shut the sideboard drawers and cupboards and turned off the electric fire in the dining-room he will go back to the drawing-room where the log fire still smokes and pick up and read the *Daily Telegraph*. In the morning he will leave at eight and drive to the far side of Huddersfield where he is currently applying his skill in business efficiency to a firm who make industrial boilers. He will spend a day closeted in the boardroom with directors and accountants who will consider his completed report.

Soon, in a week or so, he will travel a long way further than Huddersfield; to Sidney via Rome, Athens, Istanbul, Bombay and Singapore to advise his Company's prize account of the efficiency of their world-wide business.

Not many sons of dentists from minor public schools and with no university degree could have done so well as Meredith, professionally, in industry. By travelling rather faster and cramming more meetings with executives and accountants into each day, Meredith earns rather more than other men at the same level in the company by which he is employed. He is able to pay, after tax deduction, the interest on the mortgage on Hodsworth Hall, only partly bought with Edwina's cash share of the Havergal estate. He pays for school fees, the upkeep of the house and the upkeep of Edwina's car. He pays for Mrs Thwaite to come to clean two afternoons a week, and, in order to prevent Edwina selling more Havergal silver and jewellery, he pays for most of Edwina's clothes. He does not have what he would call real money, but he has never been deeply in debt.

Once the kitchen is clean and Meredith in the drawing-room, Edwina will sit for up to an hour reading the *Guardian*, writing letters and eating the left-overs from dinner. She spreads the newspaper on the table and spoons chocolate mousse from the edge of the cut-glass dish.

By working even harder Meredith has forecast that he may be able to save enough in the next two years to have the external stonework of Hodsworth Hall cleaned by sand-blasting, so that, when he drives home in the evening he will see creamy white pillars and pediment rising over the wall as he comes up the avenue. This is a long-term goal and will be perhaps the end of a series of improvements in the eight years since he found Hodsworth Hall. The house itself was the first goal, worked and waited for in flats and semi-detached houses where the dining-room table and side-board were wedged in passages and the gilt chairs kept in store. Meredith found Hodsworth Hall while working for Robert's company, when Robert had just bought the Dower House and the park and farmlands.

In the kitchen, Edwina scrapes chocolate mousse and licks it from a wooden spoon and goes on reading.

In the drawing-room Meredith could be any age from thirty-five to forty-five. If he is thirty-five, then his hair has gone grey early. If he is forty-five, then he looks to have more energy than is expected at that age. His hair grows not smoothly from the centre of the crown of his head like

Harry's and the vicar's, but springily and thickly from the whole surface of his scalp as if every hair follicle were of equal nurtured strength. The energy of Meredith is in his head. He used to play rugby, in the scrum, head down, forcing the opposing scrum, playing with head rather than with boots. In his twenties in cavalry regiment cap, gold braid on peak, he was impressive; while in suits at that age his arms were too long and his hands too big, cavalry broadcloth blues disguised the heavy bone structure. In better suits now his presence is less uncomfortable and the horn-rimmed spectacles he has worn for the last few years have distanced an occasional ferocity. Care with gilt chairs, occasional tables and boardroom clients have made control out of clumsiness. He has his hair cut expensively in London so that it curls close round his head and never needs combing in public. He is shocked by people who carry combs and pencils in outside breast pockets. His shoes are always polished leather and he would never wear suede ones.

In the kitchen, Edwina washes her hands, runs water into the mousse dish, fetches from the dresser writing paper headed "Hodsworth Hall, Yorkshire", and finds a ballpoint pen out of the kitchen table drawer:

Darling Alex. Thanks for your letter. Sorry about your cold. Sorry for all that is grotty and crummy. Yes Miss R did also write and wants to see me. So what have you landed me in now? Never mind. Next leave-out I'll try and pluck up courage. Or I might write to her. Or I might not. Or I might..."

Then she folds the letter across and tears it in half.

Meredith is heard closing the drawing-room door, coming along the passage and slowing at the bottom of the stairs. He comes into the kitchen carrying a left-over coffee cup to the sink.

"Writing to Alex?"

"Yes."

"I think we ought to save that paper for best; it's three pounds a box now." And he passes behind her and out of the kitchen door. He goes upstairs, footsteps spaced on polished oak treads, is heard pausing half-way up under the arched window and going on up the second flight.

Edwina takes the rings from her fingers to write more easily and stands them by their shafts in the gaps between the tongue and groove boards of the white table, and writes again:

Darling Alex. I really am most awfully sorry that it is so miserable at school. But you must try and make a go of it for our sake ... both Daddy and I feel very strongly that when you are older you may perhaps feel grateful...

She stops writing and crumples the sheet of paper. And, at one thirty in the morning, she lights a cigarette and starts again, finding this time a sheet of white paper off a shopping list pad:

Darling Alex. Sorry about the grotty and crummy (at least I'm glad to note it wasn't shitty this time) but hang on do; spring not far away they say. News? What news? Let's see. Daddy off somewhere soon, probably round the world. Harry fine. Harry's bicycle fine. Harry's rabbit terribly well. Weather not especially fine. Had dinner party, food fine. Both Mr and Mrs Golding fine. Two Americans fine, at least he was—he looked a bit like Paul Newman but squatter and stockier...

And an hour after Meredith she goes upstairs.

They moved to the small room on the south-east corner of the house after Harry was born because the big main bedroom, shaded by the pillars under the pediment and with another window exposed to the north, was too cold for the baby. They could not take the Havergal four-poster bed into the small bedroom, and left it there in what is now called the spare-room. Now they use twin beds jammed together which, under one counterpane, look like a double bed. While Meredith keeps to the side under the south window and Edwina to the side by the door they sleep well, under separate sheets and blankets, with the east window towards the motorway just open and the traffic steady at two-fifteen in the morning.

Diana will be on her knees praying on the thick Wilton carpet of her bedroom to a God, whom she argued at the vicarage Tuesdays was infinitely benevolent, and who gave her Robert and five children all in ten years when she thought she might be alone for ever. But Edwina does not pray because she supported in the Tuesday discussions an Omnipotent God to whom it is not much good talking at night.

Diana will ring in the morning and say what a lovely evening and how grateful Robert is for the way they looked after the Americans. She will say the moussaka was splendid and she may add that it should really have had aubergines in it instead of what seemed to be bits of sliced cucumber.

Edwina and Meredith stayed in the small bedroom even after Harry was old enough to have a room of his own. When Edwina's mother used to come to stay she liked the familiarity of the Havergal four-poster in the spare-room, which, since she died, has hardly been used at all.

Chapter 2

LADY HAVERGAL USED to come to stay at Hodsworth at
Christmas or just after Christmas or at Easter or just after
Easter. She came on her way home to Scotland after staying with Alberta in Devon and with Davina in London. She
came with two golden cocker spaniels which she used to
exercise in the park and pasture, walking for the purpose
in an old fur coat which she always left between visits in
the downstairs cloakroom because, as she often said, it was
colder at Hodsworth than anywhere else she ever stayed.
After she died two years ago, the fur coat remained in the
cloakroom hanging beside old coats of Meredith's and
Edwina's and with the childrens' anoraks and gumboots.

Edwina turned out the cloakroom the morning after the
dinner party and sent her mother's coat to the cleaners.
Yesterday she collected, and now she wears it, standing
in front of the spare-room mirror, looking through the
window under the pediment towards the park and over
the avenue trees where Lady Havergal used to walk with
the spaniels at Christmas and at Easter.

The coat fur is silver white and speckled grey. It fits
neatly at the shoulders and narrows at the waist. Lady
Havergal used to say it was "nothing very good" and
"probably only rabbit", but she bought it before the
Second World War "when you got good things". It reaches
to Edwina's knees and could be worn with skirts or
trousers. It slips easily on and off and is in good repair. She
bought new buttons for it, but it looks best hanging open,
and she wears it to walk up to the Dower House at lunchtime.

"Tuesday will be hectic," Diana said. She is having a

38

lunch party for a friend of hers who is on the County Council and what's more there is a meeting at the Village Hall this evening, which could well be the last straw on such a hectic day, Diana says.

The way to the Dower House is along the drive which is an extension of the avenue, but curves round between younger trees and hedges and through the evergreen plantation which shuts Diana's house off from the view and the wind, and deadens the roar of the motorway. Edwina's boots crunch on the thick gravel inside the cast iron gate, and she pushes open the heavy oak front door and then the inner glass door. She leaves the rabbit coat in the Dower House panelled hall, where above the waist-high panelling, Diana has William Morris red and gold wallpaper of vine and acanthus leaves intertwined.

They drink before lunch in the sunny drawing-room, six women all with fur coats in the hall. The County Councillor is talking about her daughter who is marrying a merchant banker in April, just before the local elections ... "which is the absolute end!"

Edwina looks out of the window where Diana's turquoise and green tasselled curtains fall heavily to the Axminster carpet from wooden rails, and a woman asks her if they haven't met before. Weren't they both at the concert at the Rochdales when the Amadeus played last Saturday? Or was it at some Speech Day at some school? She knows it was somewhere where people stood up and walked around. "Well it can't have been a concert, you sit down at those," Edwina says.

Beyond the window is a grey stone terrace, a rockery and a lawn which ends at the laurel bushes. The County Councillor is saying that she tried to put her daughter off an April wedding, but Fiona is romantic about that sort of thing, so untypical for the young these days, everyone agrees.

From the Dower House downstairs windows nothing can be seen of the motorway, the pits or power station, these only being visible from the attic where Diana's children and the au pair sleep. The woman who thinks she knows Edwina says, "It wasn't at Marlborough, was it? We went to see my nephew in a play. We haven't any children there ourselves." "Neither have we," Edwina says.

The County Councillor says her daughter and the merchant banker want to live in Essex, but houses cost the earth there and they'll have to make do with his flat in Kensington to start with. "It must be interesting being a County Councillor," someone says. "Fantastic fun," the County Councillor says.

They drink sparkling wine now and will drink it throughout lunch. They stand by the red coal fire with the sun slanting in on the thick patterned carpet. The woman who went to Marlborough once says her own sons go to Gordonstoun where they can ski all winter which is marvellous. Is Edwina quite sure that she wasn't at the Amadeus last Saturday? The Rochdales gave a lovely party afterwards.

There are early daffodils on the mantelpiece and huge red poinsettias in a porcelain tub. "Are you on lots of committees and things as well?" the County Councillor is asked. "Simply dozens," she says, as they move away from the fire and the sun and go through to the dark hall when Diana says it is lunchtime.

On the way to the dining-room Edwina is told that the Gabrieli Quartet is playing at the Rochdales next month and are really worth supporting. And, on sitting down, with thick damask table-napkins on their knees and *hors d'oeuvres* on plates in front of them, everyone hears Diana say: "Edwina and I have an incredibly boring meeting to cope with tonight. Have you asked the Douglases to come, Edwina?"

Dear Mr and Mrs Douglas [Edwina wrote last week]. I don't know if you've been notified, but there's a meeting of something called the Hodsworth Society on Tuesday. It's a very good thing, with social purpose and all that, to do with preserving the village and so on...

She tore it up and said to Diana, "It would be better if you asked them, since you are Chairman and I'm not even on the Committee." But Diana said, "It's really the Secretary's job, but he's quite hopeless, so I thought it would give you an ideal opportunity to call on them if you want to get to know them..."

> Dear Stuart and Christine. I don't know if you've heard, but there's a meeting...

Over the *hors d'oeuvres* Diana tells her friends that the Hodsworth Society is something Robert used to be Chairman of, but when he had his hip done he had to give it up, so it's one of those things, she says, that one takes over until he's up to it again.

> Dear Stuart and Christine [Edwina wrote]. If I may call you that...

Then she tried "Dear Douglases" and finally she wrote with no opening address but a note as if scribbled in a hurry and signed "E.M.S.". But, after all, if you have exchanged views on life with and looked into the eyes of someone in a jolting buffet bar over miniature bottles of whisky which contain more than you expect to drink, calling someone "Mr Douglas" re-erects a barrier. So she tried again:

> Dear Stuart. Have hardly crossed your path for months, not since the Intercity Bar in fact, but have now been asked to notify you ... it will be incredibly boring in fact ... and am not certain what topic is on agenda ... but nice to see you ... and your good lady ... [she crossed that out] And your wife ... [she crossed that out] And Christine of course ... [but never posted it].

The Hodsworth Society, Diana says to the County Councillor and others, is pretty straightforward on the whole, pretty easy-going because luckily hardly anything comes up in Hodsworth to threaten the already pretty seedy environment. In fact tonight will be the first time they've had anything really to talk about. Mostly it's a matter of having jumble sales and so on, should money be needed when a threat arises ... She turns to Edwina: "Did you have a word with the Douglases then?"

Yesterday would have been the day to call because Monday is the day he is at home alone until lunchtime. On Tuesday he is out all day, returning at six as she noticed last week, following the tail-lights of his car through West Hodsworth and over the railway bridge and the canal.

"I rather tend," Diana is saying, "to play down the fund-raising side of things. We've already got one fund going for a new Village Hall and the last thing one wants to do is to divert money from that, so I've told the Treasurer..."

The women round the table drink while the au pair brings the main dish in. If Tuesday is a long day at University for Stuart Douglas, Wednesday is a short one and he goes to the new library in West Hodsworth in the afternoon, where he can be seen accepting specially ordered books across the counter. He does not hover around the fiction shelves, but sometimes glances in that direction across the polished floor, leaning his head on one side as if to read the titles taken out by those who do indulge themselves in that section.

Diana is serving from a casserole and telling everyone about the Treasurer of the Hodsworth Society who talks about neighbourhood and community and never about "village", and really is a pain. The County Councillor says that no one need tell her about people like that ... there is this man on one of her committees...

Stuart glances sideways at book titles across the library floor. "It figures," he said, the week she took out Evelyn Waugh and Nancy Mitford, but the following week when she selected with care and carried out slowly, Alan Sillitoe, David Storey and Stan Barstow, he left quietly and before her.

After lunch she will write another note. "In haste ... just realised was meant to notify you ... probably no good ... probably too late ... but still the invitation is extended in the nature of a gesture..."

Diana's room is thick carpeted like her drawing-room and panelled like her hall, and as she sits down, after serving from the casserole, her chair sounds not at all, and she switches on the fringed lamp which hangs close above the table. The time to deliver the note will be on the way this afternoon to fetch Harry back from school.

Lady Havergal would have said about someone to whom you had talked briefly in libraries and shops and streets and lengthily in trains: "I know you'll say it's silly to ask, and I know people think it doesn't matter any more these days, but where does he actually come from and what does his father do?"

Information about Stuart comes mostly from Mrs Thwaite. His father was a miner, Mrs Thwaite believes, from somewhere the other side of Doncaster. Of his mother nothing is known except that she is still alive and came to stay at No. 38 at Christmas. No one has mentioned even in passing whether he is an only child or not, but Mrs Thwaite believes Christine is. Lady Havergal, however, was always happiest on all occasions with information about aunts and cousins as well as with the number in the family.

What more is known about him as Edwina walks home at two-thirty to fetch the car and leave a note at No. 38? Except that the cigarettes kept on order at the shop for him are French, that he drives a yellow car, drinks at the Bay Leaf sometimes as well as carrying cans of Long Life across the road, and is doing some kind of Degree in Education?

He wears a black anorak in the rain and argues with his wife, Mrs Thwaite reports. His wife is a teacher at a primary school in Wakefield and they are both rumoured to be somewhere in their early thirties. She wears neat coats

43

and court shoes, has piled-up auburn hair and a very white neck. He has never been seen to wear a suit, but rather chooses different combinations of needlecord or denim. His shirts are mostly blue. About his wife, Diana says she is sorry for her because, living in a terrace house in the village people don't take notice of you like they take notice when you live somewhere like the Dower House or the Hall. But Lady Havergal would have said how nice it was to see people like that doing well for themselves these days.

His voice is low. You have to lean towards him to hear what he is saying. His voice would only be recognisably northern to someone from the south whose ears are not accustomed to hearing "but" pronounced like "put". Christine's voice has not been heard, but Mrs Thwaite says you can tell she comes from down south somewhere, and it is believed that her parents have a market garden somewhere near Bristol, or it may be Bournemouth. And on some Saturdays he plays soccer for East Hodsworth in black shirt and white shorts in the lower park. And in the summer was to be seen painting the woodwork of his door and windows white. Stripped to the waist with the sun on his back; the woman in the shop said he was making a right professional job of it.

All this might have satisfied Lady Havergal, but then her interest would be only social curiosity. She would not, for instance, have gone to buy whisky in the buffet/bar of the Intercity Train as it passed through Peterborough.

Edwina was on her way to Victoria to meet Alex off the boat train from a school trip to France, and Stuart was going to the wedding of a friend of his he'd been to college with. Eyes met across two miniature whisky bottles and he said, "I thought you'd travel First Class." "Well did you then?" "Or have a carriage to yourself." "Like prisoner and escort you mean?" After Peterborough and before Stevenage he said, "Well how are we going to bridge this gap we find between our social statuses, or rather stati, should it be?" And between Stevenage and Hitchin she suggested that her Fall Proudly motto could be of help, and he re-translated it from the Latin into "Fall in a Big Way". He also added that she could now dispense with respectability which used to be the criterion for membership of the middle and upper classes, but was no longer a requirement. Instead there was decadence. "I like it," said Edwina. Or there was genteel poverty. "I like that less, much less."

"And as for me," he said, "I'm rising in society anyway, so we have no problem." "Unless I fall too far," she said, "and we simply pass each other full tilt on the way." But later, after Hitchin, somewhere in the suburbs with Kings Cross twenty minutes off, she said, "But isn't all this silly? After all nowadays there is no class; everyone is classless," and his eyes widened over the miniature bottles and he picked his up. "You don't think that!" he said. "You can't think that!" "I rather thought I did think that, but..." "Well if you *do* think that..." and he carried the rest of his whisky back to his carriage and now only nods and waves and turns his head to the side in the library. "Well I must be getting back to my carriage," he said much earlier than was necessary for Kings Cross, and never gave her time to explain that, on reflection, she had been talking about meritocracy and that she knew perfectly well that there were still people who rode horses and other people who kept rabbits, that there were people who had a main meal at six and called it tea and other people who ate at eight and called it dinner. "Well I must be getting back to my carriage..." he said, and may well never know that Edwina has a rabbit but not a horse and that she and Meredith eat at seven and call it supper.

She went back along the corridor and saw him in his carriage leaning forward and talking earnestly to a man in the opposite seat, and passed again later by which time Stuart and the same man were rocking in their seats with laughter. And since then topics discussed between them could be written on a library ticket between the print; the snow outside the library when it was snowing, the rain outside the shop when it was raining, and the price of cigarettes inside. People do forget train journeys and chance meetings on them, obviously.

She went back along the corridor and walked on. Lady Havergal would have turned and smiled at him in the carriage and gone on her way to the Restaurant Car and had a three-course lunch.

When Stuart first came to Hodsworth nearly two years ago he had his hair cut in an early Beatle style. Then it reached his shoulders and he grew a beard. He had the beard in the Intercity Train and he had the beard at Christmas, but soon after shaved it off, and now his hair is short again.

On Christmas Day, with beard, he came to Matins, during which the congregation processed down the main aisle of the church two by two and up a side aisle to the tune of Once in Royal David's City, carrying candles to be placed in slots beside the crib. The Goldings were followed by the Measures-Smiths and the Measures-Smiths by the Douglases who had with them Stuart's mother and father. Harry dropped his candle and it rolled along the floor. Stuart stepped forward and bent down to pick it up. Then he helped Harry to get it in the right slot. Eyes met across the Christmas crib.

On New Year's Day Edwina drove down to the village to buy fish and chips. Alex went into the chippie and came out saying: "That man who looks like Steve McQueen is in there."

"What man who looks like Steve McQueen?"

"That man who lives next to Mrs Thwaite's daughter."

"Stuart Douglas does not look anything like Steve McQueen."

"Well anyway he walks like him."

They were nearly home when Edwina said, "If anything he looks like François Truffaut."

"I don't know who that is," said Alex.

Diana's hall has bulbous jardinieres and red glass vases

with hanging clinking crystals, fringed lamps, bronze radiators humming with heat. Edwina picks up her coat and leaves the women talking after lunch. She leaves at two-thirty when the conversation has turned to whether or not there will be a General Election in the spring. It has to be now soon in February or not till June, Diana says, because of the local elections. The County Councillor says she feels in her bones it will be June, and a friend of hers at Central Office says....

Walking down the park the wind has dropped, and still on the side of the hill away from the motorway and through the plantation you can hear yourself walking, and walk easily on account of the sparkling wine, and still taste the orange of the curaçao liqueur Diana served with coffee, and stride into the open slopes of the park where Lady Havergal used to walk fast under winter trees with the cocker spaniels running out in front of her, their ears streaming out behind them, and her hands in the pockets of the pre-war rabbit fur.

Back in her own house Edwina re-writes the message. "Hodsworth Society Meeting" on a postcard with her name and address printed at the top. Then she changes it for a plain piece of card out of the kitchen drawer, writes "Hodsworth Society ... do come ... 7 p.m." and signs it E.M.S. and puts no name or address on the front since she will be putting it straight inside his house through the letter box.

And, having done so, she runs back across the road to where she parked the Mini outside the grocer's and walks in. "There will be frost tonight," the woman at the cash desk says. "Could I have some of those cigarettes on that corner of the shelf?" Edwina asks. "Those are Mr Douglas's special order," and Edwina turns to go. "But since the rumour is that they are leaving, you might as well have some.... I don't like getting caught with a special order like that."

"Leaving?"

"Yes, when he's finished at University, they say."

Edwina stands outside the shop in the afternoon sun. Cars going through the village at this time include the County Councillor in her red sports car driving away from lunch at the Dower House, and followed by two other of Diana's guests driving in a Rover, both wearing their fur coats again.

Leaving? University years end in June or July and this is only late in January. Plenty of time surely for him to smoke the specially ordered Gauloises on the corner of the shop shelf.

Leaving? Mrs Thwaite said last week that Mrs Douglas was very homesick and had not made friends. She probably might be better, Mrs Thwaite's daughter was saying earlier in the week, back with her own kind like, you never know.

But Stuart on the train said: "I like most things about living there, except your friend." "My friend?" "Yes Lady Diana Bountiful ... boots for the poor at Christmas, soup for the indigent. Who does she think she is?"

"She just thinks that's what you do when you live somewhere like the Dower House. Diana says you never stop anywhere—that's her view of life. You go on rising, striving, like you were saying you were rising." "Did I say that?" "In any case," Edwina said, "in your world you don't have to strive socially. Your world's classless isn't it?" At which point he left.

With Diana she should have explained that it is all to do with Benevolent God who needs praying to every night to find out what He would have Diana do tomorrow. After all Benevolent God brought her and Robert together at a Young Conservative Election Victory Ball when they were both too old, strictly speaking, to be Young Conservatives.

The Mini faces north. Sitting in it, the sun goes down behind the houses. The meeting tonight will be not only incredibly boring, as Diana said, but also cold. The sparkling wine from lunch will be remembered only by a headache, and the crummy postcard posted through the letter box, a source of shame. Lady Havergal would have called days ago and taken tea, if offered, and explained about the meeting, had she truly and honestly considered it her duty so to do.

Edwina lights the first Gauloise sitting alone in the middle row of six rows of metal folding chairs in the body of the Village Hall. Only the front row of chairs is fully occupied by people who come mostly from the new private estate between East and West Hodsworth, and the rest of the hall is empty. Diana said, "If the Douglases come, Edwina, don't let them hide at the back; the second or third row would be most sensible."

Diana herself is on the stage, Chairman, at the trestle table there between Treasurer and Secretary. Derelict houses are the agenda of this meeting, six houses in a terrace leading off Main Street, all six about to be knocked down and the site made into a truck depot.

Outside the hall cars can be heard passing fast through Hodsworth. No wind tonight, and the woman in the shop was right that there would be frost; the Mini slipped and slid coming down the avenue, and the beeches that it went between and under had all their twigs coated white. The light was on at No. 38, but the yellow car was not outside. This need not signify, however, since many of these houses have garages at the back.

Inside the Hall the meeting has begun and the Treasurer put the point that Shaw Terrace must be saved by this society, remodelled, refurbished and not, at any cost to the community, demolished. And, if a transport firm has made an offer for it, the Society must take some action to prevent, preserve, protect and . . .

The Village Hall is dark and dusty, a First World War army hut brought from Aldershot, a gift from past squire to village. The floor is splintery and never quite clean. The round iron stove with pipe rising between the rafters has only just been lit, and exudes a smell of kindling wood and paraffin.

"This Society," the Treasurer says, standing on the stage, "exists to protect the interests..."

Beside him, seated, the Chairman listens in her new rich brown sheepskin jacket with bright white lining. Evening meetings at the Village Hall, Diana always says, go on much too long. It's all very well for people who have had a meal, she says, but Robert likes to eat at eight, and likes her to be there with him, eating.

"Therefore a new approach to the owner of Shaw Terrace has been made," the Treasurer reports, "in the interests of the community, and while this approach so far has yielded no response..."

Beside him, Diana, gold fountain pen in hand, stares at a blank sheet of paper, not having heard yet anything worth noting down.

"The owner of Shaw Terrace lives in Harrogate," the Treasurer announces, "and so far has failed to see the urgency and importance to this neighbourhood of a street free of heavy traffic..."

"The owner of Shaw Terrace," Diana says, still sitting, "is an elderly and arthritic lady who will naturally sell to the highest bidder..."

Edwina smokes in the middle row with a hand in the pocket of the rabbit fur, examines the toes of her patent leather boots, and hears on one hand the Treasurer speak of absentee landlords and derelict property, and on the other the Chairman speak of the needs of an elderly lady in Harrogate who will soon be living in a nursing home. And hears the Treasurer mention private medicine at the expense of the community, and Diana speak of those who have means to use them as they wish. And outside the still-distant traffic, and inside the smell of the stove and of Gauloise smoke curling in the rafters.

At least the Treasurer must admit, Diana says, that the owner of Shaw Terrace has waited all these years to sell, waited until all her tenants have died off. Of course they have died off, the Treasurer says, living in a property like that.

Before the meeting, on the telephone, Diana said: "It won't take long, but if there's any argument, you'll support me, won't you?" And before the meeting Edwina said yes she supposed she would, and ironed her velvet trousers and put Gauloises, matches and her car-keys in the pocket of Lady Havergal's fur coat.

And during the meeting, behind her now, the sound of the metal latch of the door is heard. A car passes close in the street, and then the sound is shut away. Those on stage look up, their eyes following the course of whoever has come in wearing rubber-soled shoes, and sat, with a slight scrape of chair on floor, in a row behind.

Before the meeting Diana said, "The Society has no funds to speak of, so the whole thing is theoretical in any case, but with that Treasurer, one never knows..."

The Treasurer calls him Stuart and tells the meeting that he and Stuart have often chatted about Shaw Terrace in the Bay Leaf, and Stuart is just the person to have at the meeting because he actually lives in a terrace house himself, and Stuart's terrace house is a terrace house to be reckoned with. Members of the Society could do worse than look at the Douglas residence and see what the potential could be for a renovated Shaw Terrace, were it purchased by the Society, and were tenants found of a suitable...

"I am sure," Diana smiles directly towards where Stuart must be sitting, "I am sure that ... er ... that Mr er ... that the Douglas residence is very nice indeed, but we are talking about not one house in a row of sound houses, but of six derelict..."

Edwina bends down to put her cigarette end on the floor and treads it out carefully with the sole of her boot. When she straightens up she will turn her head briefly over her shoulder.

"Stuart will tell you, Madam Chairman, that he has had offers for his house in the past few months which exceed by some thousands what he has spent on it. If all the houses in Shaw Terrace were bought by this Society..."

The brief glance showed Stuart sitting alone in the back row, face in shadow, chin in hand.

"Funds, Mr Treasurer! Funds! Where are the Funds?"

"The Funds, Madam Chairman, may I suggest, are already at hand, and when you have listened to what Stuart can tell us..."

"The Funds, Mr Treasurer, are in your care. Perhaps you could briefly inform the meeting..."

"I am fully aware," says the Treasurer, "that the funds of this Society, as they stand now, could not possibly be considered for investment in Shaw Terrace, but I am also sure that, in your own capacity as Chairman of another Committee in this neighbourhood you know that a considerable sum of money exists to be used towards the construction of the new village hall."

Diana looks down at the trestle table, shoulders drooping, hands clasped, the grey at the roots of her hair lit by the bare bulb overhead. And the Treasurer appeals to the feelings of the meeting and to their pride of place. No effort must be spared, he says, no funds left untouched to prevent not only the demolition of Shaw Terrace, but also the roaring of heavy transport, cranes and bulldozers in the village and near the primary school. With Shaw Terrace, he reminds the meeting, enough land can be bought upon which could be built a new Village Hall, central enough for all members of the community to approach by foot and bicycle on safe roads.

Diana, not raising her head, murmurs that the site for the new hall is already chosen, between the two villages, near the private estate, and on a bus route.

"But I ask the meeting," says the Treasurer, "I *ask* them what use is a bus route when the buses stop running when the working day is over? What use is that to a senior citizen wishing to play Bingo in the evening, or a little child on its way to the Wolf Cubs or the Brownie Pack, who will have to pick their way first along a street, which, unless this meeting sees its way to prompt and positive action, will be a death trap of giant wheels and diesel fumes. I propose, therefore, Ladies and Gentlemen, that this Society approach the fund-raising committee for the new Village Hall..."

"Anyone else to speak," Diana looks at Edwina, "before the vote is cast?"

But before the vote is cast Stuart has spoken, from his seat at the back, unhurriedly. He calls the Treasurer "Jack" and says that, just to support Jack, he'd like to see Shaw Terrace preserved. Seeing old buildings pulled down makes him uncomfortable always. Shaw Terrace is not beautiful, maybe, but if it can be improved and the old stones of it made good, why not see that it is kept? And, if the new Hall was built near it, it would be something to walk past Shaw Terrace on your way there, past kept gardens and so on. "Nice to keep it," Stuart says, "that's all."

Diana, addressing the meeting in general, says how nice it is, how really it is nice to have someone who speaks honestly under the colours of conservationism. "Glad," she says, "to have a conservationist in our midst."

"Not," says Stuart, "conservationist in the sense of Conservativism, I assure you Mrs Golding."

Someone in the front row draws a breath, the Secretary on the stage looks intently at the minutes he is taking, and Edwina gazes into the rafters.

Diana sighs and then smiles and says how very stupid of her, how very stupid of her indeed not to realise that this, after all, was a political meeting this evening. She really had thought, and may she be forgiven, that the assembled company here and now were all one party for the purposes of this meeting.

"Just for the purposes of this meeting perhaps," says Stuart.

"A-political, Mr Douglas. A-political, working together for mutual benefit, rationally. A rational means to a rational end."

"Politics," says Stuart, "are seldom rational."

Diana begins to glow; the meeting has come alive for her; this is what she goes to weekend schools for; this is practise for canvassing house-to-house at elections in her sheepskin coat. "Not rational Mr Douglas? Seldom rational? Well, if I may say so, if they are not rational, so much the worse for your poor politics then!"

Stuart sits easily, legs crossed, smoking. Diana sits high in her chair, hands folded in front of her on the table. Her manner is arch, but she has the composure of the practised hostess.

"Mrs Golding, we could discuss politics rationally all night, if that's what you want, and at the end you'd still be Conservative and I would still be Socialist. It's the way we are born."

Diana gives her tinkling hostess laugh. "All night Mr Douglas? Is that an invitation?"

But afterwards in the Range Rover behind the frosted windscreen she tells Edwina that at least they need not bother themselves about the Douglases any more. "Being nice to people gets you nowhere, does it?"

Under the dim street light a few minutes ago the Treasurer came out of the Hall, went along the pavement and into the Bay Leaf. The Secretary turned in the other direction and walked towards the Post Office. A woman in a long coat came out after them and locked the door behind her.

"What a disaster! Did I make a fool of myself?"

"Of course not."

Stuart left the meeting before the vote on the Treasurer's motion was cast. He looked at his watch and tiptoed out, raising the metal latch on the door quietly without looking back into the body of the hall.

"I'll resign of course. The Treasurer can run it. I never liked running it at all, but I didn't want to go like this."

When the vote was cast the hands that went up in favour of the Treasurer's motion formed an overwhelming majority. When Diana asked for "those against" only the Secretary put up his hand.

"Why did you abstain Edwina."

"The motion was so obviously going to be carried."

"A bit of solidarity would have helped, though."

"I'm sorry."

"At least you *stayed*. That Douglas man slunk out."

Cars come down from the motorway and drive fast through the village with their headlights on. Diana reaches for her driving spectacles out of her handbag. "I keep thinking of that poor woman in Harrogate."

"Which poor woman in Harrogate?"

"The owner of Shaw Terrace. Do you know, Edwina, that if she invests the price she gets for Shaw Terrace, she'll get a fixed income all right, but is that going to pay for her in a Nursing Home until she dies—the way prices are rising?"

"I suppose she'll end up on the National Health."

"Someone like that? It would kill her. She's not rich but she's had what could be called a genteel existence." Diana buttons her sheepskin jacket and puts the key in the starter. "I was going to ask you back for a drink but it's late now after all that fuss."

Edwina looked at the light from the front window of Stuart's house across the road.

"I just don't know, Edwina. I just don't know. One tries again and again to do the right thing, doesn't one? I mean is it *worth* it?"

"You'll always go on trying..."

"Sometimes trying hard is just a matter of keeping things from going completely wrong, and even then they sometimes do."

Edwina climbs out of the Range Rover to walk back along the street to her own car. The Range Rover goes slowly along the street, the exhaust from it wafting towards the open doors of the Bay Leaf. "Keep thinking of that woman in Harrogate," said Diana before driving off.

Edwina, in the Mini in the frosty street, sitting there after the Range Rover disappeared and not immediately trying to start the engine, and still sitting there when Stuart comes out of the Bay Leaf and bends down to see who is in the car, and comes round to the driver's window to ask if she is having trouble.

"There *is* something wrong," she says, "but I'm not sure what it is."

"Try turning the engine. I'll have a listen."

She turns the starting key; the engine catches once but not again.

"More choke." Stuart stands outside the car, his face in the shadow thrown by the street lamp, his hands in the pockets of his anorak, his feet stamping in the cold.

"The choke is out."

"Then put it in. Perhaps you have flooded the plugs."

She uses the starting key again, but this time the engine does not even turn.

"Flat battery?"

"It could be."

"Would you like me to drive you home?"

"I need the car in the morning."

He lifts the bonnet of the Mini and bends into it, holding up his cigarette lighter and touching parts of the engine. Then he comes round to the driver's window again. "It may only be the leads to the battery which are loose. Got a spanner?"

She gets out of the car, goes round to the boot for the toolbag, reaches in cold hands and feels there in the dark with Stuart standing beside her. With the spanner he leans into the bonnet again while this time Edwina holds the cigarette lighter flickering over his hands.

"Did I offend your friend this evening?"

"Yes rather, but you had every right to say what you did."

"I had no real interest in the matter. This man, the Treasurer, who keeps chatting to me in the Bay Leaf kept on about it, so I went. Not my scene at all really."

"Nor mine much."

"A pity about that time on the train."

56

"What about it?"

"That you had to get off before Kings Cross."

"It wasn't a stopping train."

"Try that now." This time the engine starts and roars under the pressure of her foot on the accelerator while Stuart bangs the bonnet shut and holds his thumb in the air. She leaves him like that on the pavement.

At home Meredith will have gone to bed already; tomorrow at six in the morning he leaves for London Airport. The house tonight will be quiet to wander through and wonder at the engine's aptly timed failure and wonder again how battery leads get loosened in the course of an only slightly longer than usual evening meeting at the Village Hall. But loose they must have been; the word was given by a self-described mechanic more trained in Fords than in Austin Minis he said as he held the spanner, in the time before he became an academic. More at home with the mechanical tonight, he had decided. "Did I say on the train that I was rising in the world? Forget it if I did. If I had that confidence now I might have been as nice as pie to Mrs Golding."

So it is not the way we are born but the way we feel on Tuesday evenings. People like Stuart, then, whether anti-hero, Ford mechanic, post-graduate student or fellow traveller are various. They say people get off non-stopping trains, they are confident in September and morose in late January. They tiptoe out of meetings early because they do not want to be seen abstaining. They can speak emphatically, even dogmatically about things like classlessness and conservation, but are as indecisive as anyone else in other areas, and like anyone else they probably wait for things to happen. Saying yes to life, as Lawrence the American prescribed, is unlikely to be operative until there is something to say yes to.

"I rather thought," Edwina said, "that you came to the meeting tonight because of the note I wrote."

"What note?" Stuart slammed the bonnet of the Mini. "Oh yes there was a note."

Chapter 3

THE LAWN TO the south of Hodsworth Hall stretches flat
to a ha-ha. The field beyond dips out of sight, then rises
again, its furthest boundary marching with the plantations
which surround the Dower House. From the small study
french windows lead on to the lawn. This is a narrow
passage-like room where Edwina stretches on the chaise-
longue, feet towards the french windows, facing out along
the lawn, the thick trees in view round the Dower House
beyond. The motorway, from the chaise-longue, is out of
sight.

The study is behind the drawing-room. Officially on the
old floor plan of the house it is marked "ante-room", but
is now the television room, and, having only one short
outside south-facing wall, the warm room. For the last
year Edwina has been saying to Meredith that it should
now be a room where Alex could entertain her friends,
that it should now be Alex's room and that they should
put the television in the drawing-room. But Meredith has
rejected the plan, and said no to the television and a
stronger no to any of Edwina's belongings that would also
have to be moved.

The linen-covered chaise-longue is Edwina's favourite
piece of Havergal furniture. On top, where she lies, it is
faded summer-blue, but where the upholstered parts curve
in to meet the wooden frame the joining braid has frayed,
and you can see the deep Prussian blue that the cover was
in Havergal days.

The telephone table is to the left at the head-end of the
chaise-longue. Here, beside the telephone and for blank
moments, Edwina keeps a book of Bridge problems, also

Thorenssen on Defensive Play, and, for bright moments, the vicar's copy of *The Hypothetical Creator*. But the telephone table is mostly piled with old letters and magazines and packs of playing cards and toys which Harry leaves there. Nothing like this, says Meredith, could conceivably be kept in the drawing-room.

Edwina lies on the chaise-longue. Across the room is the electric fire, red hot spiral bars glowing horizontal between a curved burnished steel framework on claw feet. Heat is thrown across the narrow room to warm her knees, but even so she wears thick navy blue jeans, a sweater to match, rather, two sweaters to match.

Opposite on the marble mantelpiece above the fire there are unpaid bills, unfinished mending and last summer's picture postcards. And over the mantelpiece is hung a row of small photographs identically framed. Central in this row and slightly larger than the others is a soft-focus view of Grandmother Havergal, the wife of the fourth Baron, hair drawn back, wearing shirtwaist and belt, just before the First World War, just engaged to the fourth Baron. Dark hair, full mouth, she brought to the Havergals not only the gilt chairs but also the four-poster bed to which it is believed distinguished visitors found their way. Were this a painting and not a photograph Meredith would have welcomed it in the drawing-room.

To the right of grandmother Havergal are photographs of Edwina and her sisters; first her own wedding picture all blowing bouffant organdie and cold bridesmaids; then there is the *Norfolk Life* frontispiece of Alberta at the time of her engagement to Dick, Alberta in strapless evening dress and early fifties bright lipstick, clutching and peering through a trailing pot plant, dark hair like Grandmother Havergal's, heavy chin, full mouth like Alex's. Davina, the youngest sister, never having got engaged or married is represented by a Press photograph taken in her modelling days on the Rialto Bridge in Venice, wearing a shift dress and dark glasses.

The fourth baron, Edwina's father, sits at a desk in the

British Museum, in wide-lapelled pin-stripe suit, with thin hair brushed over bald patch and a small moustache. And to his left, his two sons-in-law, Meredith and Dick, both in uniform. Meredith says they ought to take Dick down now, not that one would want to replace him with Bruce or whatever his name is. And, in any case, it would spoil the symmetry of the line of photographs, he says, and make the room more untidy than ever.

"Alex," Meredith has said, "would fill it with even more rubbish and play records very loudly. That sort of thing must go on upstairs."

The photograph of Edwina's mother is one of her grinning in Red Cross uniform with a white nurse's veil over her blonde hair in 1942 when the Royal Army Medical Corps took over Havergal House for the duration of the war.

"The fact that Alex is growing up means that she will be here less and less over the next few years. Even in the holidays she goes away from time to time."

Last summer Alex went to France with the school to improve her French. There she met not many French people, but spent the time with boys from an English Public School who were staying in the same town. She came home talking of Simon who was quite brilliant and looked like Ryan O'Neal in *Love Story*, but with longer hair. When Simon came to stay he called Meredith "Sir" and gave a balanced and eloquent account of the school he was at. It rained while he was at Hodsworth and he and Alex spent most of the time upstairs. Edwina hovered on the stairs or sent Harry up from time to time to interrupt whatever was happening. After Simon went home Alex said he was hoping to get expelled from school during the autumn term. "There's too much homosexuality, he says, and Simon is completely hetero. Also it is an all-rugger school and Simon supports Liverpool." Edwina bought Alex a book on sex education and told her about all the unmarried mothers she could think of and how nasty and expensive abortion was. Alex said, at the end of the holidays, "Don't worry. I'm not going out with Simon any more anyway."

Edwina, propped on the chaise-longue on the day after the Shaw Terrace meeting, writes letters in the afternoon looking on the lawn which is grey with frost, and listening to Mrs Thwaite in the hall sweeping up the dust.

Alex went back to school last autumn having promised Meredith she would stay two more years. Her first letter said "School is shit", but she had crossed it out and put "bloody awful" instead. "Two girls have run away already this term, so wait for it..."

Meredith said, "I hardly think one can consider giving Alex a room to entertain her friends when she writes like that."

There was a drug scandal at the school Simon was at and eight boys were expelled. Alex wrote that she had heard that Simon had failed to get himself caught and was not so lucky.

At Christmas Alex went to stay with her aunt Alberta and her four girl cousins. "Smashing," she said. "Alberta lets them go to the Comprehensive and they know all the in-crowd in St Ives. Bruce is really dishy and thank goodness she got rid of Uncle Dick."

"Well that has not done her any good at all," said Meredith.

Home for the rest of the holidays Alex went to the parties she had always gone to but said she had gone off public-school boys in a big way and on the days after parties spent until lunchtime in bed.

Dear Miss Rogers [writes Edwina]. I'm so sorry to learn that Alex is causing trouble to you and your staff. I have written to her about this and will be coming over as soon as possible to the school, but, with my husband abroad...

The last week of the Christmas holidays, after they had seen Stuart outside the fish and chip shop, Alex bicycled to the village most days and bought chips. She said that was brave of her, considering that children down there stared and shouted shitty things at her; it would be better if she knew them and went to school with them. At St Ives with her cousins it was different—they used to shout shit back. She went to a party at the Rochdales with Maria Golding on the last day of the Christmas holidays. Meredith fetched both girls at midnight and said he thought that Alex was "rather the worse for wear". Alex said the Rochdale boys were particularly weedy but at least there was plenty to drink.

When Mrs Thwaite has swept the stairs with a dust-pan and brush on Thursday she usually goes through the hall with the big broom. Then she moves to the study where Edwina sits, Hoovers it and puts the paper and letters in piles on the mantelpiece, and the toys to one side; this she calls sidening the room.

It was Diana who arranged for Mrs Thwaite to clean for Edwina two afternoons a week, explaining that one had to give Mrs Thwaite lunch first. Edwina never had lunch in term time, but she cooked it for Mrs Thwaite, and, not liking to put it on the table without sitting down, she sat with Mrs Thwaite, ate with Mrs Thwaite and made conversation.

Diana says that, what with the au pair girl and only one child not at boarding school, Mrs Thwaite is now superfluous at the Dower House on Tuesday and Thursday afternoons.

Mrs Thwaite's daughter has a little boy the same age as Harry who has a rabbit like Harry and sometimes forgets to feed it like Harry does. Mrs Thwaite's daughter's little boy, however, goes not to a private school twelve miles up the motorway, but to the East Hodsworth Primary. Mrs Thwaite's daughter has colour television and is going on holiday this year to either Morecambe or Majorca but Mrs Thwaite is not sure which.

Mrs Thwaite's daughter rents the house next door to the Douglases on the main street of the village. She and her husband have been on the waiting list for a council house ever since her little boy, who is called Constantine, was born eight years ago. Now there is another baby on the way and they are moving into a council flat near Mrs Thwaite in the summer. "That will be better for our Constantine and the new baby," says Mrs Thwaite. "It's not healthy down there with all the traffic."

While Mrs Thwaite sidens the narrow study, opening the french windows in the freezing afternoon, Edwina goes to the kitchen to make tea and can still hear Mrs Thwaite talking. Our Constantine, she says, goes in next door sometimes because he knows Mrs Douglas; she is a teacher and he likes teachers and our Constantine is very bright and that at school and most teachers like him. But he doesn't care for Mr Douglas all that much though.

While Edwina boils the kettle Mrs Thwaite switches on the Hoover in the study. To hear what she is saying you have to go back into the hall and stand in the draught from the french windows. Above the roar of the carpet sweeper you can hear that Constantine's mother doesn't care for Mr Douglas all that much either, and Constantine's father says he's been heard to use foul language in the Bay Leaf and on the football field as well.

Mrs Douglas comes from down south somewhere, but is quite nicely spoken and always says good morning. Mr Douglas only says good morning if he feels like it, Mrs Thwaite's daughter says, but some days he is right maungy and slams the door of his car. They say he is a student, but some sort of student at that age, and, seemingly, if he is a student, Mrs Douglas must be bringing all the money in to the house. *He* comes from beyond Doncaster way they say which is where Mrs Thwaite's sister married and went to live and her husband can be proper maungy too.

When Mrs Thwaite has finished the study she comes to the kitchen to drink her tea. She says she wouldn't wonder if Mr Douglas was not one for the women. Her daughter has had one or two right funny looks from him, even since she was pregnant this time. He came into her garden once last summer after his cat and looked at her

63

right cheeky. Nor was he wearing more than shorts and one of those vest things with writing across the front. "Sometimes I say it's a pity that people like that haven't got kiddies of their own," says Mrs Thwaite, "and sometimes I say it's thank heavens they haven't."

When Harry comes in, dropped at the drive gate by Diana in the afternoons, Mrs Thwaite says, "There is our Harry," and makes him bread and butter before Edwina drives her home.

"Last night," says Mrs Thwaite, "my daughter said next door she was playing Hamlet with him for being over at the pub. I said those walls are thick—you can say that for old houses—so you can tell what a noise they make. And, when he does come in, like as not, he's up in the roof. They see the light up there you see. Working they say. Lying around with books my daughter says."

While Harry watches the children's programmes on television Edwina writes letters again:

Darling Alex. Believe it or not I've just written to Miss R to say I will see her soon. Christ knows what I'll say when I do. Meanwhile, chin up in best tradition please. Not for nothing was grandmother Havergal the toast of the court of Edward VII when he was still Prince of Wales. Nor must you forget your grandfather was the most painstaking numismatist the British Museum has ever seen. Bear in mind also that your grandmother knew a General in the Second World War and that your mother herself once went to Buckingham Palace and curtseyed to Princess Margaret...

Grandmother Havergal gazes in soft focus towards the curtains of the study, now drawn.

...What more? Harry is watching Blue Peter. His rabbit is having more babies by Mrs Thwaite's Constantine's rabbit we borrowed the other day. Daddy left this morning—now in Rome at a guess. Oh yes—and tonight—wait for it—Leeds United, no less, in the 4th round replay. I've bought Harry a poster of Billy Bremner and one for you of Norman Hunter (or is Peter Lorimer your favourite?), which I enclose . . .

When Meredith goes abroad he leaves behind certain papers in a green box file which is labelled "All you need to know while I am away". The first document, on opening the box, is a carbon copy of his flight schedule prepared by his secretary. Two foolscap sheets stapled together predict that Meredith will stop off at Rome, Athens, Bombay, Hong Kong, Singapore and Sidney. He left Heathrow this morning and will now be in Rome.

Lifting out the flight schedule, a file called "Home Affairs" is revealed, which contains such things as notes concerning the re-ordering of fuel for the boiler and a warning that the poor condition of the fire bricks requires that the boiler be kept well below boiling point. There is also a reminder that a stone mason is coming to consider the condition of the second pillar from the left under the pediment, and that some flagstones will be delivered during February for the new terrace Meredith plans for the south garden. Then there is a folder called "Finance" which includes cheques for gas, electricity and school fees, made out before he left and with written instructions for their posting on certain dates.

Edwina found the box file on the Havergal teak desk in Meredith's upstairs office, a small square north-facing room he finds too cold to work in, but where he hangs his school and army group photographs and keeps his filing cabinet.

Also in the box file are to be found an Insurance schedule, addresses of solicitors and accountants, and his Will, stiff paper, folded, sealing-waxed and ribboned, never opened nor ever read by Edwina.

She carries the box downstairs to the study on the evening of the day Meredith left and opens it while Harry watches Leeds United in their fourth-round cup-tie replay. She finds and puts to one side a file containing past "While I am away" instructions and last year's flight schedule. The next file which she opens is called "Education".

Two years ago Meredith wrote a piece, which is still in the file, entitled "If I should die...". It is still here in his steady italic handwriting in black ink on the large lined sheets of paper he brings home from work, headed "Inter-Office Memo".

'Harry," wrote Meredith two years ago. "I want him, as I have always made clear, to go to prep school as a boarder. The list of possible schools, all of which we have discussed, is enclosed. I think on the whole, however, we must now exclude Grantley Hall, partly since Robert's children will be there, and partly since it is in Yorkshire which is not only too close to home, but also will not offer Harry the breadth of outlook we want for him and which is notably lacking in some wholly Yorkshire-educated people of our acquaintance. I would, moreover, like Harry to see as much of England as possible. Of the six remaining schools it is impossible, at this stage, to select one finally. One must keep an eye on their progress, their changes of Headmaster, and in touch with other parents. All six of these schools have entrance deposits paid and will, I feel sure, write and remind us of Harry's claim to entry when the time shall come."

The schools' list has been amended yearly and two of the original six have had their names deleted: one went broke and closed down, and at the other a remarkable number of boys failed their Common Entrance exams and did not get into the public schools their parents had chosen for them.

Under the prep school list is a bundle of Prospectuses, large expensive booklets with glossy photographs of buildings, swimming pools and playing fields. Here also can be read descriptions of the kind of education offered, subjects taught, leisure activities followed, plus details of the boys' daily routine, the uniform they are required to wear and the equipment with which they must be supplied by their parents.

"I think," wrote Meredith, referring to the prep school list, "you will recall that we have visited four of these

66

schools. For instance—Milton House (see Prospectus)."

The Prospectus of Milton House, which Edwina lifts from the file, writes of maroon-coloured blazers and socks, soccer in the autumn term and rugger after Christmas; boys are expected to be orderly but not regimented and the family atmosphere is preserved. When they visited Milton House, the Headmaster wrung Edwina's hand and remembered Meredith in the army. Meredith looked at a list of present pupils and recognised a cousin of the Rochdales. Edwina thought the baths were dirty but the central heating good. There were toy animals on each bed in all the dormitories. Edwina and Meredith saw the school and stayed at the nearest good hotel. "A bit far south," she said at dinner, "and teddy bears on every bed! Not all boys like teddy bears, it makes you think they are there to impress."

They also visited Grafton Manor. The Prospectus said, "Anglican worship in own chapel designed by Chantrell, forward-looking and progressive, concerned with the development of the individual, but always keeping in mind the terms of Common Entrance requirements ... uniform grey and blue." The Headmaster was an unmarried clergyman with a slight handshake and had been to school with Edwina's uncle by marriage. Meredith commented afterwards at dinner in the local hotel, "Not, perhaps, very forthcoming with the parents, but probably excellent for the boys."

"Homosexual," said Edwina. "And grey doesn't suit Harry." Meredith found a name on the list of pupils which suggested kinship with the Queen Mother. Edwina guessed that one of the boys was the son of a front-bench Socialist Member of Parliament, and admitted that the tuck shop, open three times every day, was a point in favour of Milton House, albeit the only point.

At High Legh Hall, where they play Rugby Union both winter terms, there was an indoor heated swimming pool and an unbroken successful record of entries into Eton and Harrow. The Headmaster looked like Donald Sutherland and the boys were allowed home every third weekend.

Meredith's Managing Director's son had been there and had been in the British long-jump team at the last Olympics. Edwina was fairly sure that the small boy who showed them the swimming pool was the son of a famous woman novelist, but said to Meredith afterwards that a school which played no soccer was definitely out as far as Harry was concerned, that being the only sport in which he showed an interest.

"You mean Leeds United?" said Meredith. "He'll grow out of that. It's a very provincial attitude which one should not encourage."

"It's very good for people to have local pride."

"That's simply a red herring," said Meredith in the hotel dining-room. "Just something you thought of. If you do not approve of the school we saw today you should be honest and say so frankly."

"It should be quite clear by now that I do not actually approve of any of them."

"We have had all that before and resolved it. You agreed."

"Perhaps while the balance of my mind was disturbed?"

"How was the balance of *your* mind ever disturbed?"

"Temporarily, by childbirth. I agreed to prep school for Harry within days, no hours, of his birth. I even voted Conservative at the election when he was three weeks old."

"But you have come to see three schools with me! Thereby implying agreement to the matter in principle."

"Then I am not coming to see any more."

"At Grafton Manor you may remember..." said Meredith.

"At Grafton Manor," said Edwina, "they specialise in choral singing, cross-country running, golf and nigger-baiting! Great!"

Meredith picked up the wine list. "We will not discuss it any further for the time being," he said.

"And at Milton House the matron is always in attendance at the sick-bay when she's not clearing up the vomit from the homesick."

"I think we will have half a bottle of no. 48 if that is agreeable to you," said Meredith.

"Or when she herself is not under the weather or the headmaster."

"Shut up," said Meredith in a whisper, waving away the wine waiter.

"If God had wanted little boys to go away from home at the age of eight," said Edwina, "he would have sterilised all upper class mothers."

Meredith closed the wine list, folded his napkin and walked out of the dining-room. Edwina followed him and said in the hallway, "Man invented the prep school Meredith. Man invented it, in the days of the endlessly extended Victorian family when women couldn't stop having children before birth-control, and one boy child more or less in the house was barely noticeable."

They drove the one hundred miles home, hungry and in silence. The next time Meredith spoke to her was to say that her God logic was ridiculous, and that as far as local pride and Leeds United went, did she not realise that many of the players for that team were Scottish? or came from Northumberland? And in future they communicated on matters of education through the box-file, a one-way system by which Edwina read but never commented on what was in it.

With the box-file on her knee she sits on the floor and leans against the chaise-longue. Harry curls there in his yellow pyjamas and blue dressing-gown, head on folded hands, eyes flickering after the soccer ball.

Edwina lifts from the file another folder titled "Public School" and reads that, if Meredith should die, she should continue to give the closest attention to Marlborough. But Meredith is aware, he writes in his level manuscript and weighty prose, that, in the case of his death none of his wishes are enforceable. "I, you might say, can only ask. Whatever my own experiences were, and I have bored you often enough with those in the past, Edwina, I would not be where I am today, without my education."

Where he is today is now in Rome, flying first class in the night while Harry eats crisps and keeps a lemonade bottle on the floor and watches Billy Bremner, Norman Hunter and Peter Lorimer, and reminds his mother that this may be another draw, and, if so, when will the next replay take place?

"There is another point I would make," Edwina reads, "and I make this, may I say, on Harry's behalf. Accuse me as you have in the past of being too absent a father, too rigid in my life-style, too purposeful in my objectives, I am, in every way, the only father he has ever known."

The green box-file is two years old now and too full of folders for the lid to shut properly. Edwina sometimes adds to it bills which arrive while Meredith is away, or messages about telephone calls.

"Pre-Freudian I may be, as you so often phrase it, but I understand well enough a child's need for what you would call a 'father figure'. And it occurs to me that a dead 'father-figure' is better than no 'father-figure' at all. In the unfortunate event, therefore, of my death (and I assure you that I have no intention whatsoever of precipitating such an event) at least Harry could still stand up and say 'My father was' and 'My father did'."

"Could it not be," said Meredith, "that such a figure would remain all the stronger in Harry's mind were he to follow in my footsteps, with the promise, moreover, of going further than my footsteps ever reached. He would see around him, both at prep and public school, boys of similar backgrounds and would say to himself from time to time, I like to think, 'This is what my father wanted for me . . .'."

"A goal Mummy. Peter Lorimer. A goal."

Edwina puts the papers down, Peter Lorimer scores a goal helped by Norman Hunter, the study curtains move in the draught. Meredith's prose was a dying fall. She will replace the papers, in order, in the box-file, put sellotape across its lid to keep it shut and carry it back upstairs to Meredith's office. Then, when half-time comes in the cup

70

replay, she will send Harry to bed, promising to run up with the final score in case he is not asleep.

There is another page to be picked up from the floor. A recent piece entitled "Alex": "Finally I would say that, while I feel less entitled to express any firm wishes in the case of Alex, I know as well as you do how much she means to Harry. Were she to take the 'hippie' road, we should consider, I feel, the effect of this upon him. She is closer to you and I can only suggest that she will, inevitably, follow you rather than me. I ask you to set her an example. She is, after all, a girl."

The box-file is for serious matters like finance and Harry's education. No wonder there is no more room for Alex. It is time to pile the papers in, turn up the television, to hear the half-time whistle and send Harry up to bed.

Yet another sheet of paper, dated Last Monday:

"Time is short. Less than a year. He must go after next Christmas. Are you still of a mind for Milton Hall? Your reaction to that was, I recall, somewhat evasive, but I must ask you to consider, weigh the pros and cons. Dispassionately. Remind me please to discuss this upon my return."

Upon his return he will find the box-file, spilling papers and prospectuses, under the chaise-longue, where she pushes it, while on the television a voice says that Norman Hunter is having a very good game so far, and the telephone rings, sounding louder than usual, echoing into the hall and up the stairs because Harry has left the doors open.

The loud ringing of the telephone becomes a familiar signal, ringing this way for no one else; right from the first short ring. "I have your spanner."

Afterwards Stuart said that he half expected Meredith to answer, in which case he would have been quite prepared to give the same explanation for his call. An urgent call—people need spanners quite a lot; some people keep the only spanners they have in their cars.

"Oh well, I'd like it back ... some time, that is."

Later he said that he had been watching the fourth round

replay and felt something heavy in his jacket pocket. Yes, he knew he had been wearing his anorak last night, but at some time he must have moved the spanner thoughtlessly into his jacket and walked around not noticing it all day. "Car all right today?"

Later still he said he'd known about the spanner since last night and had been meaning to ring up all day, wanting to ring up all day. But there was something too obvious about ringing at a time you guessed someone's husband would be out. Even when there was something obvious involved. "I was thinking as you drove away. You might do with a new battery."

Months later he said he had kept the spanner for this very purpose but had thought he would never have the guts to ring. Something about the goal Leeds scored inspired him to lift the telephone, though God knew what. "Or at least with topping it up?"

"Topping what up?"

"The battery. I could do it for you."

He bends into the bonnet of the Mini once again, but this time in the shed by the field which Edwina uses as a garage, and with the headlights of his own car shining on the work in hand. The battery lid is prised open and he tips in drops from a bottle of distilled water which he always keeps in his garage. He reminds Edwina, "This car is not exactly in peak of maintenance condition."

"It goes O.K."

He wonders if she's had it serviced recently and how much mileage it has done. "About 48,000 I should say." From a dark corner of the garage he fetches a sack. This he lies on putting his head underneath the car, pointing upwards with a torch. 48,000 miles is considerable mileage for a Mini, he says, time to change cars perhaps it might be said.

"God knows I can't afford a new one."

Washing the oil off his hands at the sink he looks round the kitchen, at its height and contents, as if assessing whether it belonged to someone who, God knows, cannot

72

afford another car. He does not look particularly like François Truffaut at this moment, nor did he walk up from the shed like Steve McQueen might walk. But this is not why she hands him the towel at arm's length, makes coffee and fills the cups too full, and sitting at the table has to anchor her hands round the cup, take it off its rattling saucer and hold it quiet on the wooden surface of the table. And say politely: "This has made you miss the second half of the match."

"I wouldn't have thought *you* watched soccer."

He sits across the table. A man whom you now know to be about to become a Master of Education and not just a Bachelor of it. For this man you got out cups and saucers instead of mugs and considered the possibility of taking him into a cold drawing-room, or at least the study, if it were not so full of Meredith's plans for Harry's education and of family photographs. That he is in the kitchen now with oil on his hands and the cuffs of his white sweater is a coincidence and must not be thought to be the result of his offered mechanical services and advice: "You could treat yourself to a new battery at any rate I would have thought."

Perhaps his other expertise should have been consulted before he had a chance to turn mechanical. He could have been asked about some of Alex's O-level problems, except that he would consider in all probability that those whose education is paid for can have no real problems.

"It must be interesting," she asks him, "being at University. Do you ... do you specialise in any particular subject—or is it just education generally?"

"You can't do anything generally. Everything is finally particular."

"Oh I see."

"Although it is possible to give broad descriptions."

"Yes?"

"Well there are such things as behavioural studies included, the sociology of learning processes, the psychology of ... and in the first year ..."

Or perhaps cars and batteries are easier when ears are deafened with a ringing which began with the half-time whistle on television and the telephone bell, and the problem of how to convey the information that Meredith is in Rome.

Stuart has stopped talking, stopped smoking, but still sits crossing and re-crossing his legs. Shortly he will excuse himself and drive home, to lie around with books, as Mrs Thwaite's daughter says, in his attic where people see the light burning until all hours of the small hours.

Diana, while praying nightly to Benevolent God after meeting Robert at an Election Victory Ball, spent all her savings and had her teeth crowned, and at the same time made discreet enquiries into the nature of Robert's business, its profitability and where he could be bumped into accidentally. Alberta never prayed as far as anyone knows, but, once having started attending Bruce's life-drawing class in Plymouth, learnt to draw very well indeed, without which she sometimes says in her now Australian-tinged accent, "He just *might* not have noticed me so much."

Edwina, back on the chaise-longue in the evening, gazes at Grandmother Havergal gazing back, and at her mother grinning on the steps of Havergal, having had, as she so often claimed, a very good war indeed.

Meredith appeared from nowhere sixteen years ago in uniform. The memory is that at some stage shortly after that something was said to lead you to think that you had probably agreed to marry him. Before that things were said to boys in Havergal and thereabouts, but things in those cases happened wordlessly. A dialogue must have taken place in the flat in Birmingham with the man who sold encyclopaedias while Alex was asleep in her cot, but the dialogue must have been brief in the short space of Alex's afternoon nap. And at parties in recent years men as tall and stately as Miles Rochdale have danced wordlessly thigh to thigh; conversation on such occasions has seemingly prevented closer contact rather than encouraged it.

Back in the vicarage on Tuesday afternoons the choice was for Omnipotent God, who, the vicar said, having the world the way He wanted it, could not to some minds be described as Benevolent. To this version of the Hypothetical Creator you do not pray; you only report on what has happened, which is that Stuart, when he arrived in the kitchen, took the spanner out of his anorak pocket and put it on the table, but it is not there now.

So the spanner must be the link with the mechanic and the man, and if that is the only link, too bad. If you cannot meet the academic on the common ground of the general and the particular and try to understand the nature of behavioural studies, then accept the spanner link. Accept that he got oil on his hands and lay on the garage floor, and likewise accept the role which cannot ever be entirely disassociated from that which Lady Chatterley had with Mellors, which can't be bad.

"I'm in awe of that bed."

"I'm sorry, it's the only spare bed we've got. The only double one that is." The four-poster has its head against the north wall. It juts into the spare-room between west window and fireplace. Here on winter afternoons the electric fire is carried from the study. The four posts of the bed are in fluted mahogany, narrowing at the top where they vanish under the flowered and faded chintz canopy. "I'm just as much in awe of everything to do with you."

"It's difficult to see it that way."

It is not cold for early February, but wet outside with raindrops on the square pains of the sash window. "Don't be in awe. It's worse for me."

"In that case I might as well go home."

"I mean it feels very ... very cataclysmic."

"It always does."

"But something can't be both cataclysmic and commonplace."

"If you mean that it cannot be repeated, then we'll do it once and say goodbye."

"No I didn't mean that actually."

There was never any doubt two days after the Shaw Terrace meeting who was at the door in the bird-twittering half light while Harry was watching television. From the passage the outline of Stuart was seen beyond the glass door. His head was turned away from the house looking down the avenue. As the door opened he said, "I took the spanner back last night."

The bottle of Scotch was waiting in the larder together with four cans of Long Life should he choose that. He followed her along the hall past the doors into the drawing-room, dining-room and study, while she said, "It's warmer in the kitchen."

After two drinks Harry came in, shook hands and sat at the table, firmly rejecting the suggestion that he might find something still interesting on television or go and feed his rabbit. Instead he found Edwina's white writing block and drew pictures in bright coloured felt pens while they drank. And while drawing, he told Stuart that his father had been in Rome yesterday, would be in Athens today and next week in Istanbul.

Harry draws houses best and asked Stuart what his house was like. Stuart told him it was, "Very small, with one window on the top floor, two windows in the middle, a front door and a big window on the ground floor." Harry drew it in green with black windows and roof; Stuart said it should have No. 38 on the door.

"I don't know anyone who lives in a house with a number," said Harry. "Except Mrs Thwaite and her daughter and their Constantine."

"Of course you do."

"I don't. Well who then? Apart from him." He looked at Stuart. Across the table Stuart's hands with long fingers curl round the whisky glass. Hands like that should sprawl romantically over keyboards or lie fragile on death-bed sheets. Today the oil stains have faded and the spaces between them are as clean as if rubbed with pumice stone.

76

"I'll draw our house now," said Harry and he drew it from the front first with red pediment and yellow pillars and with green balloons on stalks coming out of every window. Inside each balloon he wrote the name of the room: Harry's room, Spare-room, Drawing-room, Dining-room. Stuart leant over the picture and at the same time stretched his right hand across the table as if to shake Edwina's, his wrist emerging from white shirt cuff. "O.K?" he said, still looking at Harry's picture.

"O.K.," she said, looking at the picture, but did not take the proffered hand until they were outside on the tarmac, iron hard in frost and looking up at the house itself, having left Harry drawing under the kitchen strip light.

Stuart felt exactly as expected, like himself and no one else, and the prediction after that was that they would be somewhere in bed together within a week, which prediction they are now fulfilling.

The spare-room did not seem the probable place in which to fulfil predictions. A car, a lay-by or the flat of a friend he must have would have been more likely. He must, she suggested, have more experience of finding such places than she had.

"You've heard that, have you?"

"Not at all. I just guessed. If it's true it makes you more of a prize."

"A Prize? I'm going home."

"More wanted. More desirable."

"All right then. But as far as places are concerned, I assumed that you would supply the place just as you supplied the spanner."

But this is not the time to mention that he took the spanner in the first place, and took it in the second place as well. This is rather the time to close your eyes and think of England as the saying went, and consider that whoever Grandmother Havergal brought to this bed before the First World War and whatever happened on it in the second one, the third generation is doing its best to keep

77

the standards up, and complimenting it with the top people of the day. Alberta rejected a country gentleman whose name is in Burkes Landed Gentry for an artist, and Davina had a fashion photographer and an African from Tanzania to name but two, and Edwina now says yes to life and a working-class intellectual under the canopy and in the square contained at its corners by four posts.

Diana always says sex is for procreation, but is made to seem like recreation for some people, she has heard. Love is something, says Diana, to do with keeping the children quiet for Robert and having remote control on the television so that he does not have to reach or move to switch channels. Sexual skill, Diana would say, is only for keeping your husband happy.

Close your eyes and think of England. Whatever Diana always says, whatever Alberta and Davina do, what some call foul language best describes what is exactly right and proper at the time.

Sometimes in bed Stuart will say, "We working-class people have our uses." Or sometimes he will say, "I expect you tell all your friends that you know a marvellous little man down the road who fucks superbly." He camps an upper-class voice such as Edwina has only ever heard on television. At other times he is unquestionably the superior intellect, although as he often points out, while you are actually studying such things as the theories of development of cognitive processes in close-up, you tend to lose a grip on the broad moralities of life, not that he ever had a lot of grip on those before.

And on other afternoons the mood softens and it is childhood memories week when he describes being driven back from a coach outing to York when he was about ten, about the time you first begin to feel poetic about spring and summer, looking forward to seeing his mother and telling her about what was, in retrospect, a perfect childhood day, sandwiches by the river, a boat trip to Bishopthorpe, stopping and climbing in trees hanging over the

78

water. When he is old, he says, he will look back on these afternoons like that, sitting on a park bench. And Edwina stares into his eyes and listens and manages to remember a day at the age of about ten, bicycling along a flat road in Norfolk, pale willows for miles parallel and ahead. But not, she adds for the sake of honesty, an entirely idyllic moment because of going back to boarding school that afternoon. And when she is old she will drink a great deal of whisky and play Bridge both afternoon and evening she supposes.

On this kind of afternoon he says, "I feel I've always known you." And she says, "I don't feel I've always known you, but I do feel I've always wanted to. Or someone like you." And wonders if behavioural studies are about people like her or about real people. But asks him other questions.

Looking out of the window between the pillars, to the tops of the avenue trees due west, you know there to be high-rise blocks and factory chimneys on the skyline but they are obscured by cloud and rain. Stuart says he has never been asked before to analyse the success or otherwise of sex. Just as long as it was good was all he asked. Chemistry? A cool word that. His watch ticks on the bedside table and when he straps it on his wrist and goes home there is this permanent resounding silence of the electric fire switched off.

If behavioural studies are about people like Edwina they reveal no superficial change. To the casual observer she will look the same. She may take to wearing different clothes, changing her hair style, losing weight, looking tired, looking desperate, looking extraordinarily happy and buoyant.

To her question he said that whatever it is between them is good, is excellent, in fact, and needs no further analysis, does it?

She will drive the same car, look after the same children, except that she will sometimes call them kids, write the same letters, drink the same drinks and cook the same meals. She will watch the drive for the post and

79

listen for the telephone more urgently, stare out of windows, stay awake at night and not hear what other people say. Her ears will be tuned to one channel, others having bad reception, scrambled, bleeped and distorted by something which is like a long low cello ground bass held indefinitely.

She said to him, "But you said everything is finally particular."

"I was not talking about us then."

Diana would say that the sound Edwina hears in his absence is a clarion call to found a family, and that, when it goes on sounding, the family founder's attention is guaranteed to be henceforth and steadfastly directed towards the general good. Those who have heard it once towards this end, Diana would say, should never listen to another sound. But Edwina would say, as she remakes the bed and switches off the fire, that this is the first time she has heard it properly.

"Will we be all right, do you think?" she asked him. "Not hurt ... and so on?"

"Who can hurt us?" His clothes and her clothes on the floor in the mid-afternoon and promises of Wednesday and Friday afternoons throughout school terms. There is not much you can do about the times in between except enquire, "What will you do when you get home?"

Sometimes he says he starts work directly he has had his tea. Then he goes to the Bay Leaf for a bit. Sometimes after that he does not feel like going home, so he walks along the village street and into the park where there are teenagers groping and fumbling and he realises there is only home to go to. Which is sad, he says, because home is where you ought to look forward to going.

"Isn't it ever like that at ... at No. 38?"

"Oh well ... you know ... not good."

Edwina says that she only wants to get home on any occasion to make sure it has not burnt down or anything awful like that. She has bad dreams about driving in and seeing an ambulance outside the front door. "People don't expect to be happy at home do they?"

"Yes. I think most people do."

"But the ones who don't expect to, like me, what would you say they can do about it?"

"People don't leave people, do they?" Stuart says that sometimes he and Christine are friendly and sometimes they fight like dogs. They did not want children until a few years ago, but he does not think they will have any now. Christine sometimes says she will put her name down for an adoption, but can never quite make up her mind; they don't discuss it much any more, perhaps because it's too important.

"But you keep on hoping you'll have some of your own?"

"Trying you mean? Not often. And you?"

"The same, but not for children; two's enough." She watches him dress in the afternoons in the red light of the fire. This room is never a light room, except on summer evenings when the sun shines in directly for an hour or two. A tall dark room of which the ceiling needs painting white again.

"Should we ever draw the curtains?"

"Unless someone was standing with a telescope on a branch of a tree in the avenue, we are always unobserved."

In this room the District Nurse, the morning after Harry was born, said how little light came in and she drew back the curtains and held the baby near the window for Edwina to see what he was really like.

"People don't leave children," she says. "That's the trouble."

"It's just as difficult when there aren't any."

"How can it be?"

"Someone is left really alone."

"Does she love you?"

"Not in the way most people understand it. Does he love you?"

"I don't think about it all that much. But I shouldn't think so."

81

"I wish I didn't think about it all that much," Stuart says.

If she wants further analysis of what it is between them she could always call it love, he says. "It's a bit early for that isn't it?" she answers, but follows him downstairs every Wednesday and Friday to say goodbye on the stairs, in the kitchen and, if dry, by his car.

On days when Harry is home from school with a cold they have to make do with a telephone call which Stuart makes from his house while Christine is at work or from a call box at the University.

"What would happen if she found out?"

"I don't know. She'd be hurt. What about Meredith?"

"It's nothing to do with him."

On the telephone, whatever the analysis, it is necessary to hear a loving tone.

"Does Christine have anybody else ever do you think?"

"I think she'd tell me. She is dead honest."

"You must be rather close to each other in some ways then?"

"Close locked. Closely combative you might say."

"I'm sure she must still love you."

"When Christine says she loves me it's as if she was saying she hasn't finished with me yet."

"That's awful!"

On the telephone or off the telephone, in bed or out of it, the long-held note always returns afterwards. Christine and Stuart have been married for ten years and she still hears something which tells her that she needs him.

"Does it ever wear off Alberta?" Edwina writes on a Thursday afternoon and tears the letter up again.

"Are you coming to Bridge on Tuesday?" asks Diana on the telephone.

"Dear Alberta..." But tears it up again. After all no one knew about Bruce until it was *fait accompli*.

"Yes. I am playing Bridge on Tuesday."

Chapter 4

SHE SITS OPPOSITE Victoria Rochdale in Victoria's drawing-room which is longer than any room in Hodsworth, twelve tables of four, forty-eight women in Jaeger, Chanel and Susan Small suits. Scent of freesias mix in the air with the scent from expensive bottles. Two fireplaces mix wood-smoke and floor polish and reflect on Fabergé, Rocking-ham, Ormulu, Lely, Gainsborough and Turner.

Victoria rattles her bracelets: "Shall we play that convention where I say two clubs if I have a super hand and you answer two diamonds if yours is rotten?"

"Why not?"

"And two hearts if yours is super too?"

"Right."

Stuart rang this morning, and she let Diana drive her in the Range Rover on straight white roads across flat green country with the sun on dry grass verges.

"It's good to be opposite Edwina. She has such smashing cards." Victoria, tanned from ski-ing, wears a deep brown velvet waistcoat and trousers with a billowing sleeved cream silk shirt. Victoria believes that clothes are what you buy in London or in Paris; she wears half a dozen bracelets and as many rings, one of which, sold, would re-mortar every pillar of Hodsworth Hall and pay two years of Harry's education.

Stuart this morning said, "Enjoy yourself my darling," and she said: "I don't much want to go. If there was a chance of seeing you instead..."

They play against two older women who say they come from Ilkley and Skipton and are used to playing duplicate games. Victoria sits with her back to the window, the sun on her rings and Miles's deerpark dotted with trees beyond.

Stuart said: "You go and play with your noble friends, my love. And I'll see you tomorrow." My love, my darling all in one phone call. There is, after all, nothing quite like Bridge in the afternoon. "I think I'm in love with you," he said last week in bed.

Upstairs she left her rabbit coat with minks and beaver-lamb and sealskin in a bedroom with a huge gilt mirror. "Well that's all right then," she said last week in bed.

There is certainly nothing quite like picking up and fanning out thirteen cards and seeing a rich row of aces, kings and queens. "Two clubs, Victoria."

"Two hearts."

And then there is nothing like bidding to game, promising to make four tricks, or three if it is no trumps, and being kept bidding up by your partner to little slam, all the tricks but one, and grand slam, all thirteen tricks. And Stuart is "in love".

Victoria is dummy and spreads her hand of cards on the table, and watches Edwina under the Adam ceiling play the game doubled and re-doubled by the ladies from Ilkley and Skipton, challenged and re-challenged.

Lead from an ace/king in your hand but never from an ace/queen, the saying goes. Draw out your opponents' trumps. Always, always lead trumps first; many a man walks the Chelsea Embankment at night, the other saying goes, because he did not lead out Trumps. The four-poster at Hodsworth fades as if it was swung into a dark recess with the naked bodies on it and a door closed. Hearts are trumps, and, holding nine of them from ace to six is as good as slam already. The experienced player automatically counts them as they fall. Then plays top cards from the other suits at top speed, giving Ilkley and Skipton no time to calculate, forcing them to discard their few feeble defensive jacks and tens uselessly on tricks. Hodsworth now is not twenty but two hundred miles away and the telephone you wait to ring, a dust-covered piece of someone else's history. Stuart is a man with arms and legs and a head, the back of which, when he walks down the street, moves uniquely to stir the observer. He drives a Ford car, was once a mechanic and improved his accent at college to attract more girls.

The woman from Ilkley says even Thorenssen would not use defensive play to any effect on this occasion. And Victoria says: "Oh Edwina how absolutely super. You're going to make them all."

There is no need on this occasion to make a neat row of tricks which can be counted easily. No need to count at all since they are all made but one. That Stuart is married matters not at all as long as he is "in love". That he sometimes leaves early in the afternoon to fetch Christine from school in Wakefield only suggests how considerate he is, how loyal and how concerned.

Hearts are her lucky suit, she always says. Some people give their winnings back to the charity of the afternoon, but this will buy whisky for the spare-room, and a map of the new counties of England for Harry's room. Stuart may say this prize is soiled with the hands of the rich and extorted from the poor, even though the game is being played to give Dewsbury children a holiday in Scarborough. But Stuart will be told, "I don't care if it is top people being decadent in the afternoon; there's nothing like it."

"Absolutely super. Jolly well done Edwina." But this time Victoria's mouth seems to be staying open, as on Edwina's ace of Clubs in the final trick, the Ilkley lady places slowly and with long drawn out pleasure, a heart trump uncounted and sweeps all four cards into her corner of the table.

"Oh Edwina. How ghastly," says Victoria.

"Poor you," says the lady from Skipton.

"How too grim for words."

Stuart would say Jesus Fucking Wept, Edwina.

"I always think," the woman from Skipton says as she deals for the next game, "that having consistently good hands is simply no good for anyone."

85

At four tea will be served in porcelain cups from silver teapots and biscuits handed round. Then at six there will be a choice of sherry, gin or dry martini. Victoria's long finger-nails tap the We/They score pad and her ash tray is piled with gold-tipped cigarette ends smeared with red lipstick. Next week, she says, she is going to the West Indies because Miles can't stand February in England.

Edwina says she didn't think anywhere was called the West Indies any more, and rolls up the sleeves of her T-shirt in the growing warmth. Stuart will be discussing the disadvantaged pupil in a seminar at this moment, but he said on the telephone that he had a row with Christine yesterday and would have to hurry home to patch things up.

"Whatever it's called," Victoria says, "it will be hot and gorgeous, but I'll miss Guy terribly. It's his last term at his little day school."

Edwina's hand is of hearts, diamonds, clubs and spades. The cards are new and shiny and slippery. Someone says her daughter is going to do a Cordon Bleu cookery course and has been offered a job in the summer cooking for a house-party in Scotland. Someone else says how sensible, and *her* daughter is unfortunately going to one of those Universities in Essex or Sussex or somewhere.

Stuart said that Christine, after a row with him, has bad days at school. Having been a teacher himself, he knows how rotten that can be. So fair was fair, he said, and reminded Edwina that tomorrow was Wednesday.

"But Nanny is over the moon about our going away," says Victoria. "She loves having Guy to herself."

Down the room Diana's voice says she has not had a good hand all afternoon. Stuart said Edwina must not worry; Wednesday would be a long afternoon together again; for his sake and for her sake and for everyone's sake, she must always say goodbye, smiling.

"It will be miserable when Guy goes," says Victoria, "because Nanny will go too and it will be hell in the holidays without her."

Edwina said goodbye, smiling. She looked for him on

Saturday in the park, but he was not playing soccer.

"When is Harry going, Edwina?"

Stuart took Christine out on Saturday to cheer her up. What more could anyone ask than having someone give up their footer?

"Edwina. When is Harry going?" Victoria enquires over her hand of cards and Edwina looks back across the table. The woman from Skipton plays the hand thoughtfully.

"I don't know when Harry is going Victoria."

"It's awful when they go, particularly one's youngest."

"I don't even know *if* Harry is going, come to that."

"I'd *adore* to keep Guy at home for ever and ever. Then Nanny would stay."

The Skipton lady says her son loved every moment of prep school and is now in the army in Northern Ireland.

"The only other solution as far as Nanny is concerned would be to have another baby."

The lady from Ilkley reminds them that she has just made three No Trumps.

"I'd like Harry to go to the school in the village."

"It's incredible how they take to prep school, Edwina. And stop missing home after a bit."

"It's brain washing, Victoria. From what I've heard either they have to cry every night or they just have to shut off all thoughts of home."

The Skipton woman says Edwina is right, but prep school works in the long run. "I think being thrown in like that when they are seven or eight equips them for anything later on. It's hard, but honestly I think it works."

"Oh honestly it does, Edwina."

Cards falling, ash trays filling. A voice says she thinks Women's Lib is dying a natural death. Another says her au pair girl has bought a bra at last.

"If my son needs equipping," says Edwina, "then I'd rather equip him myself."

"But that's such fantastically hard work, having them at home, and jolly well cramps your style, I wouldn't wonder. Miles and I would have no fun at all if ours were at home

87

all the time. The sort of parties we have are absolutely out in the holidays, if you know what I mean."

"My sister," says the woman from Skipton, "is terribly hard up and can't afford to send her three away. She says they come in from their Grammar school or whatever it is, in filthy tempers and slouch round grumbling and smoking all the evening."

"You just can't have children hanging around when you're having your own fling, Edwina. And God knows we deserve a fling don't we?"

"The point about prep schools I'm trying to make," says the woman from Skipton in her loud round voice, "is that they really are good places. Has anyone ever known an ill-intentioned headmaster I'd like to know? I think they really *like* children at those places."

"And there's little enough chance of a fling one way and another; ours keep getting expelled or suspended from school or simply leaving and you have to send them away on art courses and things or to Switzerland or somewhere."

Down the room women are leaning back in their chairs, smoking and talking. Some have moved and are standing near the fireplace. In another room there is the sound of tea being prepared and wheeled on trolleys in the direction of the drawing-room. Then there is silence at the moment Edwina happens to be speaking.

"I don't mind," she says, "if Harry slouches around or grumbles. He'd be all right. He'd have a bike and ride around in the village, have fish and chips when he felt like it, or go to the pictures if he felt like it, get on a bus when he wanted, go to the Youth Club or play in the beck at the back."

Victoria stares at her and says how funny that Edwina is rejecting her background. She herself went through that stage once when she was pregnant, with Guy she thinks it was, and it was simply too boring for words for everyone until she got over it. Victoria gets up from her chair and blocks the low sun from the window. It's time to have tea, she says, and to have the lights switched on. Then she turns

88

back to the table and says: "If you feel that strongly, Edwina, you'll obviously have to do something about it."

"Like what?"

"Well I've always understood that mothers have the final legal say-so about their children."

"Legal?"

"So if it's a difference with Meredith, and if it's that deep, presumably you'll take some action."

Victoria moves away. Edwina stays scribbling in the We/They columns of her score pad, while the others add up their score so far.

"The thing I adore about Bridge," someone says behind her, "is that it makes one forget all one's problems. Every single one of them. That is why I adore it so much."

She lights a Gauloise at the empty table.

Diana drives home in the dark after sherry. The butler who poured it looked like Stuart from the back. In the dark, the grass verges look white as they are picked out by the headlights of the Range Rover.

"Good cards, Edwina?"

"O.K. to start with."

"Yes I heard about that. What were you all talking about when the rest of us were waiting for Victoria to get tea going?"

"Oh . . . schools and so on, flings and orgies etcetera."

They drive on dark roads. Diana hesitates on every corner, dazzled where the road is narrow by oncoming lorries. They will go straight to the Dower House where Harry had tea with Diana's Matthew. Diana says: "Victoria can be rather silly sometimes I always think, pretending to have flings and orgies."

"Oh she has them all right." Looking back across dark fields and low hedges you can see the wide Adam front of Victoria's house with all the windows lit.

"Well we've never been asked there when they had one."

89

"Nor have we, but last time I fetched Harry from having tea with Guy, he said that Guy's Mummy and Daddy were upstairs in a bedroom with some other people having a party of their own. So I thought lucky things."

"Your children always have strong imaginations. Miles and Victoria are extremely fond of each other."

"I didn't say they weren't. Miles told me at a party once that they smoke pot together except when Victoria is pregnant."

"Miles can be rather silly sometimes too, at parties."

They cross under the row of pylons with red lights at their pinnacles and head along the flat road towards the motorway.

"Funny isn't it," Diana says, "I've hardly seen you since the Shaw Terrace fiasco meeting, not for more than a moment, that is. What's all your news?"

"Oh nothing special."

In the village, lights shine out from No. 38 behind drawn curtains. Stuart's car is under the street light.

"By the way, Edwina."

"Yes?"

"Did Mrs Thwaite tell you about the Douglas man this week?"

"No."

"Well it bears out everything I have ever thought about him. Obviously the trouble in that marriage is that he has someone else."

"Oh I shouldn't think so." A figure is silhouetted against the curtains at No. 38 and a window on the first floor lights up. "Most unlikely."

"Apparently Mrs Thwaite's son-in-law is working on the new buildings at the University and saw him holding a girl's hand in the road."

"Oh well ... yes ... perhaps ... something like *that*. Anyway I don't think they *are* all that unhappily married."

"What makes you say that?"

"Oh just a hunch. Reading between the lines."

"I simply refuse to worry about that *menage* at No. 38

90

any more. After that meeting when he was so rude I wrote her a note and said if she ever felt like having a chat to give me a ring. I feel very sorry for her being married to someone who may possibly have a very coarse streak in his nature from everything Mrs Thwaite says and from his behaviour that night. As if there wasn't enough people who *do* want helping."

Out of sight of No. 38 the Range Rover turns into the park, its lights swinging to pick out the iron play equipment and the white football posts, then it clanks over the cattle grid and heads up the avenue.

"Of course he will have friends at the University, Diana, but holding hands means nothing."

"Sometimes you are surprisingly naïve, Edwina."

The beech tree trunks light up silver, one after the other, and are left, when passed, black as before.

"On the contrary, Diana. I always suspect everyone of having it off everywhere all the time."

They drive directly towards Hodsworth Hall where the windows are unlit, but, reaching it, turn right and drive on up the lane to the Dower House where Harry is waiting.

"You should not worry about Meredith, Edwina. I'm sure he is faithful to you while he is abroad."

Later in the evening Diana will ring up and say wouldn't Edwina like to come back to the Dower House with Harry and stay the night since she must be rather lonely.

They lie face to face on their stomachs, their legs stretched behind them beside the electric fire in the study. Harry's legs point to the french window and Edwina's towards the door. The unfolded board of the game of Risk is between them, a map of the world scattered with plastic cones representing armies over the coloured continents; North America is yellow, South America green, Europe blue and Africa red. Australia, which is mauve, Harry says is not really a continent but only an island and is the only thing he has won so far. Edwina, without trying, has her brown pieces of army massed over the pale green of Asia. Apart from occupying the whole of Australia, Harry also has some pieces of Africa which would also be an island but for that bit joined on to Asia in the corner. Edwina looks at her watch, lights a cigarette and tells him about the Suez Canal. Lying on the floor you can see under the chaise-longue, Meredith's green box-file where it was pushed the night Leeds United won their way to the fifth round of the Cup.

"It's not fair. You've got nearly all Europe."

"You can have two turns running then."

"I don't want to. You didn't have two turns running."

"Yes, but I want to get a cup of coffee, so you have two turns running while I'm out of the room and I'll have two turns running later if I remember."

"Anyway, you can't have turns on your own in this game when the other person isn't there to throw their dice as well."

"You throw it for me then."

"Anyway, I looked in the rules. It doesn't say you can do that."

"But it doesn't say you can't, Harry."

Harry regards the Risk board and with one hand sweeps the fringe out of his eyes. Victoria said this afternoon that one thing she didn't like about prep schools was the way they sometimes cut little boys' hair without asking you.

"Anyway, I've only got one rotten island."

"Why not attack me from it then, there in South-east Asia?"

"Anyway, you shouldn't have to tell me what to do."

The woman from Skipton said of course they cry all the way to school, her son always did—all the way to somewhere in Sussex.

"Anyway, this game makes me very angry."

"All right. We won't play it again."

"That makes me more angry."

But, said the woman from Skipton, you can be sure

they've stopped crying two minutes after you've left. "Two days more like," said the woman from Ilkley making her only contribution to the conversation.

"The thing to do, Harry, the way I've found out not to be angry about this game is to pretend that those armies are not really mine, but that I'm just playing the game for someone else."

"That's weedy. That's weedy. That's very very silly."

The thing to do after Harry has gone to bed in tears is to pack the Risk game away carefully and put it under the chaise-longue next to the box-file. Then the thing to do is to smoke a cigarette, have another cup of coffee and remember that it is only three hours until Wednesday, and, whoever's hand Stuart holds in the road by the new building site, he has never failed to arrive exactly on time on Wednesday.

From upstairs Harry calls out from time to time that he can't stop crying.

The thing to do is to play the game for someone else, to lie on the chaise-longue and think coolly and on behalf of that someone else that Stuart has spoken of people at University called Pete, Andrew, Phil and Paul. He's spoken of girls more often by describing their figures and faces rather than by their names.

"If I'm not playing it for myself," said Harry, "what's the point of playing it at all?"

Once he mentioned a girl he brought home to have lunch one Sunday in his first year; she was ill and homesick but Christine didn't take to her and wouldn't ask her out again. "Was she jealous?" asked Edwina "Maybe so." "Did she have reason?" "Not really." The girl might, on reflection, have been called Ursula.

"Anyway, it doesn't make any difference the way I think about it. I lost and I shall probably cry all night."

The way to think about Ursula, if it was Ursula, is that she may still be homesick and ill in her third year and still need a helping hand across building sites on the way to lectures. Or was Ursula the one who wore very mini skirts and showed her knickers in tutorials? And the way to think about Stuart is not to listen to Diana in the Range Rover since she is no authority. Although she may be right about the coarse streak in his nature, luckily. And, Victoria, for all her orgies while her children are away, never had a lover like that for certain.

Stuart is short because his father and mother were short. They came, he said, from a line of small hungry people; he does not remember being hungry, though, except for yearning for sweets in the Second World War. Before Stuart grew up he was the first generation to have National Health orange juice and vitamin pills and his teeth filled for free.

Edwina is medium height although her parents were tall. She does remember being hungry because her mother only learnt to cook in the Second World War and Edwina could not eat the early experiments. She did not have National Health orange juice and vitamin pills before growing up because her mother had not heard of them. Her skin just survived acne and her teeth have been lucky rather than well cared for.

But standing back to back on Wednesday by the electric fire in the spare-room and lifting their hands to feel the tops of their heads, they agree they are about the same size. And ideally suited, they add, turning towards each other.

Stuart has the coarse streak of which Diana spoke and would call it sexual frankness. Edwina learnt the frankness from playing in the village and under the hedges at Havergal before she went to boarding-school.

Stuart tells her about the girl on the coach trip to York when he was ten, the girls at the school he left when he was fifteen, the wife of the owner of the garage where he worked afterwards. And many others. Neither Meredith nor Christine are mentioned in this context.

"You haven't said anything about Ursula?"

"What about Ursula?"

94

"Once you said something about her. Wasn't she ill or something?"

"Never mind about Ursula. I have you."

"Do you still see her?"

"Oh yes. Chatted to her the other day. She lives with some post-graduate in one of the old houses they are pulling down for the new Administration Block. I walked up there with her—nice houses they are—you ought to come and see them. They are like Shaw Terrace but brick with stone arches round the doors."

"She's got a boy friend then?"

"Oh yes, a bio-chemist I think ... these old houses I was telling you about ..."

They climb to the top floor of Hodsworth Hall because Stuart has not seen the view from here before. An eighteenth-century visitor to the site claimed to have seen from the house that stood here then both York Minster and Lincoln Cathedral on the same clear day. The window in the single attic room under the ridge of the pediment which faces east over the motorway is seldom opened. You can, with difficulty, wrench the rusty catch and open the casement, lean out and look north down the pasture scattered with elms and sheep to the backs of the houses in the village.

"No wonder top people built their houses on hills."

Far down in front of them on the motorway a coach of football supporters going north passes with flying scarves blowing horizontally out of it.

"You'd never have looked at me, Edwina, if you'd lived all your life up here."

"We played in the village at Havergal."

"Nice clean country kids suitable for his Lordship's daughters. I was a snotty-nosed town kid."

Nearer the house, against the fence between garden and field is a bright red spot where Harry left his bicycle last night.

"We were very nice to the children at Havergal. We were very nice to everyone."

"Of course you were. You could bloody well afford to be."

Diana's horses, along the inside of the paddock fence, have their heads down eating hay thrown there by a man in breeches from Robert's Home Farm.

"Perhaps we were too nice to survive. Perhaps being nice was what finished the Havergals, apart, that is, from not marrying into the merchant classes."

"Social historians would say that that was just stupid carelessness."

"We were too busy being nice to know what we should be doing."

Beyond the motorway, the ploughed fields, rolling and patchy with the pylons which lead to York and the coast, and the power station on the far side of the village. "Perhaps now we cannot afford to be nice any more. Perhaps now we've got to be positive and get things going the way we want them."

"If standing up here makes you talk like that, we will go downstairs at once."

"Oh it's nothing to do with you and me. Not really, that is."

If Stuart had spoken as meaningfully and guardedly about some plan of his, she would not have slept all night.

Chapter 5

IN EARLY MARCH it stays light until six o'clock and the crocuses on the far side of the lawn make patches of bright mauve and yellow. No primroses, but the daffodils could soon flower and stay flowering, frozen in suspended animation with continuing cold and rain into April. You never could hear a cuckoo over the roar of the motorway and spring here is mainly to do with it getting lighter and lighter for longer and longer and cars driving through the village and under the flyover to the coast on Sundays.

Edwina reads a letter from Alex and listens to Diana on the telephone. Diana says that the Easter holidays are less than a month away and that she has already started filling the deep freeze with shepherds pies and trifles and arranging social events, and that "People who say having children at boarding school leaves you free all the term are talking nonsense".

Lying on the chaise-longue it is possible to see, outside the french window, the piles of pale stone slabs which have arrived by truck, ordered by Meredith before he went abroad, for the terrace he plans to build this summer.

Diana says her plans for the holidays include sending her two eldest daughters on a nature-trail weekend in the Dales; perhaps Alex would like to join them.

"I'll ask her, Diana, but I don't think she'd say that nature-trails were quite her scene."

The terrace will stretch from the south-west corner of the house and along under the drawing-room and study windows. It will be bound on the far side by a stone balustrade, the pillars of which have also arrived and are stacked around the front of the house under the pediment.

Diana says on the telephone how nice it will be for Alex

97

and Maria to spend lots of time together in the holidays. They always used to be such good friends, and now that they are growing up they will need each other in their social life even more, although of course they are so different in so many ways, Maria being serious and scholarly, but thankfully, says Diana, extremely pretty with it.

The pale grass of the lawn spreads away to the crocuses, uninterrupted except for a narrow border in the far southeast corner. One quarter of this grass expanse will be hidden this summer under the stones of Meredith's terrace, but now it stretches, the size of two tennis courts but never now used for that or any other organised sport.

"Not," says Diana on the telephone, "that Alex is not very striking in her way."

Meredith sees the new terrace as the scene of drinks before dinner on summer evenings. Perhaps, he once said, when Alex is married there will be long tables spread with food and drink and a marquee on the lawn.

Dear Mummy. Thanks for sweets etc. and poster of S. McQueen. And letters. Doesn't anything happen at home these days, incidentally, except Harry's baby having rabbits, I mean Harry's rabbit having babies? Not that anything *ever* happens here, except people getting expelled—a third year is latest to go—under new rule that boys from the Army School must not put their hands inside our blouses . . .

"Are you there, Edwina?"

Edwina looks out at the lawn, the stones for the terrace and hears Diana say that before the holidays they must get together for a really nice long chat.

Had corny interview with Miss R who said she was "awaiting your visit", but meanwhile, etc. etc. etc. . . . in other words "watch it!" She objects, it seems, to all the Out Crowd and sees me as chief menace. "Too silly" as the Rochdales would say . . .

The lawn is dotted in places with molehills, between

which Harry cycles in the light evening, steering between them, negotiating them at speed, and braking hard at the stone ha-ha with his feet put fast on the ground. Diana says she has had a letter from Maria who is taking Spanish as an extra O-level, making eleven in all, and saying how she now goes to Sunday musical appreciation evenings in Miss Rogers' study, the only fifth-year pupil considered musical enough to appreciate. Alex writes:

> Latest indignity is withdrawal of so-called privilege of going to village shop, except for sixth-formers—on account of third year expulsion no-doubt. Miss R seems to think Army Apprentices lie in wait behind dry-stone walls at four in the afternoon. The Out Crowd theory is that she'd just love it if it was Eton or Sandhurst across the valley. Not that all this stops her from having dinner with the Colonel in Chester, so the rumour goes. Nor does it entirely stop what might be called inter-school activities!

Harry circled the lawn clockwise, then he does a figure of eight and circles it anti-clockwise. Edwina on the telephone tells Diana that she may take Harry over to the school to see Alex, perhaps this Sunday.

But she drives there, as it happens, on a Friday in the rain, climbing up and over the Pennines, down to skirt Manchester, through Chester and across the border of Flintshire which is still in two pieces administered as one, as Harry says, until local government reorganisation takes place. She drives without Harry who is left to have tea and spend the night at the Dower House. She drives shortly after midday having met Stuart at the University and told him that today is not their day together after all.

There is a neat stone village of empty holiday homes which contains the school tuck shop. Then the road rises into low hills between dry-stone walls and drops into a flat valley where high on the right is the dark grey stone mass of the Army College, and on the left is the boundary wall of St Cecilia's, with hockey goal posts on wet mown grass glimpsed between trees. Girls in green gaberdine macintoshes straggle along the road in twos and threes turning their faces as the Mini passes. Sixth-formers wear their own clothes in the afternoons, but for walking on the road they must be distinguished from ordinary people by identifiable St Cecilia's green gaberdine.

Turning left into the drive you enter a cover of pine-trees dripping, and see through them the annexe which is the sanatorium where Alex waits in confinement until her mother arrives. But the instructions are first to drive on past here and up to the front door, and the promise is that Miss Rogers will be available at five o'clock.

"Nothing to worry about Mrs Measures-Smith," said the school secretary on the telephone last night.

The Mini is parked by the gothic-arched front door next to Miss Rogers' white sports car. The instructions were to wait in the vestibule until summoned to the study where Miss Rogers is now taking a Religious Studies tutorial.

"Alex is in good health, Mrs Measures-Smith. But Miss Rogers very much wishes you to come over at your earliest convenience."

From the polished vestibule where the seating is upholstered leather, the view is of dripping pines and shrubs through diamond panes.

"No. I promise you—no accident—nothing at all like that. Miss Rogers wished to speak to you herself, but unfortunately you must have been out when she rang this afternoon and she has an engagement this evening."

The vestibule has doors at either end. A group of first formers in green jerseys and pleated skirts run in fawn knee socks and brown strap shoes. They see Edwina and stop skipping and sliding on the polished floor, whisper to each other and pass on through the far door. Edwina lights a cigarette from a packet Stuart gave her in the University car park and puts the spent match back in the box. The ash she will have to drop into the scented geranium pot plant on the window sill. More and larger girls come through the vestibule, their green jerseys bulging and the pleats of their skirts distorted by larger hips. When they have gone Edwina tiptoes to the pot plant and taps the ash off her cigarette end on to the soil. Then she takes off her coat and sits down again.

The next group of girls are out of uniform but their skirts end at the stipulated four inches above the knee and some have billowing smocks or sleeveless pullovers over bright shirts. They have long brushed hair to their shoulders, neat tights and low heeled shoes. They carry, variously, bags of books, music cases, violins, guitars and woodwind instruments. Edwina waits for them to go by and puts more ash in the scented geranium. Before sitting down again she pulls at the zip of her velvet jeans, uselessly, because the strained metal teeth have buckled. She goes on waiting with her coat on again, clasping it tightly, hands in pockets to hold it across the fastening of her trousers.

"What do you think has happened to Alex?" said Stuart, holding her hand in the car park.

"God knows! I'm scared stiff. Perhaps she's pregnant."

"Poor kid. What will you do if she is?"

"God knows! Abortion?"

"Poor kid."

"It seems incredible if that's what it is, but I can't see why else they should have had to be all secretive about it on the phone."

"What did you want to send her to somewhere like that school for in the first place?"

"It just sort of happened. There wasn't anywhere near home Meredith would agree to, and Diana's daughter liked it. It didn't seem any worse than anywhere else of its kind. It's not bad really. And the music's very good."

"Music!"

"The choir has been on television."

"Television! What's that got to do with it?"

"Nothing. I know. I should never have let her go there."

"Perhaps she's very musical?"

"No. Not at all. She's fairly good at French."

In the vestibule when another group of girls have passed wearing red overalls for domestic science, Edwina creeps towards the heavy oak door, lifts the iron latch and steps outside to draw on the cigarette in the driveway under the wet pines. Then she bends to squash it half-smoked into the earth by the roots of a shrub rose in the weedless border.

"I'm really sorry about this afternoon."

"Drive carefully to North Wales, won't you. What's Alex like?"

"Alex," she said. "Alex? Difficult to say—like anyone of fifteen and not like anyone of fifteen. Like Alex. It's like you asking me what my own hands or feet are like, or what my own nose is like which I can't see very well."

The heat in the Headmistress's study comes from three radiators fully on and from a crackling coal fire in the brass grate. The carpet is thick, fitted and protected with scattered Indian rugs. The deep chairs are covered in dark green velvet and there are piles of cushions in every corner. There is a Bechstein grand piano along one wall and bank of stereo equipment and speakers along another.

On the expanse of the flat square desk is a silver-framed photograph of an army officer in battle dress, and a tortoise-shell inkstand. On the red leather-bound blotting pad rests a grey folder labelled "Measures-Smith, Alexandra". Behind the desk is a wall full of books from carpet to ceiling. *The Hypothetical Creator* can be spotted in bright flame-red cover on the top shelf not far from editions of Bonhoeffer and Teilhard de Chardin. Then there is a whole shelf of bibles ancient and modern, a life of Wesley and something by Monsignor Ronald Knox. Below that are lives of the great composers and a complete edition of *Grove's Dictionary of Music and Musicians*.

"I am sorry to have kept you waiting Mrs Measures-Smith ... a visit to the kitchens after the tutorial took longer than expected." Miss Rogers is tall with broad intelligent cheekbones and short upswept greying hair. She has a look of the 1940's but wears a grey-green cardigan suit of a length and style which is anything but dated. Before she came to St Cecilia's three years ago there was a full-length press photograph of her wearing a kaftan and long beads. The newspapers headlined her as "Back from the jungle and into the gymslip", and reported that she had worked with Dr Schweitzer in his leper colony after having been a University lecturer and, in her younger day, in M.I.5. The framed silver photograph on her desk she has described to the girls of the sixth form as "a very close friend I once had".

"Do take your coat off Mrs Measures-Smith. This room is usually very warm."

Jennifer Rogers, M.A., Ph.D., is now said to be fifty, and came to the school three years ago, young for the job, they said, but likely to bring St Cecilia's happily into and through the 1970's.

"We are near the kitchens and the boiler here, but I could put more on the fire if you are really cold."

At her first Speech Day Miss Rogers spoke clearly to the parents and said she would find her way gradually towards a method of dealing with their daughters somewhere agreeably between the extremes of necessary discipline and a desirable measure of freedom, a *via media*, she said, appropriate to the age and era. And for a start she let the sixth form wear their own clothes in the afternoons.

"Did you have a tiring drive over? I loathe those motorways. But Yorkshire is superbly various isn't it? I have some very good friends in York ... I always go for the Festival ... I wonder if they have done the right thing for the Minster, though ..."

Miss Rogers, they all said, heralded a new era, except for the Out Crowd who called her "Roger" at once.

"... all that lightening and brightening and gold-leaf ... a rather over-optimistic gesture, don't you think? But of course the Bishop justifies ..."

The Out Crowd say she is only interested in daughters of the rich and of University Professors and that she once made the mother of a scholarship girl cry. But she is not unsmiling across the desk as she opens the grey file in front of her, leans forward and says, "And now Mrs Measures-Smith, we do have something of a problem with Alex."

Distant voices and feet in corridors mix with the sound of crockery and cutlery from the kitchen and dining-room. Miss Rogers leans her elbows on the desk: "Do you know I really do like Alex? You can't help liking Alex in all sorts of ways." She talks out across the desk into the room as if all the soft chairs were full; her voice is deadened by the carpets and cushions as much as by the rain on the diamond window panes. Alex, she says, is witty and not stupid by any means. But Alex, she says, does, as they all do at that age, make rather a play of what she thinks is cynicism...

They said, when she came, "You can say anything to Miss Rogers." They liked the way she let them play guitars at musical evenings and she even promised them a jazz group and a pop concert and a joint dance with the Army College.

She gets up now from behind her desk and walks round the room, arms folded. She walks like this on the stage at Speech Day, turning to the audience to emphasise a thought, but is as capable of stony stillness in Chapel when she reads annually the opening passage of the Gospel of St John. "Are you *sure* you are not cold Mrs Measures-Smith? I can easily put some more coal on the fire."

"No. Not at all. Go on about Alex please."

"Alex," says Miss Rogers. "Yes, Alex." She has Alex's form for religious studies, and Alex, like so many of them proclaims her atheism, expecting a surprised reaction.

The jazz group got going, but not the pop concert, and the joint dance with the Army College was held once and not again. At her second Speech Day Miss Rogers talked about parental responsibility and muscular Christianity as a bastion against the world. And at her third she said they should all be frightened of the world the girls were going into.

"Cynicism as they call it is such old hat these days.

Questioning values, questioning everything, it's all been done before. Ah yes, people say, but along with this cynicism in this generation goes love and kindness and communication within the peer group such as we have never known. That may be, but..."

More running feet in corridors, more rattles from the kitchen. It must be from there that the smell creeps into the study of something which could be cabbage boiling and sausages frying in meat dripping. Miss Rogers moves, cool in her cardigan and silk shirt and leans against the window frame.

"The boy thing is so irrelevant, so trivial, exaggerated beyond..."

"The boy thing?"

"I'm sorry. I was leaping on ... we'll come to that."

The collar of Edwina's fur coat is beginning to stick to the back of her neck. She could, perhaps, while Miss Rogers is at the window, slip her arms out of her coat and lay it across her knee. But Miss Rogers turns: "The mistake we've made is to believe that love and kindness and communication make up for loss of faith and discipline, that 'love thy neighbour' is all that's needed..."

"But the boy thing, you were saying," begins Edwina, but stops and raises her head before her sweat shows on the velvet chair, pushes her coat sleeves up her arms, unwraps the coat from stomach and leans forward to hide the gaping zip, and breathes deeply, while Miss Rogers paces in the room and says how only people who believe blindly in the goodness of human nature can agree to allow children choice in education.

Deep breathing brings the kitchen fumes of meat and cabbage more strongly to the lungs. So breathe gently and find value in cool places, the University car park in the rain, Stuart's wet fringe, the lawn at Hodsworth, Harry on his bicycle with the wind moving in his hair. Never mind the boy thing now; we will come to that, Miss Rogers said.

"It's not enough, Mrs Measures-Smith. Mrs Measures-Smith, it's not enough. Liberal education, freedom of choice and loving kindness is not enough!" and Miss Rogers pushes her right fist into her left hand to emphasise and trap her point. "Children must be told. Told to believe in something. Told what to look for in the world to reinforce beliefs, *told* what the world contains, not left to find it ..."

Harry bicycles out of sight, Stuart walks back up the hill to the lecture block. The thing is to forget all food, to pretend that the smell is something else, or, like how to play Risk without minding, pretend this nose, these lungs, are breathing on behalf of someone else.

"That's why we are here. Why St Cecilia's is here, to make them see, to tell them. That is why we have to offer excellence, shining excellence. My best dream, Mrs Measures-Smith, is that a child will one day say: 'That thing is excellent and therefore I must learn it'."

Breathe evenly and inhale for someone else. Breathe for Alex, who must smell the kitchen every day. Did Alex go to Matron and say: this smell made me feel faint and sick and therefore I may be pregnant.

Back by the window Miss Rogers has thought better of shining excellence, it seems, and calls St Cecilia's a source of excellence. A source of excellence for a few. "Elitism is a dirty word today, but there have to be some strong and excellent people, Mrs Measures-Smith, to ward off the threat of insipidity," and she talks of massive grey areas of the world where excellence is spread so thin as to have disappeared altogether, where more means worse and where Edwina breathes for Alex in the sanatorium in the pines and for Harry on his bicycle.

Miss Rogers wonders if she is being too simplistic and breaks into words like seminal, probity, didactic and eclecticism, and then turns to the room and to freedom as a concept, to great brains at work on this and to girls who, without instruction, think they know about it.

Breathe and listen and think of girls reporting to Matron in surgery, and mothers red in the face in Miss Rogers' huge soft chair, believing, without instruction, that they are also pregnant.

"As well," Miss Rogers says, "to omit to tell a crawling baby that the fire is hot, or never put a puppy on the lead, as to let girls find the world the way they see it. Because the world will use them, Mrs Measures-Smith. My message to them this term is that what the world contains..."

Considering the broken zip and considering the nausea, it would seem that the world will contain next autumn two prams on the lawn at Hodsworth or on Meredith's new terrace instead of a wedding feast, in one the child of an Army Apprentice and in the other the child of a Master of Education. Or there will be two abortions.

"My worst dream, Mrs Measures-Smith, is that not one child will listen to us, but they will all wander out..."

But babies are rare and conception barely possible, and the nausea nothing but that which stems from a nauseous smell. Conception has occurred only twice with Meredith and never, however careless, with anyone else. And it was nice to be able to say to Stuart in the spare-room that there was no risk, no risk at all, and to hear him saying, "Your child and mine! Something rather rare!" But he must never know and that's for certain, if the only child of his loins should be extracted from the womb in embryo and discarded in a sterile bin.

Words coming from the direction of the window are no longer concepts and abstractions but illustrations of how the rejection of traditional values and the use of misinterpreted freedom will result in hordes of grey-faced people harassed by extremists left and right: "Shuffling elderly teenagers," Miss Rogers says, "waiting to be mown down, undedicated to anything but each other, vast groups of them..."

Stuart's child would have pale eyes like him; it would be born probably in November. Miss Rogers walks across the room and carries her prophecies to behind her desk where she lifts Alex's grey file and, looking at it as if it were a crystal ball, admits, still looking at it, that she would rather, yes much rather, send out of the sixth form a dedicated Marxist than a sweet-faced girl who will follow the first boy out there who talks of kindness, love, and drifts away with her.

Stuart's child would have ... Miss Rogers puts down the file and regards the potential mother of that child, pale and with beads of perspiration on her forehead, and apologises for going on so long. Edwina stares. The thing to do, and the thing that must be done, is to take Miss Rogers' place at the window. Not to hurry there, but walk there slowly as if considering the argument, and opening it, swinging the casement into damp Welsh mountain air. To open the mouth to offer actual comment on what has been said would be to vomit.

Behind her, someone who is still Miss Rogers goes on talking, describing yet again the world as she sees it as of overwhelmingly deep concern for those with children or with responsibility for the future, as if anyone exists without such responsibility, she adds. What the world contains, she says, is nothing until you face that responsibility. No joy exists until that is absorbed and understood, but she still apologises for going on so long. Her message is disturbing these days she knows, her views may sound obsessive, but what with one thing and with another....

"But children today look prettier and more innocent than ever," Edwina says faintly from the open window. "And love and kindness are not to be sneezed at surely." Which comment Miss Rogers does not even concern herself to answer, but mentions Alex's name again.

The kaftan and the beads and the talk of measured freedom that first Speech Day were as nothing. The cardigan suit and the Italian shoes are simply stylish accessories to a different kind of greyness. Only the well-dressed can combat the menace to the vast shuffling groups she mentioned earlier who wear T-shirts, jeans and gymshoes and throw their green gaberdines away. "Elitism," Miss Rogers said one Speech Day, "is not in question. We dismiss it as a topic because we see it as irrelevant. It only is a concept used as a weapon by the other side. Remember all of you that it is an epithet not worth worrying about."

It would seem that Miss Rogers is now asking if Alex ever smokes.

"I've known her to."

"Ordinary cigarettes?"

"Cheap cigarettes I would say."

"Are you all right, Mrs Measures-Smith? Can I get you a cup of tea?"

"No thank you."

Sitting on the edge of the chair now, she hears Miss Rogers explain that they instituted a search throughout the school for some missing money and found a cigarette in Alex's desk which immediately aroused their suspicions, but not about the money of course. They have not had it analysed, but they showed it to the Colonel of the Army College who knows about these things and he is sure that it is no ordinary cigarette. They have asked Alex herself what it is and where she got it but she has not as yet chosen to speak upon the matter. They have been lucky so far at St Cecilia's as far as drugs are concerned. But this could be the thin end of the wedge and so, unfortunately, some action had to be taken in this case.

Stuart's baby would live in a house with a number, play football in the park in winter, and in the summer go fishing with his father.

The Colonel seemed to think that, since the cigarette had not been smoked, there would be no need to bring the police in on this. The Colonel, whom Edwina may have met on Speech Days, is highly responsible of course and an extremely nice man and nothing about Alex or the cigarette will go further than the school gates. Meanwhile, perhaps it would be better...

"I'll fetch Alex then. Is her trunk packed?"

"Yes, but first wouldn't you like a drink or a cup of ..."

"I'll fetch her then..."

"I discussed this with all the staff. We all agreed the measure was not too strong..."

"I'll go then..." It will be dark and wet and they will stop for food and drink if such things can be faced, on the other side of Chester.

"And we'll be in touch before next term. I'm sorry that..."

"Just as long as no one thinks she stole the money..."

"You can depend on that. Please don't misunderstand me, Mrs Measures-Smith, this ..."

She walks beside Edwina and talks along the corridors clearly for all to hear about the new Science Block which is scheduled for next spring, past the kitchen and the dining-room while Edwina walks facing ahead, hands in pockets, coat still clutched around her. Zips break after all, zips do break. She hears Miss Rogers talking still, even after she has started the engine of the Mini to drive through the pines to the sanatorium.

"Of *course* I didn't smoke it."

They drive in the wet fast towards Chester, the Mini swaying with the weight of Alex's trunk in the back.

"I'd had it for ages—in my knicker drawer and most of the grass had fallen out of it. I was going to sell it to someone in the sixth form but she hadn't saved up enough money. Simon gave it to me last summer. He smokes but I didn't like the smell. Actually it's probably stale by now and lost its power or whatever it had."

They face east and skirt Manchester to get on to the M.62 which takes you over the Pennines. On the motorway Edwina drives steadily into the rain and sees signs coming up telling her that this is the way north west to Carlisle and the Lake District. "Fuck!"

"Can we stop for fish and chips."

"No."

They leave the motorway driving down a side road which takes them back towards Manchester and into busy traffic and flashing lights in suburbs.

"Thanks ever so much for coming and fetching me. I'd no idea I'd get expelled. Everyone reckoned that it would be suspension until next term and that they'd give me work to do at home."

The road back to the motorway is fast, a dark dual carriageway. The Mini accelerates north-east again with the windscreen wipers working. Then it bumps and grinds and comes to rest on the edge of the grass verge. "Fuck."

"I was expelled, wasn't I?"

"Get out and thumb someone down to help us change this tyre."

It will be after midnight when they get home. Edwina put a hot water bottle in Alex's bed before leaving this morning, and filled the boiler with enough fuel to give them baths tonight. She switched on a heater in Alex's room and locked all the doors of the house. Tomorrow she will fetch Harry from Diana's and tell Diana something of what happened today. It may be Monday before Stuart will telephone and learn something more of what happened, but not everything.

Alex stood in the rain, her thumb pointing in the air and her green school gaberdine over her head. The first thing to stop was a heavy truck whose driver got out and took the rusty jack from Edwina. As he fitted it into the slot by which it lifts the Mini, they both noticed that his oily hand had three fingers missing. "How did you lose your fingers?" Alex asked.

"Changing a tyre on a car. It slipped off the jack."

They stopped again on the motorway. Edwina drank coffee and Alex worked the slot machine; coins and tokens poured into her hands and were stuffed into the pockets of her gaberdine. "I was expelled, wasn't I? I saw you drive up to the school, but you were hours with Roger. What on earth was he on about all that time?"

"What's in the world and so on."

"Oh that old thing. She was practising for Speech Day I expect," said Alex, and went on talking about the man with a thumb and only one finger on his right hand and about other disfigurements she knew about.

Chapter 6

To WAKE UP in the morning in a four-poster bed is to see the two end pillars like uprights of a goal mouth beyond your feet. This is the view of the world first thing in the morning, the pillars occupying the view to the left and the view to the right, the left hand and the right, on this hand and on the other hand. To have moved to the spare-room and to be occupying the bed on your own is to lie in the middle of it, equi-distant from the foot-end of the fluted mahogany pillars.

Soon Harry will appear, as he does every morning, in his yellow pyjamas to ask, as he has every morning for the last three weeks, why you are sleeping in the spare-room. He usually sits on the end of the bed between the pillars, but one morning he stood, arms outstretched, to see if his left hand could touch the left pillar while his right hand was holding the right pillar.

When he is sent to wake up Alex he jumps off the bed and is heard across the floor of the spare-room and the boards of the landing, opening Alex's door and telling her exactly how many minutes his watch says before she must leave. Then Alex is heard in the bathroom and then going downstairs, then in the kitchen. Then she shouts up the stairs that she is going, and there is another five minutes in which you can lie half-awake and hear Alex push the bicycle across the cattle-grid and know, dozing, that Harry is dressing. There may be a further five minutes after that of real sleep still to come. Turn on your right side and hear Diana say, "You're not sending Alex to the *High* School? Surely? She'll have a terrible time there. Have you written to Meredith about it?" So turn to your left side and hump into the pillows where you hear Stuart saying, as he has said on a Wednesday afternoon in this same bed, "Christine said the other day that from what she's heard on the grapevine about that school she wouldn't send kids there if we had them." But remember that Alex went off whistling across the drive this morning and said yesterday that it's best at Hodsworth High to keep quiet about yourself when you are new. Only about a third of her form come from East Hodsworth and know the sort of house she lives in; the others will only get curious if she draws attention to herself, so she's saying nought, she says, or playing it very cool like any other new scene. Luckily, she says, people at the High don't know about titles and that, and wouldn't understand her mother's Honourable if they read about it.

Stuart said: "Well anything would be better than that loony and elitist place from which you rescued her."

"Elitist, I agree, but not entirely loony."

The High School is on the far side of West Hodsworth, set in rolling greensward, in a white building which stretches out wing after wing on top of a hill, concrete and plate glass reflecting the sun. Nor is there a single elderly shuffling teenager to be seen in the central hall of it which reaches up to the roof with open stairs climbing to class-rooms up a high wall decorated with an abstract design in deep red and green mosaic tiles.

Stuart said: "And at least it sounds as if Alex will remain unharassed by left and right extremists."

"Of course she will."

Also in the central hall a fountain plays, surrounded by ferns and foliage, and there is a signpost which shows visitors and new pupils the way to the Theatre, the Concert Hall and the swimming pool. There is also, Alex says, a Sports Hall with trampolines and badminton offered among other choices of physical education. Out of doors you can put the shot or throw the javelin or do track events like they do in the Olympics. A track suit is not compulsory but it would be great to have one.

Getting Alex in to the school was as easy as making an appointment with a dentist or an optician. The Headmaster's study is like an executive suite with fitted carpets, more ferns, charts and time-tables on the wall next to his framed degree from Oxford. He has four telephones on the desk and four secretaries in outer offices.

Alex says the work is dead easy but you must not do too much of it in case you get labelled as a swot. The laboratories are fabulous, especially the biology one where there's a moving diagram of a baby being born. A boy and girl in her biology division had a baby last year; the girl says it's not as easy as it looks on the diagram.

Between the pillars of the four-poster turn from left to right and left again before getting up in the morning. After all today is Friday. Drive to the Dower House half an hour after Alex has left for the High School, stand in the wind with the car door open to let Diana's Matthew climb in beside Harry. Shut the door, drop back to the village, drive through it and on to the motorway in growing wind and under swinging pylon cables. The smoke from the massed funnels of the power station is carried east this morning and the radio has warned pantechnicons and heavy vehicles to keep off the motorway.

The west wind began two days ago by blowing down two beech trees in the avenue. Men from Robert's farm were dragging branches off the road with a tractor when Stuart arrived, and the spare-room sash windows rattled all the afternoon. The electric power was cut; bed was for huddling in while twigs blew against the window.

And today it is still blowing dust off the dry fields and across the windscreen. The steering wheel must be firmly grasped. She stays on the inside lane behind an open truck stacked with bales of paper bound in sacking, torn at by the wind so that fragments of newsprint flap like old flags flying.

Two days ago they sat up in the four-poster in sweaters. They warmed their hands on cups of tea before touching each other. He said it was like having breakfast in bed together, very domestic and cosy and tucked away from the elements. She said that the way it struck her as that Omnipotent God was banging at the window.

"I thought it was all over between you and Omnipotent God."

"It never is, is it?"

"Let's have Omnipotent Man for a change."

"What about Omnipotent Woman?"

"All right then. Man including woman. Or, if you like, Man embracing Woman."

"I like that, but call it man embracing woman embracing man."

On Wednesday last, man embraced woman who in turn embraced man, both being in the four-poster raised out of the draught. And on Friday, with only four hours until he arrives again, she drives behind the truck with torn shreds of paper blowing and getting stuck on her windscreen wipers. She switches on the wipers and the shreds dislodge and get swept across the road under the wheels of overtaking cars.

"Edwina?"

"Yes."

"Are you happy?"

"Yes."

"Not worried about anything?"

"Not a thing except Meredith coming back next Tuesday and the holidays after that when I shan't see you."

After he left a pantechnicon blew over and slid into the paddock fence. The furnishings of a house in South Shields which were being moved to Derby spilled on to the grass verge. The driver who had a broken arm and his mate who was bleeding from the head were taken away by the ambulance, but the pantechnicon stayed there for twenty-four hours with its buckled doors gaping open and an upright grand piano and a double bed pushed on to the grass verge.

"The day you went to fetch Alex ..."

"What about that day?"

115

"You were going to come round the University with me. I wanted to show you those terrace houses they are knocking down."

"I'll see them another day."

It took a crane to get the pantechnicon upright and a team of men to stack the furniture ready for collection by another pantechnicon. Harry, yesterday after school, sat on the fence watching them in the freezing wind. Today he says on his way to school that perhaps another truck or removal van will be blown over. But today the tallest vehicles are parked in the Service Area behind the transport café just before you leave the motorway to take him along the road to the gate of his school.

"Those houses," said Stuart on Wednesday. "Made for us."

"For us?"

"I never thought about choosing houses until now. Christine has always chosen where we live."

"So did Meredith."

"It was always easier in the end to say yes."

"But always possible to say no."

"The story of my life."

"And mine."

Today it will be warmer since the power is on and the electric fire waiting in the spare-room because that is where she sleeps these days and will go on sleeping. "The only way to say no without actually saying it."

"You shouldn't do that on my behalf," he said.

"It isn't on your behalf, but on mine."

He went on talking about the terrace of houses near the University, kids playing in the road. "Not ours," she said.

"Oh we'd have at least five."

"In that case thank God this is a fantasy.'

He stopped talking about houses and talked about the concrete future such as whether he would persuade Christine to stay in Yorkshire, and if so, whether he would get a grant for more post-graduate study, and if not . . .

"Stuart..."

"Yes?"

"The day I fetched Alex..."

"Yes?"

"There was a moment, but it's over now. It was fantasy like the rest."

"What was it?"

"I wouldn't be telling you if it hadn't turned out to be fantasy, luckily."

"Tell me."

When he went home on Wednesday she followed him down in the roaring gale to his car. "Why wouldn't you have told me, if it hadn't turned out to be fantasy?" he asked.

"It would have been my problem, not yours." She went into the house and put coke on the boiler which was glowing white hot in the down draught far in excess of Meredith's instructions.

"And why luckily?" said Stuart.

Sometimes on Fridays he rings up in the morning to say what time he will be arriving, especially if he is going to be late. He has a two-hour seminar in the morning, but this is an optional sitting-in on undergraduate discussion, and he only takes up the option when the topic discussed touches on the subject of his thesis, which concerns broadly and in general the disadvantaged pupil, but for which a considered and particular title has not yet been given.

But this morning he will not consider the option, having promised to take Christine to the optician and get her back in time for afternoon school. She already has reading spectacles but needs new ones. Also, since she is learning to drive, he believes she needs driving spectacles as well as reading ones. She is very bad at dealing with people like opticians and dentists, nervous he supposes, so he has always taken her to appointments, and will do until she has learnt to drive. He is also teaching her to drive; they can be seen sometimes on Sunday in quiet lanes; each lesson he says ends in tears, and, if they could afford it he would send her to a driving school.

This Friday the visit to the optician may include a driving lesson if there is time. Edwina stands in the study near the telephone and sees that the wind is still high by watching the plantation trees around the Dower House bending. Then she sits on the chaise-longue opposite the mantelpiece where cards from Meredith have been arranged by Harry in order of their arrival from Rome, Athens, Istanbul, Bombay, Hong Kong and Singapore.

When the telephone rings it is Diana to say that her Range Rover is still at the garage, although promised for this afternoon, so can Edwina fetch Harry and Matthew from school?

"No. Sorry, Diana. Friday is always hopeless for me."

"Yes. I've noticed. Why, if one may ask?"

"I'm ... I'm ... waiting for a telephone call for Meredith —very important—so that I can tell him ... give him the message directly he comes home. Business."

"Can't they ring through to his office?"

"No. His secretary is off ill and this is an international call and highly confidential. Let's get a taxi for the boys from school this afternoon."

"Are you all right, Edwina?"

"Yes. Fine."

"It's a long time for you to be alone, I always say to Robert."

At lunchtime Edwina stands in the hall outside the study and sees through the glass panels of the front door and between the pillars outside it the tractor towing a trailer of sawn-up branches from the two trees blown down in Wednesday's gale. Half an hour later she stands in the kitchen where a jug of coffee and two cups are laid out and two cans of beer were taken from the fridge this morning.

Again from the study window she sees the plantation trees still bending but against a darker-clouded sky, the lawn a deeper green and the patch of mauve and yellow crocuses, although nearly over now, stand out purple and orange. Nearer the house a clump of daffodils still in bud lean towards the motorway.

At first lift the receiver of the telephone only to make sure it is working and can receive calls. Then dial Stuart's number in case he has called in at home on the way. Dial it again fifteen minutes later and then at intervals of ten minutes. Across on the mantelpiece the latest postcards from Meredith to Harry are of Sydney Harbour and of an hotel in Wellington, New Zealand. On the back he wrote that it was very hot and that he had been swimming in the Pacific Ocean and that he hopes Harry will travel here one day when he is a man.

Large raindrops splash on to the french windows. The daffodil stalks lean towards the house; the wind must have gone round to the south-west. Switching on the lamp on the mantelpiece, Edwina gets out the telephone directory and looks up the number for the University. The lamp also shines on Meredith's latest postcard to Alex, forwarded from St Cecilia's. He wrote that he hoped she was being good at school and working hard; he told her that it was very hot and he had been swimming in the sea and that he would be home before she broke up for the holidays.

With Sydney Harbour bridge spanning bright blue water across the room Edwina dials the Student Health Centre and hears that they have no patient by the name of Douglas and who is asking for him please? Under the bridge, with white bow wave, curving up against the waters of the harbour goes a speed boat. In the distance is a three-funnelled liner and beyond that the shell shapes of the new Opera House.

The Education Department can only take messages for students and put them on a board in the foyer. If it is urgent they suggest a call to student flats or any of the boarding houses.

She leaves the study and the telephone and looks out of the kitchen window from where you can see the south-bound traffic. Perhaps if he was still giving Christine a driving lesson it would be possible to spot his yellow car. But Learner Drivers cannot go on motorways. So wait in the study, walk in the hall, sometimes in the spare-room from which window you can see cars coming up the avenue.

"How," she asked him on Wednesday, "can Christine be so sharp at choosing homes for you and yet be afraid of opticians, dentists and driving instructors?"

"Perhaps," he said, "because I've always done those things for her."

"And she hasn't had what you would call the advantages I have?"

"You said that. Not me."

The rain buckets down and runs to the side of the drive. It pours over the empty plinth in the middle of the circle of grass and gets cupped in the hole where a statue would be fixed. Three-thirty is always the time Stuart leaves, half an hour before Harry comes in and a whole hour before Alex. In the study Edwina makes a stack of the postcards, shuffles them and arranges them in order again.

Alex puts her wet school satchel in a corner of the kitchen and stands with the rain dripping off her anorak; her tights and knee-length boots and her mini grey school skirt are soaked.

"How long have you been here?"

"Just come in."

"You're early aren't you?"

Alex takes her anorak off slowly and hangs it over the back of a wooden kitchen chair. She goes to the fridge and takes out a bottle of milk and pours some into one of the glasses next to the beer cans on the table.

"What's the beer for?"

"Why did they let you out early today?"

Alex finds a biscuit out of a tin and leans over the table reading the newspaper which has lain there unopened all the day.

bedside table. Hear Alex talking in the evening through television programmes and a can of beer.

She'd seen it coming for a long time—ever since she started at the school three weeks ago. Even her friends—well not friends really, but the people she went around with, said she'd have to have it sometime before the end of term. So she had played it very cool and kept away from the Janice gang who had it in for her. She kept in crowds in the corridor, moved from room to room for lessons with other forms, never been on her own. She'd used staff toilets when no one was looking—that was a slant no one else had thought of. The Janice gang used to wait by the fourth year girls' toilet, so Alex would never use it. All that gave her quite a few days' grace. And it was probably that which drove the Janice gang to fight in public.

Diana rang up again in the evening: "Have you completely burnt your boats, or rather Alex's boats at St Cecilia's? I mean, as you have said, she *may* only have been suspended. Shall *I* have a word with Miss Rogers?"

"I wrote telling Miss Rogers that Alex was withdrawn from the school. That is that as far as St Cecilia's is concerned."

"Oh dear. Oh dear. I do feel for you, Edwina."

Alex said that being brayed in the Sports Hall made it very difficult for people to sneak away like they could in corridors. People *do* sneak away at brayings, naturally not wanting to get involved; anyone would if they could. If you join in like as not it will be you that gets it next time. But in the Sports Hall this afternoon when Janice and three others came at her behind the trampoline end, everyone stayed. Quite a few watched, cheering and that.

"I was saying to Robert how brave you were about it all, but he pointed out that it is one thing being brave on one's own behalf, but quite another thing being brave on one's children's behalf."

Alex said over the beer that it was really weird. Really weird that suddenly it only counts how strong you are and having long nails and wondering how long you can stand your hair being pulled and at what point it will come out at the roots. Things that counted at St Cecilia's don't count any more, not that you'd expect them to would you? At St Cecilia's you could impress some people simply because your mother was an Hon. and all that. Or by having an aunt who was divorced and living in sin, until Alberta actually married Bruce, that was. Or having a photo of Simon who everyone thought was dishy. Or, if you were feeling unpopular you could always try and do well in some subject like French and get at least *someone* smiling at you.

Diana said: "Do watch Alex carefully won't you? Delayed shock can be so traumatic."

At Hodsworth High, said Alex, opening the second can of beer, they think that just because you aren't going out with a boy you are soft or scared. It's no good being seen talking to boys; you have to be going out with one, officially. And it's better if it's one from the school so it can be seen to be official, like Susan and Mal which has been official for ages, since half-term Susan says.

"Thank goodness for your sake, Edwina, that Meredith will be back next week."

Susan who came to Alex's rescue in the Sports Hall really did the thing for Alex; they both fought together. Susan is fantastically strong, five foot ten and forty inch hips. She'd been brayed years ago and no one dares come near her anymore. She just waded in and pulled Janice and the others off, while Miss Aykroyd the games teacher was having hysterics and running for help from more staff. Susan says what sparked it off was Janice seeing Alex talking to Chunkey Thornton who used to go out with Janice but officially finished it last week. No one in their right mind would go out with Chunkey Thorton anyway. Susan thinks it was Chunkey, who lives in East Hodsworth, who told Janice, who lives in West Hodsworth, what sort of house Alex lives in. Chunkey set it up, as it were, maybe because Alex, who could be said to be an East Hodsworth girl, wouldn't go out with him. But you never know. You never know—Susan says everyone gets brayed; it's just something you have to go through.

In the very early morning before Alex's alarm clock goes off, the four posts gain shape, cease to be shadows round the bed. Turn to the left where Stuart used to lie, and may lie again. Nothing has officially finished. But then nothing officially began. You have to be seen together, Alex says, and not only in school for it to be considered official. Sometimes people write to each other and fix it up, or pass notes in class to finish it; the girl and boy in biology who had a baby finished the other day in chemistry, (but he still goes round to her mother's and takes the baby out for walks).

Turn away from Stuart's side of the bed and sleep again. Wake up to find Alex gone and Harry with letters in his hand saying it is time for him to be taken to school. The letter with the East Hodsworth postmark may be like a note passed in class:

Forgive me. Things catch up on me. I love you. Miserable day in the rain. C wanted to do shopping as well as optician as well as driving lesson. Got her back to school late. But I mind about letting you down and will ring as soon as possible.

And are there cans of beer still in the fridge?

It strikes me that man embracing woman embracing man also embraces so many other things that I can't give you. This struck me forcibly when it started to rain this afternoon and I was in a traffic jam and C was panicking about being late. But you can never say to someone else get out and walk, can you?

Chapter 7

HARRY STANDS IN his royal blue anorak in the late afternoon low sun with a pair of binoculars pointing at a
Citroën which he says must be going to Scotland because
it has Perthshire number plates. It is followed by a Rover
which has come from Buckinghamshire. The next one is a
Fiat; he is not sure where it comes from, so he will have
to fetch the AA book and check.

"Harry. Are you coming to the station with me this
evening to meet Daddy?"

"Is Northampton the county town of Northampton-
shire? Is Daddy coming home today?"

Alex eating a sandwich in the kitchen is dropping
crumbs where Mrs Thwaite has swept and washed. "Does
it matter, by the way, if I don't come to the station? I'm
going out with Susan. Is that all right?"

"Yes, but be back by half past nine."

"Daddy doesn't even know I'm at home, does he?"

"I'm not sure whether he will have got my letter."

"So you'll be telling him when he gets home?"

"Yes I suppose so."

"What do you think he will say?"

"We'll see."

"He won't say that."

Harry reads from the AA book that there are two four-
star hotels in Southampton and two in Northampton. Alex
says it would be difficult to put off going out with Susan
now, because Susan is not on the telephone. And Susan
can't get out very often because she has to stay to look
after her sisters and brothers and the baby. Harry says
that you would have thought that Southampton would be

a county town like Northampton but Winchester is the county town of Hampshire and not Southampton. But Southampton has more AA hotels in it than does Northampton even though Northampton is a county town.

Edwina clears the table and puts used cups and plates in the sink. Alex says it is difficult with Susan because Susan has a bad scene at home with a stepfather and mother out at work. She says she will be back at half-nine without fail and that is a promise. That is all right isn't it? Isn't it? She'd forgotten about Daddy coming back. No one had said much about it really. "You look nice in that coat."

"Oh thanks. You've seen it hundreds of times."

"Susan thinks you look nicer than most people's mothers ... younger too. Has ... has Daddy seen that coat?"

"Is your bicycle light working Alex?"

"Yes. I got new batteries, for both front and rear, as you suggested."

The station used to have a curved canopy roof of glass set in wrought iron like Waterloo or Paddington or Kings Cross. At dusk such stations echo with people hurrying under the canopy, with steam shunting and porters pushing luggage trucks on metal wheels. People departing or arriving, carrying things, shaking hands, kissing, coats over arms and suitcases in hands. There was a smell of steam, slamming of doors, waving and whistles of guards.

The old station had a curved canopy arched above like a rainbow. In that sort of station you greeted people you had been waiting for, or you left from it excited about the meeting you would have at the other end. In those covered, light, dirty places there were platforms jutting out into the fresh air for exceptionally long trains.

Homecomings have been exceptionally good, with Alex dancing on the platform, Harry held in arms, presents and surprises and news exchanged. Meredith, then, tanned from foreign parts drove them home chatting, thrilled with what he had been doing and what they had been doing and how they had been growing. In the past, home-coming good humour lasted for a week or more.

Not that anyone is suggesting for a moment, in the flat new grey station where the trains are diesel and the porters' uniforms changed, that the removal of the glass canopy has the remotest connection with the arrival of Meredith on this last day of March.

In the new station you park underground and an elevator takes you to platform level, into the main concourse where the floor is of ribbed rubber tiles and a closed circuit television tells you which trains have arrived or departed from which platforms. Warm air blows through swing plate-glass doors to the street outside. You walk quietly, not raising your voice, between people doing the same—over there by the café, or there by the newspaper stall, or outside the tobacconist's.

On the way to the station Harry said that, whereas East and West Hodsworth are clearly divided by having fields between, you can't tell in a city whether you are in this suburb or that suburb. How do people know which bit of a city they live in? Perhaps, said Edwina, when they get a letter with their address on it. What a silly answer. Daddy will know. Daddy will also know how many miles he has been round the world in the two months, that is actually sixty-three days, he has been away. Which is longer than Guy Rochdale's father and mother who went away for two weeks' ski-ing and three weeks to the West Indies this term, but they came back in between, so it does not really count.

The urban clearway is raised high over confused suburbs where people have to discover by post where they live, and cars look down on small streets, empty streets where people who have come home in the rush hour are having tea.

Harry will tell Meredith about Northampton, South-ampton, Citroëns from Perthshire and Rovers from Buckingham. Meredith will tell Harry about Istanbul, Athens,

Rome and Bombay. Above the clearway are green lit-up signs in a sky of no colour. Lights on stalks bend over by tall office buildings. Drive easily with not many cars at this hour. Flash indicator that you are leaving the clearway, go down to the roundabout, take the road to the station which passes under the railway bridge. Outside the station wait until the green light flashes which tells you that you may enter the underground car park.

Harry takes coins for the platform tickets. He reaches up to the red machine, head back he studies the closed circuit television. He leads the way to the barrier, shows the tickets and looks in the eye of the man who lets him through. Edwina follows him through the barrier and along the platform. She tells him not to stand too near the edge, but positions herself back in the doorway of the Ladies' Waiting Room.

There is not much waiting to be done. The digital clock moves to 18.45, the train which is due at this minute appears around the bend of the platform, soundlessly. In its passing windows people are getting up from seats and lifting suitcases down from racks. Harry stands carefully watching all the carriages marked First Class and Smoking; at one of these he points and jumps, then he runs beside the moving train, weaving through porters and passengers in his Clarks sandals like a dashing Rugby forward heading for touch-down. While his mother stands, hands in fur coat pockets, holding the coat tightly round her.

Over there, dividing his attention between Harry and the luggage-porters, standing between the door of the carriage he got out of and the Guards Van, is Meredith, a tall broad-shouldered man with curly hair and horn-rimmed spectacles who puts down the briefcase he is carrying and puts out his large hands to hold his son under the arms and lift him from the ground. And put him down again on the platform in order to be able to pick up the briefcase again.

Tall, broad-shouldered, curly-haired. Or heavy, with

receding frizzy grey hair. Genial, you would say at this distance across the platform. Expansive it would seem at this arrival—almost jolly. A man who talks on trains and at board meetings. An upstanding, jolly, genial, expansive man who talks on trains and lifts his son in the air when he gets off them. Or a heavy tired man with receding frizzy grey hair, grey suit and polished black shoes, who puts his head back when he laughs and whose mouth stays open after the laugh has finished, whose gestures look large, but in whom small mannerisms of subtlety have failed to develop. The talents he lacks are on the small side. Talks in trains and at board meetings and not much elsewhere. Is good in stations, walks confidently, a huge mass of travelling Meredith with porters pushing a trolley of his suitcases, camera over shoulder, briefcase in one hand, Harry's hand in the other. Towards Edwina comes a processing wide-load of Meredith and what is Meredith's from the other side of the world and of the platform.

Clumsy, but not entirely insensitive, he notices her in the doorway of the Ladies' Waiting Room. Perhaps she was the first thing he noticed when the train pulled in. Just as he turns pages of reports and reconstructs from words on paper the circumstances and conditions of a business firm, he operates towards Edwina the same constructing glance, and observes his wife standing, reads the evidence of her positioning and knows immediately how she wishes to be greeted. Which is not to be greeted at all.

All he need say is "All right?"

All she need say is "Harry spotted you then?" and follow the procession of man, child, porter and luggage along the platform under the flat unarched roof.

There has to be some acknowledgement of the sixty-three days and ten or so countries and that this is not the end of an ordinary working day. Supper in the dining-room, food somewhat special, but to include egg and chips which is Harry's favourite and will ensure that he stays at the table which is laid for three and not two. When Harry wants to go and watch television say, "What a good programme it is, and let us all watch it."

Harry kept talking all the way home and talks throughout the cooking and the eating.

"How's Alex?" Meredith asks.

"Fine."

Harry's present from India occupies the centre of the table, a brass replica of the Taj Mahal which plays a metallic Raga.

"Let's see ... when does she break up from school?"

"Let's see—today's Tuesday, isn't it? By the way your stones have come for the terrace." Lift the roof of the Taj Mahal and watch the revolving brass cylinder pick at tin notes with spikes; let Harry play it through supper and in the distance during the Tuesday Western. Then let it play its way upstairs with Harry. Suggest to Meredith that he can go up with Harry and see what's wrong with the electric trains which haven't worked since Christmas. Hear Meredith upstairs talking, carry the supper things from the hatch to the sink. Visit the larder when all is clear and inspect two new cans of Long Life beer kept in trust for Stuart and so that a letter could truthfully be written ending "Yes there is always beer, but in the larder actually."

Meredith has come downstairs and gone back to the study. The warm air from the kitchen, wafting into the cold larder, carries the scent of a cigar wafted to kitchen from study. There always will be some beer in the larder actually, even if now she prises off one metal tag and goes into the kitchen to find one glass.

So how did you break the news in the end grandmother? Well my dear, she says, grasping a silver-headed cane in elegant ringed and bony fingers, and looking at the upturned face by her knee, and then into the far distant corridor of her infinitely boring memories, counting with taps on the floor with her cane, the garden boys of her youth, the summer fields of Scotch and Long Life, the heads of her children, the lithe frame of her favourite lover, the view from the four-poster bed, the Ford car, ponies chomping grass in the field, the pantechnicon which fell into it in the gale, the smell of Gauloises and engine oil. And turning back to look at the grandchild who should not, she hopes, be born for years and years, she says, "What news my dear?"

Leave the kitchen. Walk to the study and say "Meredith". Say "Meredith". Do not say "Darling" as you used to or "Er ... Meredith". But just "Meredith", firmly.

Or, on the other hand, arrive in the study as if by accident or as if you wished to watch the news importantly and wait for him to ask again about Alex. And if he does not ask ... there is always another can of Long Life in the larder actually.

Meanwhile there is the chaise-longue; lean back as if you were leaning, or sit as if you were sitting on it. Seem to lie or seem to sit with the *Sunday Times* Bridge Problem across your knees.

There is another door into the study, one which is nearly always shut, but has led into the drawing-room ever since this was the ante-room. Only Meredith uses this door. He gets up from in front of the television, opens the door and goes into the drawing-room where he can be heard drawing the curtains, undrawn all of the sixty-three days. After that he can be heard going out of the drawing-room and into the hall, footsteps on stone, moving slowly, then not moving at all as if he had found something of interest on the Havergal oak chair. What he has found he is bringing back, coming into the study the long way again through the drawing-room, entering through the same seldom-used door between the mantelpiece and the french windows, carrying by its loop by which it should have been hung in the coat cupboard under the stairs, Alex's maroon school blazer with four white roses of York on the pocket, a blazer which should have been dark green with one scarlet dragon of Wales emblazoned on the breast.

"Where is she?"

"Out."

At half past nine, by which time Alex said she would be back, but called it half-nine, Meredith stands in front of the curtains of the french windows and says, having listened to Edwina's brief and not untruthful résumé of recent events, "How can I ever go away again? How can I ever trust you to carry out my wishes? Why do I write long pieces for the box-file? How can I know whether the same thing will not befall Harry one day?" Then more urgently. "Is this decision about St Cecilia's irreversible?"

During the first half-hour of the argument Meredith edged towards the door into the drawing-room as if it were safer ground, and Edwina went on seeming to lie, lean and sit on the chaise-longue, having fetched from the mantelpiece the letters from Miss Rogers and copies of her own replies. Meredith took the correspondence and gesticulated with them throughout, having long since put out his cigar.

"And this! This letter from Miss Rogers completely and absolutely belies the suggestion that she expelled Alex in the way you have told the story. Surely you do not wish me to believe that you mistook the word 'suspension' for 'expulsion'?"

Edwina, as the argument began, lit a cigarette and placed an ashtray on the newspaper which covered her knees and repeated that neither word was used in the headmistress's study on the day in question.

"And this! This letter from you to Miss Rogers explicitly states that you are withdrawing Alex! You! Withdraw Alex! It even offers to pay next term's fees in lieu of notice. And who will pay those fees one asks oneself!"

She watched the smoke curl high above beyond the picture rail and along the moulded plaster lines of the ceiling and said that everything happened exactly as described.

"And you! I suppose you think you have some special

133

powers where Alex is concerned, to dispose of her educational chances in one fell sweep?"

At the next inhalation she blew the smoke across the room. Some went into the fireplace and was drawn out again past the electric fire and in front of the row of photographs. She said that she supposed that Meredith meant one fell swoop.

"But a contract has been broken, a contract made between us and between Miss Rogers and Alex, a contract discussed and decided upon five years ago, and, if my memory serves me, agreed upon, and now broken in the most underhand fashion in all of my experience."

The thin veil of smoke drifting across the face of Grandmother Havergal hovered and spread outwards to waft along and across the faces of her daughter and her daughter's daughters.

"A contract to which you were party, having agreed that this course of action, this, I may say, very expensive education would be the best education for Alex."

The smoke dispersed by the time it reached the photographs of the husbands of Grandmother Havergal's grand-daughters, and Edwina said that it was very difficult to be sure that anyone's choice of education for anyone else is the best for them, and, since you cannot be sure in that way, it seems sensible to take the education offered in the district in which you live.

"A typical answer if I may say so, a very typical, utterly unconstructive answer, in the same vein as the broken contract. And a contract broken for the worst of reasons, an education which was chosen supplanted by an education which is second-rate."

Meredith stepped forward and placed the letters on top of the television set. He walked down the narrow room passing close to Edwina on the chaise-longue and made his next speech while walking back towards the curtained window with small steps and with his hands folded behind his back. Edwina blew smoke at the ceiling and said, perhaps as they were discussing Alex they could talk in terms

134

of Alex herself, Alex, and not in terms of broken contracts.

"All right then. All right. Since you say we are talking about Alex and not, as I half believe, talking about *you*, and, since you wish to evade the issue of the broken contract, I will now ask you, Edwina, what possible benefit Alex can derive from spending her time at some second-rate Secondary Modern, mixing, as I think she will be mixing, with the..."

A draught from the door still open into the drawing-room blew the smoke down from the study ceiling so that it travelled nowhere. Edwina said that she supposed Meredith was about to say that Alex would mix with the hoi polloi, and added that the school was called a High School and not a Secondary Modern.

Meredith stood in the open drawing-room door with his hands behind his back and spoke of the contract again and its tragic breaking. Moreover he spoke of a two-fold tragedy for Alex, both educational and social. Moreover he said that, since Alex was a girl the social side of it was the more tragic, the predominating tragedy and the great one. "What chance is there now," he said framed in the drawing-room door, "what chance is there now of Alex meeting and marrying someone, well someone, well someone...?"

"Of her own kind you mean?"

From a little way inside the drawing-room Meredith could be heard to say that Alex would suffer because Edwina had failed in her social rôle as mother and not encouraged her to be friends with people like, people like...

"The Rochdales?"

"Everything you say," Meredith's voice carried from the dark drawing-room to the lamplit study, "everything you say is nothing to do with this, nothing to do with the central problem, nothing to do with anything we are talking about. Everything you say is cheap jibes and irrelevant. Everything. How can anyone expect Alex to

135

grow up with any respect for all the things other people believe in?"

"Decent people you mean?" said Edwina, as the draught blowing through from the drawing-room increased in volume and then decreased, suggesting that somewhere an outside door had been opened and shut again without sound.

Alex, coming in late, would push open the back door and push it shut again, listen for voices and distinguish whether they came from the television or were spoken by people in the house. Then she would go to the kitchen to make herself coffee, or, hearing no raised voices, she might make coffee for three and bring it into the study on a tray with downcast eyes as if caring most of all that it would not spill. Or she might stand in her gym shoes at the bottom of the stairs within earshot of the rooms down the hall and the rooms in the rest of the house. Not that there is ever complete silence under the motorway hum, but the lack of voices Alex might interpret as either an interval in conversation or as uncommenced strife, or even quiet harmony which, in Alex's experience, will be the most unlikely reading of any pause.

Alex aged seven said she wished they would not shout so much all night and keep her awake. Alex aged fifteen said Susan's mother and step-father go at it hammer and tongs all night and wake up the baby, which is rotten for Susan because she is the one who has to get it to sleep again when they have been screaming and belting each other downstairs. Once Susan had to carry it outside and into next door to get it away from the noise.

"I have noticed," says Meredith across the pause, "that you do operate, to some extent, a kind of social selection; that you spend more time, say, with Diana, than you do with Mrs Thwaite."

"Oh yes? You've noticed that have you?"

"Yes I have noticed that, and, deny it as you most certainly will, I find it difficult to believe that it is the case that you would rather have Alex mix with and marry

136

someone from Mrs Thwaite's walk of life than with someone from Diana's..."

Edwina removes the ash-tray and the *Sunday Times* Bridge Problem from her knees. She sits up on the edge of the chaise-longue and puts her feet on the floor. "Alex," she says to the invisible Meredith somewhere in the drawing-room, "Alex will marry who she wants to, if she marries at all. Alex will be someone who could know anyone and marry anyone anywhere. I want Alex to see everyone from everywhere, but I don't want her to see them as coming from what you would call a walk of life. I want her to see them as people with their own value and never ask them what part of the world they come from or what their fathers do for a living."

Edwina stands by the mantelpiece and says, "I don't pretend that I wouldn't like to be the way I want Alex to be. I'd like to know people like Mrs Thwaite or like Mrs Thwaite's grandson; I'd like to feel the same as them, not as they are now perhaps, but I'd like them to feel the same as me. Instead, what I feel about Mrs Thwaite is guilty that she sweeps my floor and sidens in my kitchen. That's what I feel about Mrs Thwaite. My social hang-ups are bred in me by my environment."

She assumes now Meredith's position in front of the curtains and goes on talking: "Alex won't have social hang-ups like that. She'll have other hang-ups for certain, but she won't have the sort that get her stuck with nitwits like Diana and not the sort that make her guilty about Mrs Thwaite cleaning her floors and stairs. Alex won't get stuck with anyone she doesn't want to be stuck with. She won't have a myth perpetuated around her of big houses and boarding schools. Alex will have seen so much of everything that she will know when and how to say no to some of it. You talk of choice of education, but Alex will have a choice of life-style and of life. Whatever else happens to her she won't say yes to what somebody else chooses for her."

Inside the drawing-room it is just possible to see the

137

back of Meredith's head unmoving above the frame of a gilt chair. To avoid this sight she moves down the study and back again slowly as Meredith did earlier. "Alex," she says, "won't have a house chosen for her because it is a better, older house than someone else's and behave like people who do live in such houses. Alex won't wince when someone says toilet instead of loo or pardon instead of what or what did you say, or ta instead of thank you, and pleased to meet you. When Alex says 'pleased to meet you I am sure' she will mean it. Alex will have kids not children and swear in front of them when she feels like it. She won't tell them, blushingly, about the birds and the bees and let them look at the medical dictionary—she'll say fuck and screw and wank with the best of them and go into pubs and listen to dirty stories and not only want to be seen in the best company. She won't have to find an Out Crowd to belong to and giggle in corners about the Headmistress and the Colonel of the Army College. She'll know that for people like Miss Rogers being screwed by the Colonel would be the best thing since sliced bread."

And since Meredith may or may not be still there in the nearest gilt chair to the door in the drawing-room, she goes on.

"This isn't about Miss Rogers, Meredith. I like Miss Rogers. She knows more about some things than either of us, and I wish her well. What she doesn't see is that you have to give people something of what they want before you get anywhere with them. Then you can be tough. Then you can tell them what to do. Then you can shout at them when they come in late. And since it is me that has given Alex what she wants, it's going to be me that's going to shout at her, and I'm going to shout at her right now."

The fight is as it should be now, as it is done in real life and at Susan's where they wake the baby up and have to take all night getting it to sleep again. The door between the study and the hall is banged open and banged shut and the door into the kitchen is banged open. Alex sits there drinking coffee and reading the paper and eating

138

sandwiches. Her mother shouts that she might at least have come and said she was in. And how long has she *been* in by the way? And she might consider that mothers worry about people coming in at the promised time. At least at St Cecilia's you didn't have to worry for three-quarters of the year what was happening to silly children, silly kids, who ought to get to bed right away and bloody well leave the kitchen with every crumb of bread removed, every coffee cup washed up, like no one had ever used it or been in it tonight.

Back in the study she finds Meredith standing ready for her, fist clenched on mantelpiece.

One foot rests on the brass fender. He moves his fist slowly up and down on the marble mantelpiece. Meredith has often spoken of his ability to swing a board meeting his way, to address an executive body, to persuade both board and executive as well as lower ranks, of the wisdom of a course of action. He does this simply by standing still and going on talking.

Meredith could have gone into his father's dental practice when he left the army. There he could have talked to gagged patients, persuaded them of the poor condition of their teeth and sold them the expensive benefits of advanced dentistry. He could have stayed in the army, had the cavalry of his time not been a regiment of rich young men all richer than the son of a dentist who retired before the post-war boom and the high-speed drill.

"I see," he says from the fireplace, "from that little scene that you have already adopted the life-style you wish for your daughter, but I infinitely regret to have been witness to it."

Lady Havergal used to say that, in the past, people would not have looked at sons of dentists twice and would have treated them like they treated vets. But that was all ridiculous these days when everything was so lovely and democratic, and when girls could marry anyone. And, in any case, her own mother had known a perfectly delightful dentist in Pitlochry who used to be asked to tea several times a year. People could marry anyone these days, Lady Havergal used to say. All that fuss about people being in trade was quite dead and, after all Meredith was not actually going to *own* a business, was he?

He could also, many people used to say, have been a Member of Parliament. Now he stands in front of the Havergal photographs with his foot on the Havergal brass fender and says: "I won't say, Edwina, that I have not suspected for some time that you had it in you to speak in that manner. In fact, when I consider past occasions, I suppose that it was always clear that certain distasteful elements in your nature were subdued rather than eliminated."

He has often said he would have been a good Member of Parliament, he believes. Or a Colonial Administrator in the days when there were colonies. He wished he had been clever enough at school to take the Foreign Office Exam because he definitely has a way with foreigners; now he uses his rhetoric in the study. "One knows," he says, "and has not one always known, deep in one's heart, that, perhaps one was young and easily impressed, perhaps even seduced, by the panoply of the Havergals? But since then one has learned, oh yes one has learned: there was Alberta after all, and there is Davina and we all know about Davina, and there have even been hints and evidence about ... about other members of the family. One has learnt, for instance, you may laugh Edwina ..."

Once he said he would excel at administration because he has the knack of standing back and seeing whole problems and, at the same time, their solution. That, he says, is what such leaders as Winston Churchill could do; that, he says, is what emerges as you read biographies such as Churchill's and other studies of people in power. Now, he says, Edwina may laugh, but one has learnt, definitely and painfully learnt, not, for instance, to trust one's wife with large sums of money. Also one has learnt, Edwina may laugh again, that such a trivial instance as Lady Havergal's habit of trespassing in private gardens and stealing plant-cuttings from public ones was symptomatic of deeper un-palatable traits. And, laugh though Edwina may, it is time that people like the Havergals stopped thinking they can go on doing what they like, thinking that they own the ground they walk upon.

There is something, when Meredith holds his hand up like a policeman halting traffic, which keeps the opposition quiet while he points out gradually that the Havergals do not own the ground they walk on any more. "And, Edwina, this deep-seated trait of the Havergals, whether or not it is the result of inbreeding somewhere, whether or not it is a symptom of decay, whatever is its cause, its root, its radical source, one does not intend to let it go further. It may be too late for Alex, one knows to one's cost. But it is not too late for Harry. Nor while I live will it reach to Harry. It may seem a joke to you, Edwina, it may seem a joke to Alex, but Harry will go to a prep school of my choice and stay there. Even if I never go abroad again, even if I eschew all possibility of reaching the positions I am aiming for, that, and I say this in no jest whatsoever, is how it will be."

He turns his back on the mantelpiece and leans on it and outlines his plans for ensuring the continuity of Harry's education. "Experts," he says, "legal experts are what are needed. There are ways of doing this I feel sure. I need hardly mention what such steps may involve in connection with you and in connection with Alex." He looks at the ceiling while he talks and now he keeps his hands in his pockets. Until he turns round again and clenches his fist on the mantelpiece once more to em-phasise that the thing Edwina has done to Alex will be beyond her power with Harry.

In the spare-room she shuts the door quietly and stands by the window.

When he went on talking again it was about this evening and his arrival home. What was one supposed to think as the train drew in at the station and one walked across the platform and one's wife made no move to greet one? How, one asks oneself, is one supposed to know what's what in life, when over sixty-three days one wears suits and lives alone in hotels? One knows, God knows, one is not missed. But at least Harry is pleased to see one, one is glad to say. One is very glad about that. Very glad. One feels with Harry that, even if one did not bring him a present he would run along the platform. One is glad that he can run like that, isn't one?

She stood with her hand on the handle of the study door and said she was going to bed.

One does not ask much out of life. One has learnt not to expect full return on investment. The thing is to have purpose, long term purpose and the knowledge of the way to carry it out. And the knowledge which one lacks oneself is as nothing if one knows who the people are who possess it.

At the top of the stairs he will stand and see the closed spare-room door and the strip of light under it.

One is not blind, he said downstairs, to one's own faults. One knows all too well who has the clever answers, has read the right books and owns the porcelain and some of the silver. But who keeps those going? Who protects them from being sold? Who provides? One is not blind to all that. One is not blind at all. One may be absent, but one has one's imagination because one sees what goes on when one is at home. One sees what happens at parties for instance. Oh yes one sees.

His footsteps, heavy because he will be carrying a suit-case, move across the landing to the other bedroom.

Chapter 8

THE TERRACE IN which Stuart lives is half-way along the village street and faces the Bay Leaf and the grocer's shop. It is a terrace of five houses standing a few feet further back from the edge of the road than the other houses in the main street. Stuart lives in the third house of the terrace and Mrs Thwaite's daughter in the second. "No. 38," he once said, "is just somewhere we live." Although the Treasurer of the Hodsworth Society said at the Shaw Terrace meeting that Stuart's was a "terrace house to be reckoned with".

Mrs Thwaite says good money has been thrown away on bad at No. 38 the way they have knocked it about, making the front room and the back room all one room and building a lean-to kitchen out at the back. Her daughter told her they've left bare brick in places and stripped the paint off woodwork and not painted it again.

Edwina parks the car outside the grocer's on her way home from taking Harry to school on the last morning of the spring term. In the shop, which is now a mini-supermarket, she picks up a wire basket and stands in the window looking down at heaps of bags of frozen peas, sweet corn and runner beans. Then she moves along to the section where there are fishfingers, beefburgers, ready-for-oven chickens and chicken pies. She reaches into the frost for blocks of ice-cream, economy packs which Diana says are a very good buy for the holidays. From the window over the deep-freeze you can see across the road, but not into the blank windows of No. 38. The outside paintwork still glows white where Stuart painted it in the autumn. But Mrs Thwaite's daughter says that, what with Mrs

143

Douglas being out at work the place inside doesn't get looked after much, not that it seems to be really dirty, but you can usually tell from looking at a house which people come from down south. Stuart says that Christine "goes mad cleaning" some weekends. He says that some women think a brush in the hand gives them special rights of movement around a room. Christine argues that if they went out more together, or if he took her out more often, she wouldn't be cleaning so much. Or if he'd give her more driving lessons she'd go out on her own and leave him studying in peace.

There is no sign of life at No. 38 this morning, nor is Stuart's car outside, but, since the University term has ended, he may be inside, and his car parked in the ginnel at the back. Edwina leans into the deep-freeze and picks out two packets of frozen lemon mousse which have 3p off the price this week. As she looks up again she sees Mrs Thwaite's daughter, with heavily pregnant waddle and shopping bag come out of No. 38, lock the door and walk along the street towards the bus stop. Mrs Thwaite herself will be at the Dower House this morning, sidening for Diana.

Yesterday, as Mrs Thwaite sidened for Edwina, she said that she'd seen Mrs Douglas looking right miserable in the shop on Monday afternoon. You could not help feeling sorry for her not having any kiddies sometimes and being away from her home and that, but she isn't like someone who seems to want to make friends, although she's nice enough when you talk to her.

Edwina carries the basket containing frozen mousse and ice-cream and puts it on the counter. The woman who runs the shop adds up the price on the till and talks about Alex, as she has talked about Alex and the braying in the Sports Hall every time Edwina has been in the shop since last Friday when it happened.

"My daughter says it was time someone got that Janice."
"It was Susan who did it really," says Edwina turning

144

her head having seen out of the corner of one eye a movement behind the window of No. 38.

"She's all right, is your Alex." The frozen food is packed
into a stiff brown paper bag, the money is exchanged and
Edwina stands inside the door of the shop. "I was saying
yesterday; Alex is all right. I was saying that they'd under-
estimated her. I said that you and Mr Measures-Smith
wouldn't have sent her to a posh school for nothing."

Outside it is sunny on this side of the street, but No. 38
is still in the shade. Edwina opens the door of the Mini
and leans over to put the brown paper bag on the back
seat before crossing the road and knocking at the door of
No. 38. You have to climb two steps to knock and then
stand waiting. If you stand on the top step, when the door
is opened, you will be almost touching the person who will
stand in the doorway. So it is better to step back down
again after knocking and look, while you are waiting, up
and down the street as if this was a casual call and you
are not at all concerned whether the woman in the grocer's
is looking across the street or not.

This end of the long room which was once two short rooms
there are cotton-covered chairs and a sofa. At the far end
is an oak drop-leaf dining table and four chairs. There is
no carpet, but the floorboards are stripped and varnished
and scattered with small bright multi-coloured rugs. This
end of the room there is a black iron grate, and above
it a Victorian lithograph of a white-faced, pale-throated
woman with heavy red hair. At the far end the fireplace
has been blocked in. The walls throughout are bricks
white-washed and the doors and fitted cupboard-fronts are
soft wood stripped to its natural grain.

"It was going to be roses round the door when we first
moved in," says Stuart.

"It's very nice."

"You don't have to say that."

"I mean it. I like it."

"Not a bad effort for poor people then?"

145

He came to the door in a white shirt, green cotton trousers and bare feet. A tie hung untied over his shirt and his hair was wet.

"Were you just going out?"

"Thinking of it."

"I won't stay then."

She sits on a chair which she knows, from outside experience, cannot be seen from the street, and picks from it the stripy towel with which he must have been drying his hair in front of the gas-fire in the black grate. He sits on the floor beside her with his feet on one of the rugs.

"They are rag rugs aren't they?"

"Yes. Christine makes them."

"You can use up old clothes and things, can't you?"

"Yes. Kind rich people give us scraps."

On the mantelpiece are two blue glass vases and at one end daffodils in an earthenware pot arranged with spring twigs and budding lime. Either side of the fireplace there are books, mostly paperbacks, the titles too small to read at this dark end of the room.

"Did you get my note?"

"Yes. I was worried though."

"Did Meredith come back?"

"Yes."

"How was it?"

"Predictable."

Cars pass in the street, people walk on the pavement and Stuart reaches out for the towel on her knees and starts rubbing his hair with it.

"Did he thump you?"

"Of course not."

"I would have, I think."

Then he says, "Excuse me," and pads across the room in bare feet to the kitchen where he disappears. Edwina sits with the gas-fire warm on her legs and picks his comb up from the floor. Out of the window across the road the top windows of the shop and the Bay Leaf can be seen; the

146

sun shines on their roofs which steam after the early morning frost. A loud, machine-like hum comes from the
kitchen. "The washing machine," says Stuart coming back,
"I promised Christine I'd switch it on."

"Mine's broken."

"I know an awfully good little man down in the village
who would mend it for you."

Returning he sits down again with his toes stretched
towards the fire.

"Now tell me what Meredith said."

"It doesn't matter."

"It matters if it affects you."

"It won't."

"Does he know about us?"

"Is there any *us* still to know about?"

The bedroom faces on to the ginnel at the back where
Stuart and Mrs Thwaite's son-in-law both park their
cars. The room has a fitted white carpet and built-in wardrobes. He made the wardrobes and Christine made the
patchwork bedspread. A fawn skirt is folded over the back
of a wicker-work chair under the window. A matching
fawn jersey is likewise folded on the seat. Stuart looks in
a drawer for socks, reaches under the bed for shoes and
takes his needlecord jacket from a coathanger in the wardrobe. "You think Friday was to do with more than just
taking Christine to the opticians and being late, don't
you?" he says.

"It seems to be."

She followed him up here to sit on the edge of the bed
when he said they could talk while he got ready to go
out. There is a pile of old copies of the *Times Educational
Supplement* on a table beside the bed, and a pile of books.
A spectacle case suggest that this is Christine's side of the
bed and that she is reading *Lady Chatterley's Lover*. Also
on the table is a tin labelled "Sewing", and folded on top
of it the sweater Stuart wore last Wednesday in the gale.
He counts loose change into his pocket from a pile of it

on the dressing table. Christine keeps no make-up there, only a brush and comb with no long red hairs in them. On the floor underneath she keeps her Dr Scholl's sandals.

"What you said on Wednesday was a possibility I hadn't considered."

"I wasn't telling you about a possibility. I was telling you an anecdote about myself."

"An anecdote!"

On the dressing table to one side of the mirror there is a photograph of Christine, taken perhaps ten years ago, but the tightly permed hair makes her look older than she is now.

"I shouldn't even have mentioned it I realise now."

"Shouldn't have mentioned it! Christ!"

Stuart stands back from the mirror, knees bent, to brush his hair. Christine looks out from the photograph with confidence, as she may be looking at this minute, out over the heads of her class at junior school.

"So what do we do now?"

"Well, you are never at a loss for practical solutions."

Downstairs, Christine's automatic washer hums and vibrates, circulating in her absence her clothes and his.

"I seem to be at the moment, at a loss I mean."

There are two rooms on the top floor, at the back a junk room lit only by a skylight, and at the front a larger room with a dormer window where people in the street see the light burning into the small hours. His work table is under the window, but his books are on the floor. Contrary to rumour and speculation he does not sit up here working all night, but lies up here on this pile of cushions and works on his thesis stretched along the length of the radiator.

This was the only practical solution Stuart could bring to mind and is not, he admits, in keeping with his frame of mind since Wednesday. He says his mother had an abortion once. She had six children, three younger than him and two older. No one thinks maybe she should have gone on having kids because she hates to be alone, pathologically, and will do anything to have grandchildren with her, and when they are not around, Stuart's father, or such of his brothers and sisters who live near home take turns to go out with her.

"You don't think I would have *enjoyed* having an abortion, do you?"

Stuart says his father left his mother once for a year and lived with a woman a few streets away, but his mother nearly went out of her mind, so he came back.

"What happened to the woman a few streets away?"

"He still sees her I think."

There is nothing up here of Christine's; Stuart hung the curtains and carried up the cushions, the work table and the books; he sweeps the room himself and empties out his ash-tray. He has no pictures but one round poster on the wall, a hectic bright commemoration of the Woodstock Pop Festival which he said Ursula gave him, and which he did not like that much and had been meaning to take down for months. It had been put there as much in defiance of Christine as for any other reason.

The cushions were the only location for the practical solution, Edwina having said no to the bed with the patchwork quilt. The washing machine could still be heard at first, but now has switched itself off. "Supposing I gave you a poster to take that one's place?"

"Of your coat of arms, emblazoned with mine? The pelican eating her young?"

"All right. Point taken, but it's a crest and it's feeding her young, not eating them." People like Stuart go on teasing and being aggressive for quite some time and then they forget and return to practical solutions, which is temporary forgiveness. The weekend of waiting disappears, the Saturday when he was not to be seen playing soccer, the Sunday which was a series of hours passed clock-watching and the Monday which was a day of listening for the telephone but not daring to make a call. Tuesday was only incidentally the day Meredith came back, and chiefly the day marked down as the last possible to remain out of touch with No. 38.

But this is an anonymous day time. Shut your eyes and think of nothing else, only opening them to affirm and receive affirmation that all is at this minute well, and if not as well as it has been, it must be better than the last minute. What the world contains, you would insist to Miss Rogers, is in this instance worth discovering for yourself. Be grateful for the practical solution which came to Stuart's mind, and do not repeat, repeat do not repeat, previous mistakes. The Havergals, Meredith said last night, no longer own the ground they walk on, as if you ever thought they did. The world is Stuart's, and if you did not think that, you would not be here now. And his world contains more than a mere Havergal pelican can provide. He has, on his own admission, fucked as much out of marriage as within it, and he may still fuck within it more than somewhat or why does Christine read *Lady Chatterley*? But never the direct question on such topics; remember that, but for glances or more he has given Ursula probably, and the looks he gave Mrs Thwaite's daughter certainly, you might not be here either. Consider Christine who must conjecture about his glances but looked trusting and unconjecturing in the photograph on the dressing table. She accepts or seems to accept the share she holds in him and does not need to consider and be nice about the other shareholders.

Around the cushions are his books and files and his table is at the window through which only blue sky can be seen. "You would have gone off," he said earlier, "you'd have gone off, or awf as you say, in that car; you'd have paid for it by selling spoons or rings; the car would have broken down fifty times on the way, but you'd have got there. And if anyone asked you where you were going, you'd have said 'I'm just going out; I may be some time.' Isn't that so?"

You must never accuse people like Stuart of not loving you any more. Months ago he announced that you never really stop loving anyone. "Good God," she said. "Not him either," said Stuart.

The washing machine has not stopped but only paused in its programme. It vibrates through from two floors down and is still spinning clear water out of white clothes while Stuart makes coffee in the kitchen. He makes real ground coffee in a royal blue enamel pot. Through the plate glass windows of the kitchen is a rose-bed and two small borders, raked and with seed-bed labels. While he pours the coffee she opens the fridge to get milk and sees a bacon joint soaking in water, which will be his meal tonight. On the table a pile of recipe books and an engagement diary open at a page for this week and next week.

"I could have destroyed the only thing we'd ever really shared," she says.

"*I* don't believe you could have in the end."

The writing in the engagement diary is large and round and even, not Stuart's. Christine has noted that she breaks up on Friday morning and is going to the dentist in the afternoon. On the Saturday space she has written in capital letters "Away" and followed this all through next week by writing "At Mother's" diagonally across the page.

"Are you going too?"

"I have to . . . I said I would drive her down."

"Is it nice down there?"

"She has friends there."

"Doesn't she have any here?"

"Not really."

They sit to drink coffee back where they started in the long room in front of the gas fire, but this time both on the floor.

"Legally I'd have had no share," says Stuart. "Legally it would have been Meredith's."

"But mothers always get custody don't they?"

Stuart puts his cup down on the floor beside him and reaches for a cigarette. "Was custody mentioned between you? Custody and things like that?"

"Oh no. Good heavens no. No such thing."

Drive north again, not looking back, to fetch Harry from school at lunchtime on the last day of term, with ice-cream and mousse slopping in the bag on the back seat of the car. Leave Stuart to put on his jacket, socks and shoes and get ready all over again to go to the library. Say good-bye and go out of the back door of the ginnel where his garage is, so that when you come into the street again the woman in the grocer's may believe you have been to any one of the houses in that part of the main street.

Upstairs he tore down Ursula's poster. "Those days are over."

"But not ours."

"Oh no."

"But why does poor Ursula get chucked out now?"

"It's sick. Was sick. Like your friend said, elderly shuffling teenagers."

"When I told you that, you said Miss Rogers was both loony and elitist."

"She may also be prophetic."

"Alex isn't elderly and shuffling."

"No, Alex is demonstrably unharassable by left and right, but then Alex..."

"I know. Alex is advantaged!"

"*Very!*"

But before they went downstairs again and heard the washing machine start rinsing he said he would write to her from Bristol because it would be pretty dead boring there. And she said she would write back. He even gave her printed envelopes so that Christine and her parents would believe they were from the Department of Education.

When Lady Havergal used to come and stay in the Easter holidays she used the four-poster in the spare-room and kept her false teeth on the table where Stuart puts his watch, his cigarettes and his lighter. In those days the holidays were times for outings to Fountains Abbey and

Flamingo Park, evensong at York Minster and drinks with Diana before lunch. Also for meals in the dining-room and having the silver polished. Stuart once looked at the Havergal photographs in the study and said: "Your mother looks as if she knew all about life, love and laughter."

"Yes she did. She definitely did."

Holidays then were predictable. These holidays are not, except that Meredith will start work on the terrace, slicing up turf, laying foundations of rubble and thinking the while. Harry will bicycle round him while he works, and Alex will be off, out down village as she calls it. Meredith will eventually and inevitably hear about the braying in the Sports Hall and stop digging or go on digging as the case may be.

Stuart's letters, it has been agreed, will be posted to arrive on Mondays and Fridays throughout the holidays and the other days will be like weeks cancelled diagonally on an engagement diary. Some would say the letters should be placed under glass and framed with silver and have lights shining on them, but they will be kept variously between the pages of Thorenssen on Defensive Play and under the four-poster bed. They will be answered. It would be easiest and most genuine to send pages covered from top to bottom with "I miss you", but that would make boring reading on the outskirts of Bristol. "This sort of correspondence needs practice," you will write. "This sort of emotion is best expressed horizontally on cushions."

So letters are to be carefully composed, sometimes running to two and three drafts each time, to emphasise the emotion and the missing, but with no reference to what people like Meredith are doing and thinking. Just as no reference is made to it by Meredith himself. But he is observed.

Meredith keeps newspaper cuttings held together by a bulldog clip in one of the drawers of the kneehole desk in his upstairs study. He writes the date of the newspaper, from which the cutting was taken, in ballpoint pen, and the latest cutting is always at the top.

The clipful of cuttings almost always contains a number of photographs of houses from the property pages of *Country Life*, eighteenth-century mansions surrounded by greensward and with ten master bedrooms, five reception-rooms, more suitable, it sometimes says, for conversion to flats or an institution. From *Country Life* Meredith also collects articles on the modernisation of such mansions and on landscape gardening. From the *Sunday Times* he is more apt to cut advertisements for military biographies and reviews of books on Neo-Classicism. The news items he cuts out are generally about people he has known at school, in the army, or in business. And recently the clip has contained a number of reports of the activities of the Sealed Knot and photographs of their mock Civil War battles. Meredith has often said that he could not but help enjoy the thought of becoming a Cavalier in the Sealed Knot, which is odd he says because he has always had little taste for the seventeenth century.

But the slow dedication with which he removes squares of turf from the space to be occupied by the terrace suggests that he will not become a Cavalier for this season's battles. Manual work, physical struggle, he has often suggested, feeds the purposeful brain, and to the re-tarmacking of the drive last year he attributes his success with Brigstock Boilers this. And the increasing light of April evenings gives him more time for the maturation of whatever plans he is now working on.

On the chaise-longue Edwina writes the final draft of a letter to Stuart. Meredith scrapes earth from his boots outside the french window, and the letter is closed inside the pages of a Colour Supplement.

"Perhaps Meredith was right," she wrote just now. "Perhaps Havergals still do think we own the ground we walk on. Perhaps the element in me still exists and made the gap between us widen ..."

The french window opens. "I'd like to talk to you."

"Oh yes?"

Stuart's last letter said: "Realise now just how much the last few months have made up for other lacks, and I don't mean just the obvious one. It's not that I don't care, but that I care too much. Man embracing woman embraces man caring for woman don't forget..."

The french window closes and Meredith takes up his position by the mantelpiece: "No action has yet been taken..."

"Oh yes ... no action..."

"But we are both aware that it could be..."

"Um ... yes..."

"And it is not to suggest that enquiries have not been made..."

"Enquiries?"

"Yes enquiries into possibilities ... we both know what I am referring to, I think."

Sometimes he works outside until it is as good as dark. He shuts the french windows again at twilight and walks back towards the upturned area of soil.

Will an enquiry agent hover by the beech avenue or in the shrubbery? Can long shots be taken with the interruption of the pediment shadow into the spare-room window? Or was the agent in the grocer's or the Bay Leaf at the end of March, or has he already crept down the drive and written in his notebook the registration number of Stuart's car? And if so, what of it? Mothers always win, Victoria said, and she must surely include in the category of mothers, adulterous ones.

She turns back the pages of the Colour Supplement and completes the draft. "I think the summer is going to be exciting." Then adds, "No reason for this, simply the sap rising I suppose."

Meredith's office contains his desk and his filing cabinet, a chair and not much else. There are photographs on the wall of the teams he was in at school and the regiment he was in in the army. Here he also keeps a gun he used in the days he belonged to a shooting syndicate with

Robert, and a fishing rod which belonged to his father and which he is keeping for Harry. The papers on the desk are all open to view and weighted down by glass paperweights, and none of the drawers, neither of the desk nor of the filing cabinet, is locked. It would appear he has nothing up his sleeve; the only letter to his solicitor in all recent correspondence is concerned with his contract of employment as South Yorkshire representative of his Company, which says that he intends extending for a further five years. And a letter from his mother asks how he is and how Edwina is and how the children are.

The newspaper cuttings, checked last week, perhaps deserve another glance. Still on top is the *Country Life* article entitled "Eighteenth Century Grace Updated", showing in a photograph architect and lady owner standing in front of a temple built in the grounds of the Warwickshire manor to commemorate the renovations. And under this is still the advertisement for an "Entire new rose-garden this summer" from the *Sunday Times*.

There is nowhere else to look, except on the bookshelf above the desk where Meredith keeps catalogues, the annual from the Country Gentlemen's Association, *Who's Who* and *Whitaker's Almanac*, all books whose backs would not grace the shelves downstairs. Private correspondence can be kept in books, but these are dusty and have not been touched in months. Nor is it worth looking in other drawers where there are very old letters and bank-statements done up in rubber bands. Nor among receipts and cheque-stubs. Which is to discover nothing about what can at any stage be spoken about on telephones or dealt with in his other office.

Stuart wrote: "Something of an itch to get home, something the behaviourists call deferred gratification, to which they say a middle-class (or since I am writing to you, an upper-class) child/kid responds to, but the working-class kid responds better to a boot up. So Christ what have you done to me that I am responding to it now?"

Edwina wrote: "Christ has done nothing to you; perhaps I have. And deferred gratification, as it happens, is something I would rather do without."

In the garden at the end of April it is almost hot. The field beyond the ha-ha dips and rises again to the evergreen clump around the Dower House. Elsewhere it is a winter landscape in summer sun. The ponies are strung out in the dip moving slowly, heads down grazing in grass which a few weeks ago was waterlogged. They move in line skirting the promontory. Across the motorway clouds blown a long way from the south make shadows on the ploughed fields and change their shapes high up to make variable dark patches on the expanse of land.

Mrs Thwaite's daughter's new baby is home from hospital and gaining weight nicely. It seems a long time, says Mrs Thwaite, sidening in the kitchen and talking through the window, since she was up at the Hall and she can tell by the dirt that it is a long time. She didn't like staying down at her daughter's to look after our Constantine while his mother was in hospital. But it was quiet with the Douglases away most of the time; they got back two days ago and look right cheerful now.

This garden was once the servants' quarters of the house. The paths between beds of vegetables were once passages and corridors, but now are trodden grass leading up to the back door which was once the door between servants and gentry. It is warm enough to stand, coatless, on the grass paths in the early afternoon; and the sun throwing a bare shadow across a carrot patch of a leafless apple tree. Stuart's last letter a week ago said spring was well advanced in Bristol. Mrs Thwaite says when they got back they called in to see the new baby and said they'd had a lovely holiday.

Three stone steps lead up to the back door where the stone hall is still the temperature of winter. Mrs Thwaite in the kitchen uses clear water to wipe surfaces clean and does not believe in detergents. A clean damp cloth is all you need; her daughter thinks the same. Mrs Thwaite leans over the white kitchen table; she has done the walls where they are white and the glazed white tiles on the window sill. Her daughter doesn't use detergent for the baby's things either. Just pure soap, and boiling, and in the dry weather makes sure they are out blowing on a line. Nothing but pure soap. The new baby is called Carey and his nappies are as white as driven snow, says Mrs Thwaite, as the telephone rings down the hall and she cleans and whitens in an empty room.

Chapter 9

IN EARLY JUNE it is sometimes warm enough to sit in the evenings with the french windows open on to the lawn seeing across the newly dug earth which will soon be the terrace. Or, if you are Harry, you can sit on the piled stone slabs with the binoculars, or bicycle around the grass paths of the vegetable garden, or circle the statue plinth in front of the pediment. Or you can go down the slope past the horses and hang over the motorway fence and watch the traffic with the wind warm round your ears and the rise behind you.

There is also the pasture sloping down to the village with groups of oak, beech and elm gracefully spaced, some with branches low enough to climb. There is a copper beech tree near the fence which is straight and strong enough to swing a rope over a branch, and if you get someone to swing the rope and tie a knot in the bottom of it, you can sit on the knot, stand on the fence and then jump off so that you swing out towards the village and back towards the house.

From June onwards through the summer, occasional motorists explore the park and stand outside the drive wall looking in. Or people in old vans come with a tent and ask if they can camp in the park, and they come into the house to fill their water containers. You can watch them pitch tents and if you are Harry, go out there first thing in the morning with fresh water for them and maybe get a piece of camper's breakfast bread or a drink of strong tea. You get tramps sometimes, on their way north wearing long coats tied at the waist with string. They ask for cups of tea, sandwiches and old trousers and tell you they are walking to Scotland.

It is all right in the summer to be on an isolated promontory because it is light enough and fine enough for people to find you there, people who remark on the space and luck of those who live there with all this space and light, fences, ponies and swings to themselves. And this June you are even luckier to have others to share this with. Alex's friend Susan comes to tea, and, because she has to look after the rest of the family while her mother is on afternoon shift at the Golding Trouser Factory, she brings them with her: Kevin, Tracy, Nigel and the baby Joanne.

When Susan comes to tea, Edwina goes out and comes back at seven to find the kitchen swept and the tea cleared. Susan is a sidener like Mrs Thwaite and is even teaching Alex the art of sidening. No crumbs, no biscuit wrappers and even the drying-up cloths are dry and folded.

Coming up through the tunnel of the avenue at seven o'clock in June you break into the circle of light at the end and see Harry, Kevin, Tracy and Nigel balancing on the wall, and the red and chrome bicycle leaning below them. The pediment above them reflects the yellow of the overgrown laburnums in the shrubbery. Susan and Alex, holding the baby, stand by the open front door.

Susan, as Alex has always said, is a very big girl, taller than Stuart and wider, with frizzy blonde hair and apple cheeks. She sways when she walks and blocks doorways into rooms. Within Edwina's hearing she never speaks, a huge and silent presence. But in the garden calling the children, and upstairs in Alex's room she can sometimes be heard talking and laughing. Her boy friend, Mal, as tall as her but thinner and with long straight hair, left school last term and works at the filling station by the flyover at the far end of the village. Alex says Mal is not allowed to visit Susan at home, but he comes here to Hodsworth when he finishes work, and plays on the lawn with the others or pushes them on the knotted rope out over the pasture.

It seems a very reasonable and happy arrangement to have things this way when you want to go out in the afternoon. Alex says Susan's Dad—rather her step-father —does not get home until seven, and, if Edwina can drive them all home to West Hodsworth he won't grumble. And it's much more fun than her being stuck with Harry on her own, and since Susan cooks them a proper tea, all you have to do is leave sausages, fish fingers, or a tin of corned beef for hash and several loaves of bread. It is not, after all, a permanent arrangement. They are smashing kids, says Alex, and always do what you say, at least what Susan says.

Behind the trees of the Dower House, Diana is having an absolutely hectic summer what with running the Conserva-tive Gala in the village in July and going to the Great Yorkshire Show and very much hoping to take Robert to Wimbledon if he can manage it, but his hip is playing him up so badly that she has even had to put off a dinner party to which an invitation had been accepted by the Rochdales.

But the Rochdales to Edwina this summer are something else; the place where she waits in the Mini for Stuart in the late afternoon. Rochdale Grove is a street of red-brick houses with cobbles and plane-trees and it runs at right angles to Rochdale Road which climbs the hill from the University and up which Stuart walks carrying his brief-case. Rochdale Grove and Rochdale Road are all that is left of the area of Victorian housing called the Rochdales. Demolition is taking place, cranes dangling swinging iron balls are flattening and have flattened Back Rochdale Grove, Rochdale Terrace, Back Rochdale Terrace, Roch-dale Avenue and Back Rochdale Avenue.

While Susan cooks tea at Hodsworth, Stuart walks up and under the crane which is battering the lower houses in Rochdale Road, and appears at the lower entrance of the Grove carrying his briefcase and with his jacket slung over his shoulder. He looks up as if inspecting the top windows of the remaining houses, or he could be sniffing the dusty air of diesel fumes and powdered old buildings, or he could be looking up at the air above the city or the tower of the blackened stone church on top of the hill. He walks towards the Mini which is parked next to his car, and Edwina sees him coming through her rear mirror, along the broken pavement and between the plane trees and the red-brick houses.

The demolition dust in the air has fallen on the road and pavement and mixed with pink blossom blown from a flowering cherry up the hill. Outside the city it will be sunny, but here it is not quite like summer anywhere else; warm enough for Stuart to have rolled up his shirt sleeves, but if he stood for long in Rochdale Grove he would put on his jacket again.

Alex's Dad comes home at eight when everyone else has gone. He has dinner at the dining-room table, facing north out of the window while eating, and when he is not looking out of the window he reads the *Daily Telegraph* propped on a brass lectern. Across his knees is a thick white damask table-napkin, and he drinks his soup from a Havergal pelican soup plate, while, through the hatch in the kitchen, Edwina cooks his next course. When he has finished his soup he can be heard moving his chair to bring the empty plate to the hatch, by which time Edwina has cooked his chop or his steak or his plaice. Aware of him standing by the hatch she brings him the second course of his three-course meal. While eating this he can sometimes be heard fetching the decanter of wine from the sideboard and pouring it into a glass. Then he usually asks if Edwina herself has eaten and she usually says that she was too hungry to wait and has eaten with the children.

This afternoon, before leaving for the Rochdales, she stood in his office holding the clip of newspaper cuttings while Susan's Nigel, Kevin and Tracy shouted in the shrubbery with Harry. There seemed to be nothing new, except a report from the *Sunday Times* about inherited criminal tendencies, which was next to "Eighteenth Century Grace Updated". But between these two was a smaller folded piece from *The Times*, a Law Report, beginning "Litigation could have been avoided . . ."

The date of the cutting was February, when Meredith was abroad. The creases in it suggest that it must have been kept folded since then in somewhere small, a pocket or a wallet.

But litigation did take place and under the general category of Matrimonial Causes, according to the article. Tiptree v. Tiptree were the litigants. The children concerned were not named, but ages were given, ten and twelve, and sexes, both male. "Litigation could have been avoided," said Mr Justice Rigby on the 12th of February this year, "had Mr Tiptree's solicitors at the time of the divorce hearing two years ago inserted a clause into the decree. This would have given Mr Tiptree the right to insist on private education for his sons . . ."

Meredith eats his dinner at eight-thirty. From the kitchen you can hear the knife on the plate as he cuts the meat, the movement of the vegetable dish on the table as he helps himself to more potatoes and peas, the folding and refolding of the newspaper and the wine being drunk. There may be only silence to indicate that he has finished eating and that the pudding course can be brought to the hatch.

"Father's Rights Upheld" was the heading of the article which told how Mr Justice Rigby ordered Mrs Tiptree's sons, although still in her custody, to be sent to the school of their father's choice. This, said Rigby, was in accordance with certain clauses of Matrimonial Causes, usually only applied in cases where there was a difference in religion between the parents.

The stage of the meal which Meredith is at is always evident, just as it is always evident where he is in the house day and night, whether he is walking around straightening pictures and adjusting the position of gilt chairs in the drawing-room, or on dry nights around the outside of the house stamping down the tarmac in the drive where it shows signs of breaking.

"Mrs Tiptree's choice of school," Mr Justice Rigby said, "was not in itself cause for concern. Rather it was the environment of the single-parent family with a mother out at work, which could not be deemed to provide the same potential academic encouragement as could be found in the environment of the type of school their father had in mind. The Tiptree males of ten and twelve will of course spend a fair proportion of the holidays with their mother."

Meredith goes to his office in the evening now. In spite of the dry weather there is a hiatus in the spreading of the terrace stones. The turf is cut, but nothing laid on it.

Edwina irons in the evening and Harry stays in the garden until nearly dusk and has to be called in over the noise of the traffic. Edwina then goes on ironing, folding sheets carefully in the growing dark until she is forced to switch on the white strip-light over her head, or abandon the ironing and sit in the study with the french windows still slightly open.

Sometimes the waiting in the Mini has lasted for half an hour before Stuart comes up the hill. Sitting in the car there are the remaining Rochdale houses to watch, where people who have been moving out carry furniture into vans and fill dustbins on the pavement. Then they sit talking on long flights of white stone steps which lead up to their front doors.

Stuart has described here in the car three-hour papers and hour-long interviews with outside examiners. "Pity," he sometimes says, "people can't go on being tested in a room and on paper for all their lives instead of having to go out there and live."

Edwina in the car reads the *Evening Post* and sees the sale advertisement for his house for which they are asking £6,500 for through-lounge, fitted kitchen, central heating, double-glazing, two bedrooms, studio attic and junkroom suitable for conversion to extra bed. Then she folds the paper, gets out of the car and walks along to the end of Rochdale Grove to an open space where trucks bring the broken doors, plasterboards and mantelpieces of houses from the other streets for burning. "A strong temptation," Stuart says from time to time, "to be the eternal post-post-graduate student, to get donnish and wear granny glasses, or would that come under the heading of elderly shuffling teenagers?"

The last end-terrace house in Rochdale Grove is already abandoned and its door is hanging on one hinge. Down the narrow passage with peeling wallpaper is a dolls' pram full of rags. Stuart thinks this is the house where Ursula lived earlier in the year with the bio-chemist, but she did not have a baby and nor did the bio-chemist, so he cannot think why there should be a dolls' pram in the passage.

In September, Stuart, in collar and tie, will be spelling out what he has learnt in the same Bristol college where he met Christine. And learn himself, he sometimes says, to mow the lawn on Sundays.

Edwina in the car reads that the house in Hodsworth is a very desirable property close to schools and public amenities. "At least," he said the other day, "I shall know that you are safe and sound and unlikely to be drummed out of the house by Meredith."

"And at least we have the summer until Christine breaks up and the house is sold."

A truck appears in the open space ahead of Rochdale Grove and tips off its load of boards and plaster, linoleum and pieces of carpet and drives off while the dust is rising.

Diana once talked about a cousin of hers who had this terribly sad thing, she said, with a man in Shell or Esso or it might be Total, and of course, as these things do, it came to the usual tragic end when he realised how his career would suffer, and she took a deep breath and deep thought for the good of her family. Being awfully sensible, Diana said, she went completely away on her own with a suitcase and left a note saying she must be on her own for a few days. To lose herself, as it were, Diana said. "These things are so awfully sad, Edwina."

Someone left a piano in a Rochdale house and the truck brings this to the open space and tips it with the other rubbish, so that it slides with its lid open and its black and white keys flapping like loose teeth and falls on its back with a percussive thump.

Diana's cousin has got over it completely and runs a play-group, works for the WRVS serving meals on wheels to old people and is learning to play Bridge again. You would never know when you go to stay with this cousin and her husband what a frightful fraught hiatus there was in their otherwise terribly happy marriage.

The man who drives the truck gets out and goes round to the piano and stamps on it. Then he levers up its wooden front and throws it to one side.

Alberta was lucky she admits. She and Bruce had been "having it off for years on and off and more on than off" when his wife went off with this potter from Camborne "and our ship came in just like that!" Alberta now says, "Jesus, we were lucky, Edwina."

The truck driver by the piano bends over it and pulls pieces from the inside and makes a small pile of bits of brass wire and lumps of lead for later collection.

And what of Mrs Tiptree of *The Times* Law Report, two years free of Tiptree but still unmarried, with whatever circumstances prevailing which made Mr Justice Rigby judge she would provide an unstable background in term-time for young ten and twelve? What is she doing while Tiptree arrives at school cricket matches in his Rolls?

If it was raining, the rain could stop when Stuart comes and cause rainbow prisms in the puddles. Or if it was windy would suddenly drop. Or perhaps a brass band could play him up the street.

It was not simply the dust of the falling Rochdales that kept the sun away from the city. Over the suburbs on the clearway the light in the sky is grey and the blocked clumps of trees, fields and hedges as you drive towards them are an alarming green lit by a coral pink ball of sun above the houses. Edwina follows Stuart's car at the end of rush hour on the inside lane of the clearway.

The interval widens between the two cars as they pass through West Hodsworth where the High School stands on a hill with its plate glass frontage reflecting pink against the surrounding playing fields and white goal posts. After that only the roof of the yellow car can be seen flashing between white hawthorn hedges and taking the rise to the railway bridge.

For Stuart, it could be argued, there will always be a car behind him or waiting for him parked in a side street, but to this he always says, "Don't count on that."

"But once you said that sometimes fucking a woman is a compliment you can't deny them."

"Perhaps I've changed."

"Not that much."

The yellow car is out of sight; the Mini pauses on the rise to the railway bridge. From the left, between fields coming away from the city, a blue diesel train heads towards the bridge, then it shoots east between more fields rustling the tops of white cow parsley and going towards the power station.

It is best to assume that the dread of parting is mutual, basing your assumption on the premise that neither wishes to hurt the other by going on about it too much.

A mile from East Hodsworth the road takes a bend and crosses a canal which travels parallel to the railway, across fields, but is unused and glassy, reflecting, like the High School windows, the pinkness of the sun. She said to him in the Rochdales, "It's not that I mind so much the idea of you fucking someone else. It's more that I would think of her thinking to herself—ah, now I've got him."

Turn into the village and increase speed, pass, without turning the head, the shops and the church and the car outside No. 38, although the door of his house will have scarcely shut on him. The beech trees of the avenue, which came into leaf within the last month are still a glossy pale mass reaching up the slope between the pastures. They are to be driven under, with flashing glimpses of the dry sky, and the village is left behind and below. The best way is to drive at second gear at top speed through the tunnel of the avenue, rising in height until the circle of light at the end comes into view. On the home flat stretch, as you emerge, change gear to third and head for the cattle grid at speed and keep the window open. Not that the smell is of hay or bluebells, but there is a freshness mixed with sulphur or whatever chemical it is that gets wafted in this direction from the power station and is said to be good for roses, someone said.

It was not the fear of a little man with a notebook in the shrubbery that kept them out of the spare-room this summer. After all, little men could find more protective colouring in the Rochdales. Rather it was Stuart's possible fear of possible little men, had he known of the possibility.

Re-reading *The Times* cutting does nothing except to confirm that it remains there between "Eighteenth Century Grace Updated" and the "Entire Rose Garden". And Meredith's life goes on; the Sealed Knot have fought a battle at Warwick Castle and a man who knew Meredith slightly in the army has got a C.B.E. in the Birthday Honours. Tiptree and Tiptree are now four cuttings deep. Meredith can be heard moving in his office and then can be heard coming down the stairs.

"I'd like to talk to you."

"Oh yes?"

"Of course, if you have anything to say . . ."

"No I don't think so actually."

"Or anything to suggest . . ."

"Not at the moment really . . ."

"Plans or so on . . ."

One late afternoon in the Rochdales, Stuart said that someone came to look at No. 38 and offered £6,000, cash down. Christine was out so he said to the man that they would discuss it, and could he come back tomorrow. But the man failed to turn up and, for some reason, Christine refuses to believe it ever happened.

Then he said that Christine's mother rang up to say there was a particularly nice house for sale in their road. So Christine dashed down one weekend by train to see it. When she came back she said the house was fine, but two nights' staying down there made her realise just how narrow her mother's outlook was. It would not do to live so close; they will have to find a house on the other side of Bristol, some other outskirt. Stuart accused her of incredible inconsistency. "Who wanted to go back there in the first place?" he said. "Of course we'll go," she said. "But people do change, don't they? People do grow up. Maybe not you," she said, "but people do."

Meredith can be heard going back upstairs. "We'll wait and see," said Edwina before he went. But he left with her a new box-file, red this time instead of green, which he opens and finds four new Prospectuses of prep schools clamped under a spring and with a note on Hodsworth Hall writing paper saying "Your comments please". The box-file also contains a copy of a letter to Meredith's mother with a section underlined which refers to Alex: "We took her away from St Cecilia's because we both think she will benefit from a home environment. I am pleased to say that she is acquitting herself well at the new school and has emerged triumphant from bullying. I believe this augurs well for Harry's school career."

And underneath, and surprisingly, another glossy booklet, like a prospectus but brightly coloured, is a brochure offering package holidays abroad, and another note from Meredith attached: "Thought something like this might interest you and Alex in August." Edwina writes underneath his writing: "Thought you knew Alex is going on pupil-exchange to France again and I have accepted open invitation from Alberta and Bruce for me and Harry. What about you? But thanks all the same." To which, some ten days later, Meredith replies: "I will stay here and finish the terrace."

169

Edwina irons in the evening and Harry stays in the garden until nearly dusk and has to be called in over the noise of the traffic. Edwina then goes on ironing, folding sheets carefully in the growing dark until she is forced to switch on the white strip-light over her head, or abandon the ironing and sit in the study with the french windows still slightly open.

Chapter 10

THE MAIL FOR East Hodsworth comes by post office van
to the village where it is sorted, divided into two and
placed in the khaki sacks which two ladies on bicycles carry
and deliver, one to the motorway end of the village and
one to the park end, Hodsworth Hall, the Dower House
and the Home Farm and cottages. The park end lady
reaches the gates of the park at about 8 a.m. and rides
as far as the first cattle grid. From there she has to push
her bicycle all the way up the avenue to the Hall, where
she leans it against the wall and walks across the cattle
grid and drive and to the front door. There is no letter
box in the door, but a mahogany brass-bound box just to
the left under the pediment standing on straight wooden
legs and with a brass letter slot. The envelopes go through
the slot and the parcels are placed on the lid of the box.
The box is not locked. When Meredith found it in the
attic the key was not with it. He polished the brass slot
and the brass corners and said it must have once stood in
the hall for the outgoing mail of the Baines-Robinsons and
their house-guests.

Whoever is first up at Hodsworth Hall goes to the front
door, draws back the bolt and turns to the right under the
pediment to open the mail box, while the post woman
pedals on in all weathers and, sometimes in the dark, up
towards the Dower House. In dry weather she wears a dark
blue serge coat and skirt and in wet weather covers this
with a heavy white macintosh. In winter you can see her
clearly from the upstairs windows, leaning forwards to
push the weight of her bicycle and the bag on up the hill.
In summer and autumn behind full trees she is only visible

171

in her macintosh, a slow moving patch of white.

On mornings when the wind does not carry the sound from the motorway over the house you can hear from the spare-room the scratch of the bicycle as it is leant against the wall and the post woman's shoes on the tarmac. By the time she has walked up the steps of the pediment you will be in dressing-gown waiting out of sight of the glass front door. Then, when she has gone, walk with bare feet on flagstones, unlock the door and step across the metal bootscraper, stand on the dusty floor of the pediment and open the box.

Meredith receives business letters in long white envelopes and once a week a letter from his mother on Basildon Bond. Alex occasionally gets smudgy envelopes from past friends of the Out Crowd at St Cecilia's. Stuart's letters used to be indistinguishable from the outside, but that was in the days when he wrote, between studying, on lined note-taking blocks in whatever ball-point pen he had to hand and found envelopes where he could. But, since he has been provided with an office at the College, his letters arrive in strong white envelopes and are addressed in thick blue-black ink. They arrive as promised on Tuesdays and Saturdays, but it is always worth listening for the post woman on every weekday in case some important development has forced him to write an extra letter.

Tuesdays and Saturdays of the late summer are days to lie back in bed and be reassured by glowing phrases which he manages to phrase variously from letter to letter. It helps to hear that there is no one in Bristol or its outskirts who could be called your equal. Nor is there, as it happens, a pub to equal the Bay Leaf. Nor is there a first class football team to follow, come to that.

Generally the first paragraphs tell you what Stuart has been thinking and the last ones what he has been doing. It seems necessary, lying in bed in the morning, to turn to these last ones first, and read that he has done the double glazing in the new house, bought a new suit and a new car and that Christine has passed her driving test. The first week at College a penultimate paragraph described a girl who showed her knickers in a tutorial. The final paragraph is always for plans. He thinks he can get away for a weekend towards the end of September, and hopes that gratification will be no longer deferred than that. Although, at the same time he has to admit that his life-style more and more resembles that of members of the class of people who respond to deferred gratification.

Edwina lies back in bed in a blue cotton housecoat, bought hopefully for the end of September, re-reading what she will re-read at intervals during the day, and is there again at night, re-reading.

"Well now that's all over, thank goodness," Diana said, drinking coffee downstairs at eleven o'clock.

"What's all over?"

"The summer. I've never known such a hectic one."

Diana sat on the chaise-longue in her autumn beech-coloured shirt, skirt and cardigan and said it was time they discussed the half-term party. Their daughters must approve the joint guest list before Maria goes back to St Cecilia's. Half-term would be an ideal time because it means lots of invitations coming for them in the Christmas holidays.

"Hectic and terrible summer," she said.

Outside, where it might rain any moment, Diana's children have been sent to play with Alex and Harry. The lawn is dark green and damp and beyond it the rain has flattened the michaelmas daisies. Diana says what you should do with michaelmas daisies, if you cannot stake them properly, is to cut them down to eighteen inches in July and then they don't grow so high.

"There was some quite nice weather in June," says Edwina.

"It poured all Wimbledon fortnight." Diana opens a notebook called Half-term Party and says one of the difficulties is that so many of Maria's friends were coming

173

from far away and would need putting up overnight. She has another list headed Hospitality.

"How's Robert's hip?"

"No better. The Channel Islands did him no good at all." She has twelve names of people requiring hospitality; Edwina can manage at least three in the spare-room with camp beds and mattresses and probably as many in the attic, can she not? That will leave six for the Dower House which they could manage at a pinch. "I think I may have to get Robert away to the South of France before half-term. Thank goodness there is now no sign of an election." She writes Drink on another page of the notebook and underneath Punch and Cider Only. If any boys want beer —that is just too bad; the Rochdales had beer last Christmas which was a great mistake.

Now she begins a page called Rules. Rules might sound silly for a party but with this particular age group and with the Rochdale experience last Christmas, it was vital to keep boys and girls dancing in the dancing room and sitting out in the sitting-out room. The secret Diana is sure is to let no one upstairs but the girls: girls' coats and girls' loo upstairs—boys' loos and boys' coats downstairs. "Agreed, Edwina?"

Edwina looked out of the french window at Alex and Maria; they walked across the lawn, arms folded, like two women who have just met and are making conversation.

"Edwina?"

"Oh yes fine. Loos. Plenty of downstairs loos for boys at the Dower House aren't there?"

"I thought the party was being held in your house ... here."

"Oh is it?"

Maria wears her long blonde hair in an alice band and walks in the wet garden in a school-uniform cardigan, cotton frock and sandals. Alex wears jeans, gymshoes and a T-shirt with 69 printed on the front of it.

"Edwina, honestly, I'm quite sure we agreed on it. If

you remember we had that party for them at the Dower House two Christmases ago."

"Yes of course you did. I know you did. I'd just forgotten. It will be fine having it here. Anyway it's months away."

"I didn't mean to land you with it. I mean, if you don't want to have it here ... but quite honestly what with Robert being so seedy ... and with all the others home for half-term ... and with..."

"I *want* to have it here Diana."

Two Christmases ago at the Dower House, Maria and Alex and their friends had sandwiches, sausage rolls and jellies at five o'clock, games and Scottish dancing until eight.

Upstairs again Edwina re-reads Stuart's letter, studying a sentence closely: "It is lovely here in autumn", which could also read "It is lonely here in autumn".

Diana took her four younger children and Harry in the Range Rover back to the Dower House for lunch, leaving Maria still walking in the garden with Alex. "Say what you will," said Diana before leaving, "Alex has changed enormously since she left St Cecilia's; but I think she and Maria are still good friends."

Maria waited until everyone else was served before starting. She ate slowly and now leaves a totally clean plate and asks first, if she might leave the table, and then if she may help with the washing up. She also says what a very nice meal it is. She says she had a lovely holiday in the Channel Islands but looks forward to going back to school where she will be in the sixth form now and working for A-levels. She heard the other day that she passed all eleven O-levels. The only thing that bothers her is that she wants to give up Latin, but Mummy and Daddy think she's quite good at it and want her to keep it on.

Alex, because of the change of school, is not taking O-levels until next summer, although she is a head taller than Maria and at least two bust-sizes larger. Her 69 T-shirt she got in France when she stayed with a French family whose daughter will visit Hodsworth next summer. Alex didn't think much of the daughter, she said, but the brother was O.K. The parents spent most of the time playing cards while Alex and the brother and his friends bicycled in the forest. They all had T-shirts with 69 on them this summer.

Maria says Mummy is having a long white dress made for her for the half-term party, but she herself will choose what coloured sash to wear with it. Alex says she doesn't know what she will wear for the party; she has not got a dress only lots of pairs of trousers.

Maria has long blonde hair, pale skin and high cheekbones and should look fairly devastating in a long white dress. Alex has dark skin, grey eyes and thick lashes. Her hair is as long as Maria's but she thinks she might have it layered into a sort of David Bowie hair-cut before half-term.

Maria says she envies Alex being at home all the time, but she knows Mummy and Daddy would never let her leave St Cecilia's yet. She will probably have a year off between leaving school and going to University and be able to help Mummy who has such a lot to do. Alex says it's not all that hot being at home all the time.

Maria says what a nice kitchen, what a nice table. "Did you have a nice holiday, Mrs Measures-Smith?"

Maria has a bedroom with a washbasin in the warm gable of the Dower House, with printed wallpaper, matching curtains and divan frill, wall-to-wall blue carpet, fitted bookcases, dressing table, desk and wardrobe. She and her younger sisters have ponies to ride in the fields, but go everywhere else by car. She has a mother who directs life comfortably and a rich father who does not quite know what to say to her. She does not know much about either her mother's family or her father's family and has lots of cousins of whom she only knows the names. Her school trunk will be half-packed by now for tomorrow; the au pair will have washed and ironed the clothes, but Maria may herself have sewn on some of the name-tapes.

Alex has a big cold bedroom over the kitchen at Hodsworth with an iron bedstead which used to be in the servants' quarters at Havergal. Her curtains are cut-down Havergal night-nursery and some of her sheets have a Havergal monogram on them. Her bedroom, like Maria's, has a washbasin, and with brass taps, but it is cracked and freezes to be unusable in the winter. She has posters on her wall of David Bowie, Alice Cooper, Che Guevara, President Kennedy, Steve McQueen and Norman Hunter. She goes to school by bicycle but is sometimes taken by car if it is raining. She has a father who does not know quite what to say to her and a mother who usually knows where she is and more or less what she is thinking on selected subjects. Alex's father goes away a lot and leaves lists of where he is going. Her mother goes out less but does not always say where. Alex doesn't know much about her father's side of the family but gets on well with her two aunts and four cousins on her mother's side. She was especially fond of her grandmother and still talks about her.

If you asked Alex what she thought of Maria she would say she was O.K. but a bit ordinary, but very nice really. She used to go to the Dower House for tea but says it is silly when you are fifteen to have to say things like "Can I have another chocolate biscuit" and "Please may I get down" when you want to leave the table. If you asked Maria what she thought of Alex, she'd say, well, she was not sure, but she thinks she would quite like to be friends with her.

Both Alex and Maria go upstairs after lunch to Alex's room and Edwina writes letters on the kitchen table.

"It's all wet end of summer here. But everything you write about is glowing—even thoughts of the double-glazing are mouth-watering. A is back from France wearing a 60 T-shirt. Diana said: 'Is it something to do with commemorating some Parisian student uprising in 1969 or something?' M is still banging away at the terrace.

Thud of spade but otherwise silence. Does Bristol know it's hovering in a rose-tinted haze?"

When the doorbell rings Edwina stands outside the kitchen and sees the looming width of Susan and the droopy shoulders of Mal through the glass panels. She sees Alex come down the stairs and along the hall. Back in the kitchen she hears them all going up the stairs.

"This morning had incredibly boring session with Diana about something called a half-term party. She thinks kids are going to fuck themselves stupid in all unguarded space ..."

Upstairs loud music, but no further movement.

"... You had been out of mind for at least ten minutes yesterday when Mrs Thwaite said that the new people at No. 38 have papered the downstairs flowery. Better not tell Christine. But tell yourself you are painfully missed ..."

At the bottom of the stairs by the banister rail can be heard percussion and brass filling the whole range of sounds which can be received by the human ear from the lowest to the highest.

"Barrage of noise here. Alex has incredibly boring Susan and Mal, plus Diana's incredibly lovely Maria. They listen to music, but I never hear them speak."

At the bottom of the stairs again, though the sense of hearing may be swamped, sniff and sniff again.

"They're all right, but what about us? End of September isn't long. When and where?"

The smell from upstairs was only the familiar smell of Gauloises brought back from France.

"For Christ's sake, when and where?"

Later with the sun out and Harry back from Diana's,

178

Susan's Kevin, Nigel and Tracy were on the lawn which was bright but still damp. The larger ones came down from Alex's room and pulled the smaller children heaped one on top of the other in Harry's old pram, and Harry on his bicycle sped head down towards the michaelmas daisies, crashed through them, breaking the flattened stalks and came out the other side of the border.

On an exceptionally clear day from the top windows, it is recorded somewhere, you can see both Lincoln Cathedral and York Minster, but from ground level, looking across the lawn and the smashed border the first high points to north and south are pit wheels which are not spinning.

As the sun moves behind the house the lawn is divided diagonally, one half dark and the other half still bright. Now on the grass people move between the sunny and the shady, but the traffic on the motorway prevents you from knowing whether they are laughing or screaming.

In the foreground an area of turf is missing. In the shade outside the drawing-room window and stretching past the study flat stones are spread like jigsaw puzzle pieces with gaps between. At weekends Meredith works from dawn till dusk and for autumn work he has rigged a searchlight against the wall of the house and works after dark. The stones must be all laid and the balustrade erected before frost can turn the cement brittle before it sets. He started digging in April and stopped in May and June. He went on again in July and stayed home for his three-week summer holiday to carry rubble dumped by a truck by the pediment and spread it on the soil for the foundations.

The terrace will stretch under the drawing-room window, but access to it will be through the french windows of the study. And the study, Meredith now plans, will return to its original function as an ante-room to the drawing-room. It will, during the winter, be redecorated and he will be on the look-out in sale-rooms for suitable furniture. The chaise-longue will go, for a start; and then the television, up-stairs to Alex's room or perhaps to Harry's, or if Edwina insists on making herself a hideaway place where she can smoke those extremely unpleasant-smelling cigarettes, at the bottom of the four-poster in the spare-room.

When they have dinner parties in future summers, Meredith plans that they will start by serving guests with drinks on the terrace and then they will process through the ante-room to the drawing-room and finally across the hall to the dining-room. There will, necessarily, have to be suitable garden furniture, perhaps the white table from the kitchen which used to stand on the terrace at Havergal.

Edwina protested that summer dinner parties, were they to be held, would be delightful she is sure, what with aperitifs on the terrace and long drinks poured on clinking ice from the Waterford jug, but it would be nicer if it was built so that it received at least some of the evening sun. As things are, she pointed out, the wind blowing round the corner and the height of the house keeps the south side of the house fairly cool, if not actually cold, on many summer evenings. And even when it is still and warm enough for ladies in thin dresses to sit in the shade at eight p.m., the mosquitoes come, and the noise from the motorway tends to echo more than usual against the fabric of the building.

Meredith went on digging and spreading rubble. By the time Edwina and Harry came back from St Ives the measured area was outlined and ready for the first laying of stone slabs.

"By the way," he said, when she returned, "you will find some new thoughts on Harry's future in the red box-file."

The new thoughts of Meredith were attached to another Prospectus, that of a school which, calculated on his milometer when he visited it, was at the most thirty miles south down the motorway and could be reached in not much over thirty minutes. In Nottinghamshire, not in Yorkshire. The Headmaster Meredith described as very sound, an Oxford M.A., ex-Parachute Regiment and D.S.O. and bar. The school has all the requirements they once agreed upon and a good record of successful entries to Eton, Harrow, Marlborough and Rugby. In fact they hold the record for successful Common Entrance candidates in the North of England. They have a most interesting and obviously efficient system of instilling in boys what Meredith called a "Winners' Instinct", by a method of rewards, privileges and withdrawal of same. The Headmaster could not have been more charming to Meredith, and informed him that they are always able to detect in the first few years of a boy's entry into the school whether or not he is likely to pass into the Public School his father has chosen for him. A few fathers, the Headmaster said, once they know their sons are unlikely to reach the chosen goal, prefer to withdraw them. After all, the Headmaster understands, an investment of school fees at the rate they are forced to scale them these days, is indeed a large investment. In a few cases boys have been withdrawn and placed in state schools where they have been able to settle, he understands, without too strong a sense of failure. Meredith told the Headmaster of a few of Harry's qualities and the Headmaster fully believed that he sounded the sort of child who would benefit from the system and fit into it. Some children, said the Headmaster, have a natural sense of order and hierarchy and the school fits them like a glove.

"That's what I'm afraid of," wrote Edwina at the bottom of the report.

"He will start after Christmas," wrote Meredith in reply.

Many boys, the Headmaster told Meredith, start off as day pupils, but they often find, after a time, that they are falling behind, missing out on the community life and choose to become boarders. "It's a long way to drive," wrote Meredith, "I fully admit, and the time may come when you will need a new car. Unless, of course, it happens that Harry chooses early to join the community as a full member."

"I am also afraid of that," wrote Edwina diagonally across the whole page of writing. "But, if it comes to that, there are better, much better places I have heard of."

At five o'clock she borrowed Alex's bicycle to ride to the

village to post her letter to Stuart and walked back slowly up the avenue.

An hour ago they had all been moving on the lawn, but now they were grouped under the pediment between the two central pillars, the tall ones standing on the top step and the short ones on the next step down, with Harry at their feet on the bottom step, a front row all of his own. Meredith stood with a camera aimed at the group and his back to the cattle grid. If this was a colour print it would be of grey stone, blue denim, Maria's blonde hair, with Harry's red rubber wellington boots making a splash of colour in the low foreground. Meredith clicked the camera and said "Stand still again please", and clicked it again. Then he waved them away and they stood around looking at each other, while he consulted his light meter and aimed his camera higher and clicked again.

Noticing that Edwina had returned he explained that he wanted a photograph or series of photographs which gave the exact proportions of the pediment, and that it was lucky that there seemed to be children of various sizes around to show comparison with the building against which they stood.

"Why on earth do you want a photograph of the pediment?"

Meredith explained that it was part of a plan to have the Havergal coat of arms carved, but the difficulty was that the 1836 took up a central position. "This stone-mason with whom I have discussed it says it might be possible to incorporate the date into the design of the arms, spreading the three suns around it, incorrectly perhaps. It is simply a question of asking oneself whether one is going to compromise in this matter or whether one is going to keep to the letter of the law of Heraldry." He stepped slowly back towards the cattle grid and lifted his camera again. "And by the way—ask Harry to come back here again. I want one of him alone, rather sentimental I suppose, but under where his coat of arms will be. Yes there, Harry. Sit there, Harry, under where your coat of arms will be, Harry. Sit there very still."

Edwina said, "I haven't actually agreed."

"To what? This photograph?"

"To that place, that school."

"It seemed to solve the problem excellently I thought. I've left it as long as possible to give you a chance to mature whatever alternative plans you might have had to propose." He lifted his camera. "I thought perhaps you had some."

"I may have."

She reaches under the pillow and gets out Stuart's letter again. "Lovely in autumn" or "Lonely in autumn"? And then there is a sentence about Christine which says "Bought a new car", but the word before "bought" could be "we" or "she". Did they go out in the lovely autumn together and buy a new car? Or was it lonely for him while she went out and bought it?

The low sun shines directly over the avenue and into the spare-room between the central pillars of the pediment; and down the avenue Mal and Susan walk away hand in hand.

But, if it was lonely for Stuart while Christine went out to buy a new car, it comes to the same thing in the end as it being lovely to go out together.

There there is the bit: "All gloomy", he wrote, "C is trying". Lady Havergal used to call people "trying" when they were what she called tiresome people, people who try the nerves. "Very trying people" to Lady Havergal were nuisances. But, for Stuart, people are bloody or smashing or mean or warm-hearted. Never trying, unless they are making some deliberate or praiseworthy effort.

Meredith passes across the drive with his spade and wheelbarrow containing a bag of cement. He stops, turns and stands looking up at the pediment. Edwina ducks down out of the beams of the sun.

Stuart did not write: "All gloomy *but* C is trying". Nor did he write: "All gloomy *and* C is trying". The interpretation can only be based on the insufficient and isolated statement that Christine is trying. Or look again and wonder if she could be crying.

It was tempting to stop on the outskirts of Bristol on the way home from St Ives, but the new home address was given for emergencies only, and not for the sort of emergency caused by the exhaust pipe falling off the Mini in the middle of a single line of traffic. They waited while a garage replaced the pipe and any moment Stuart might have driven past. But Bristol, being, as Harry pointed out, one of the six biggest cities in England, would have very extensive outskirts through which to search for Stuart's house. They drove on again when the exhaust pipe was mended and Harry slept for the last two hundred miles.

At St Ives, Alberta was finally told about Stuart in the small hours of the last day of the holiday, and said, "Hang on I should. You two may be lucky like Bruce and I."

"I'm not sure I actually want Stuart's wife to leave him like that. He'd be terribly hurt."

"Jesus," Alberta said. "You don't mean that. Or if you do you're certainly no Havergal."

"But the Havergal thing, I always thought, was to be nice."

"Is that what you think?" said Alberta, but the conversation was interrupted by the coming in of two of Alberta's four daughters and three of Bruce's four sons.

Meredith fetches a stone slab and places it edge to edge with the last one laid last night and explains how he has discovered a little man in Beauchamp Place who sells stone urns. Meredith has ordered four which will be placed at intervals over the expanse of the terrace and should have plants growing in them. Edwina, he suggests, could during the winter look up some gardening books and see what sort of things are suitable for urns.

Chapter 11

In NEW LONG boots to the knee which almost touch the hem of the fur coat Edwina walks down the stairs of the empty house carrying a small suitcase. She crosses the hall into the kitchen where there is a large sheet of foolscap paper on the table and beside it a blue felt pen. She puts the suitcase down and picks up the pen. The list reads:

1. Evening meal—sausage & mash. Potatoes peeled in saucepan, sausages in fridge.
2. Boiler. Leave damper in present position *regardless* of temperature of water (Daddy's instructions).
3. If Harry comes back from school with worse cold see that he does not play outside.
4. If Mal comes for a meal with Susan see that he leaves before 9.30.

To this list, using the felt pen, she adds: "5. If you finish loaf of bread this evening, you'll have to bike down to village to get another loaf for breakfast." Then she picks up the suitcase, slings on her leather shoulder bag, goes through the hall and leaves the house by the front door. She posts the key in the mail box and goes down the steps to where the Mini is waiting. As she leans over to put the suitcase on the back seat, the wind bangs the car door against her legs. The same wind piles dead leaves from the avenue in heaps on the steps of the pediment. She sits in the driver's seat of the Mini, fixes her safety belt and switches on the engine, but after a few seconds she lets the engine die, switches off the ignition, undoes her safety belt, gets out of the car, takes the key out of the mail box and goes into the house again. In the kitchen she picks up the blue felt pen and adds to the list: "6. See note 3 about Harry's cold. He ought to have electric fire, convector from dining-room in his room, but take it out before you go to bed. DO NOT FORGET THIS."

Before meeting the wind in the drive again she stands buttoning her coat inside the front door, and before she leaves the house again she returns to the kitchen and writes: "7. If by any chance Susan can't come for the night you are to ring Mrs Golding and say this is an emergency which I shall explain later and ask if you and Harry can go there until I return."

The Mini half-circles the drive, crosses the cattle grid and goes down the avenue through the park and the quiet mid-morning village where two women stand beside a pram outside the grocer's, the hems of their coats flapping in the wind. Edwina drives between the grocer's and No. 38, looking neither left nor right and does not stop again until she reaches the filling station on the round-about. Mal walks towards the Mini slowly in his blue dungarees and pink cap, his long straight hair blowing around his shoulders, and reaches for the hosepipe and metal filling nozzle of the petrol pump. "The usual then?" he asks. And he gazes up on to the motorway and she looks straight ahead while the pump hums. He turns to inspect the gauge, switches off the pump and comes to the driver's window to tell her that he has put in five gallons. She asks him to check her oil. He lifts the bonnet of the Mini and lets his long hair swing into the engine. He wipes the dipstick on his dungarees and sticks it back in to the oil tank. "You're not forced to put any in," he says, staring at her, holding the dipstick in the air. She asks him for water. He unscrews the cap of the radiator, looks inside and shakes his head. "Anything else?" She asks him for air in her tyres and moves the car close to the garage wall. She watches the top of his pink cap while he kneels on the ground, holding the end of the air pipe to the tyres of the car and keeping his upturned eyes on the gauge on the wall above his head. She gives him a five pound note and, while waiting for him to bring her the change, she looks at the mileage gauge inside the car which says the Mini has been 49,706 miles exactly.

"Your Alex all right?" he says putting change through the window into her hand.

"Yes. She's at school. But half-term next week."

"Yeah I know. Might see her later today."

"And Susan of course."

"Oh yeah ... and Susan." Then he waves. "Tara then."

Beyond the canopy covering the petrol pumps raindrops spot the tarmac. Edwina drives away and through her rear mirror sees Mal leaning on the cash desk inside the plate-glass window, gazing out and up at the lorries moving on the motorway. As he gazes he is licking an ice-cream.

She drives back through the village faster than before. She takes the avenue and the cattle grid at speed, runs into the house leaving the front door swinging and goes back to the list on the kitchen table: "8. Think perhaps you should not let Susan have Mal round here this evening. Not at all, I mean. Better I think, since I have not asked Susan's mother what she thinks about it, and really haven't got time to go round and check with her." Before leaving the house again she crosses out this last bit by scribbling over it, blotting it out completely with felt pen so that the list ends in a thick blue oblong block, and adding: "9. If *anything* unusual happens or you are worried about *anything* ring Mrs Golding."

The signs which stand on tall metal legs on the grass verges of the motorway are dull dark green with white writing. On the south-bound carriageway they read "The South, Nottingham, Leicester, Derby". They are read through the murky windscreen of the Mini which is splashed by lorries overtaking and cleaned by humming windscreen wipers. The Mini travels on the inside lane, dwarfed by a long vehicle in front which carries on its open back long strips of metal shelving with sharp ends.

The Mini will stay for the start of the journey and for safety on the inside lane between lorries while the road conditions are considered and equipment tested. Check petrol, oil, air and water, windscreen wipers working, indicator lights operating both left and right, and, at the touch of a lever, the car heater is on; operate the windscreen washer with a foot pedal, try the new boots on clutch, brake and accelerator. On the dashboard instrument panel the temperature gauge points to a mark called "normal", the speedometer reads fifty miles an hour and the mileage indicator is now sliding up to 49,710. Less than efficient, however, is the car radio; water has reached inside the aerial socket, the reception is blemished and the sound of music which should accompany this journey is lacking. It is only just possible to hear between static interference on the midday weather forecast that a belt of rain is sweeping from the north-west following the cold front which arrived three days ago, but this will be succeeded by brighter and more changeable weather in the late afternoon. Some sun can be expected in northern and midland districts before nightfall, and temperatures at the weekend will return to normal for late October.

As the cold front arrived Meredith announced that he would be in London until Saturday or possibly Sunday, and the list of instructions was commenced in blue felt pen, and kept in the drawer of the kitchen table along with the now near-completed other list called Half-Term Party.

The Mini coasts at a careful distance between the truck of metal shelving in front and the yellow pantechnicon behind. The road rises and becomes flat with embankments falling to either side. The sky clears of rain and in grey cloud the convoy of vehicles slides towards the converging of motorways.

Meredith came into the kitchen in his black London coat and with his briefcase and said that, while in London for business purposes he intended to see the stone-carver about the pediment and the little man in Beauchamp Place about the urns for the terrace. He had not, however, forgotten the Party on Saturday. Whether or not he returned in time depended on a great many factors operating in the prevailing circumstances. Meanwhile the study could stay as it was, and not until after the party would it be the ante-room again.

Between truck and pantechnicon Edwina accelerates down a wide hill towards Sheffield where overhead lights direct traffic to travel at sixty miles an hour and where furnace tops sending out smoke are at eye level and where on a fine day and with a working car radio you can thunder to music as loud as they play it in Alex's room.

In case Meredith did not return by Saturday night he packed all Havergal glasses into boxes and put them in his office together with the Worcester porcelain from the drawing-room. For the first time ever he locked his office door.

Up and away from Sheffield the heavy traffic slows and it is time for the Mini to edge into the middle lane and take the gradient easily at 65 miles an hour, climbing towards a dark cloud and into more rain.

Meredith said that, if the dancing had to be in the drawing-room the gilt chairs must go in the dining-room. He piled them in the corner behind the table. In case he did not return in time to see that they remained there he wrote a notice on a piece of card saying "Not to be moved". And, again in case he did not return, he gave Edwina ten pounds towards the food and drink.

To one side of the long hill out of Sheffield stands a blue notice saying "Services 30 miles" and bearing symbols representing cups, saucers, knives, forks and petrol pumps. The Mini keeps going at sixty-five while the mileage indicator reads 49,740 and enters the next downpour in the belt of rain still sweeping from the north-west.

Diana telephoned every day this week with amendments to the guest list and changes in the names of people who would be spending the night of Saturday at Hodsworth Hall. She decided to let Edwina have three boys and three girls but all on the youngish side and unlikely to prowl around at night and that sort of thing.

The rain bounces on the once-white Mini bonnet and steams with the heat of the engine which has driven nearly 50,000 miles in the six years since it arrived on a Christmas morning; Harry was strapped into his car chair to be given an early ride in Daddy's present to Mummy which would drive him to school for years and years. More recently an ex-Ford mechanic who looked at the engine on a frosty night predicted months rather than years. And more recently still Edwina has committed herself to drive it daily sixty miles there and sixty miles back until such time as it fails completely, or until such time as Harry says: "Mother you need not drive me to school daily any longer; I shall now become a full member of this community and stay here all the time."

Diana said she was fetching Maria from St Cecilia's early for half-term and together they would finish the long white dress. Alex bought black velvet trousers and a black T-shirt with a red dragon on it. Susan found a red crêpe long skirt and blouse to match and has put white embroidered braid on Mal's purple flared trousers and helped him choose a satin shirt.

A warning notice "Strong Cross Winds" comes into view as the Mini sweeps with the rain belt along the top of hills between Sheffield and Nottingham and its destination is one hundred miles away. Zero hour is six o'clock in the foyer of a motel not far from Birmingham.

On Monday Diana said this was the final countdown. She brought to the house a cousin of Robert's who is going to run the discotheque so that he could check the position of electric plugs. She whispered that she was not that happy about him; Robert's relations, unlike Robert himself, were unpredictable, and this boy was reading sociology at Essex University. Moreover Robert now said they would have to ask him to stay the night at the Dower House—an extra house-guest she would rather do without.

The car goes well at four hours from zero hour; there

will be time to sit and time to drink in the foyer of the motel before Stuart comes.

On Tuesday she made up three mattresses in the attic and three in Alex's room. She explained to Diana that she wished to keep the spare-room for all the girls' coats. On Wednesday she made Quiche Lorraine for fifty and took it to Diana to put in her deep-freeze. Diana said Quiche Lorraine was best either frozen for weeks or made fresh, and that she had expected Edwina would be making it on Friday. "Friday may be a little complicated Diana."

On Wednesday Diana said the boy who is running the discotheque would have to be put up for the night. She wished Robert had not introduced his cousin, but since it is his only contribution to the party apart from money, it would be impossible to refuse. But there just wasn't room at the Dower House, and, since this boy will bring his own sleeping bag, couldn't he squeeze into the attic at the Hall?

On Thursday Edwina, wanting a bath, moved the damper of the boiler beyond the point which Meredith had marked so that it roared white hot for two hours and then went out. She was cracking sharp volcanic clinkers out through the fire door with a bent poker when Alex said, reading the list on the kitchen table:

"Where exactly are you going tomorrow?"

"Have you altered the hem of your new trousers Alex?"

"Hem?"

"Yes. Hem."

"Hem. Hem. Yes, but the zip won't work."

When Harry also asked where she was going she said, "Leicester".

"Which hotel are you staying at?" He got out the AA book. "There is one four-star and two three-star hotels in Leicester."

"I will decide which one when I get there."

On Friday morning he stood in the spare-room doorway and sniffed.

"Harry! You haven't got a cold, have you?"

"No. Just a sniffle. Did you know that you should go to

191

Leicester down the M1 as far as Junction 22 or you could go through Nottingham as well if you wanted to." He sat under the eiderdown between the two end pillars of the bed and traced the way to Leicester with his fingers on the quilted cotton.

With ten miles to the Motorway Service Area it is still possible, just, to touch sixty miles an hour on the middle lane, and slide ahead of trucks and coaches, under the white bridges which span the road; but to keep at that speed it is necessary to press the accelerator a little harder and hear that the engine runs with effort and makes more noise. Loss of Power, you must call it when describing such symptoms to people who know about engines.

They should have met as planned at the end of September when the mileage clock read 49,000; then they should have met the first weekend of this month, October, but Stuart had to stand in for someone at a weekend course in Bath; nor could they meet the next weekend because Diana was in Cannes with Robert and left Matthew staying at Hodsworth Hall because the au pair was on holiday. Then they should have met the weekend after that, but Christine was ill. And it has to be half-term. Christine is "blooming" now, wrote Stuart, and he has told her he is going to a conference and sent her to her mother's. "Fixed it finally."

Loss of power on the middle lane means flashing a left indicator and hoping you will be made space for on the crowded inside lane, that a truck will fall back and flash its headlamps to let you in. And, having found space, the problem then is to coast at fifty and find that this requires harder pressure of foot on accelerator than ever before to achieve this speed.

Stuart wrote, "I don't have to ask if you can fix things your end."

The car inside feels hotter and smells of heating metal; suspect the radiator even though this was inspected this morning by Mal and declared by him to be full of water.

"But drive carefully. I want you whole. Wholly want you whole," wrote Stuart.

Then come jets of steam and after that jets of black smoke seeping out round the bonnet and blowing in front of the windscreen. The Mini comes to a halt on the hard shoulder of the motorway only inches from heavy traffic, refusing to be nudged a further inch to safety. Shaken by the vibrations of the stream of vehicles and near one of the high white bridges, it stays there, nose into embankment. Now is the time to leave it and stand, coat collar turned up, hands in pockets while steam and oil-smoke mix with wind and spots of rain. Back up the road is an emergency telephone; walk three hundred yards there with all sound of walking drowned by engines.

"Motorway emergencies. Can I help you?"

Listen, feeling the traffic behind you move your coat. Look down the road at the smoking Mini by the bridge. Stuart will be setting off, packing up his books, picking up his briefcase, locking his filing cabinet and office door.

"Motorway emergencies. Please state your position and the nature of the breakdown."

He will light a Gauloise as he gets into the new car; he says it's a Ford again of course but red. He'll study the map, put on his dark glasses maybe; maybe wear the new suit he wrote about.

"Please state your position caller."

He's worked out he will leave the College at four and get on to the M5 which turns into the M6 somewhere to the west of Birmingham and take the ring road towards the motel and be there promptly at 6.30.

"Caller do you know exactly where you are?"

Something in the air, he said, about this weekend. As he pointed out to Christine, conferences set you up wonderfully; it's twenty-four hours of study sessions. Study of the development of the cognitive processes he told her. Of Edwina's cognitive processes, he has not mentioned. "Forget it. Anticipation is acute and cards at last stacked in favour."

"Caller. Do you know at all your whereabouts?"

"Queue Here", the notice says. The Supervisor's office is behind the garage of the Services Area, a narrow dark room where you wait in line in front of his desk. He sits up there reading reports mechanics have written on small square bits of paper.

"Motor-cars which break down on Fridays," he informs the queue, "are lucky to be dealt with. The service we provide..."

He has smooth black hair and a white linen jacket, and under his raised desk his legs can be seen in black trousers and narrow ankle boots. Behind him are spare parts on a block of metal shelves.

A man with a Volkswagen next in the queue whispered as he came in that he'd broken down on a Friday once before and not got home till Monday.

"This service is not for ill-maintained weekend motor-cars unaccustomed to motorway demands. Rather we act as suppliers of small spare parts for the driver who, having used his motor-car, or, as it may be, his truck, throughout the week..."

The mechanic who inspected the Mini brought the ticket to the Supervisor who now holds it as he talks. Impossible to read the writing on it, however much you lean towards the desk. The man with the Volkswagen stands hat in hand.

"Some motor-cars, let's face it, on a Friday," the Supervisor says, "come here to die."

Behind his head and on the top shelf of the metal block of shelves the spare parts are in small boxes illustrated with their contents; headlamp bulbs, sidelights, switches, sparking-plugs and fan-belts.

"A driver of a motor-car on Friday, and with a major fault, does not expect assistance." He bends his neat black head towards the queue. Behind him on the second shelf are larger boxes—clutch plates, brake cables and what might be air filters.

194

"Motorists with faulty cars who risk their lives and the lives of others on the motorway, and arrive..."

To see on to the lowest shelf of all you have to stand beside the Supervisor's desk. This shelf holds large chunks of metal, each one with a tie-on label, exhaust pipes, gearboxes, batteries and some radiators.

"Motorists, rather, who are brought in, towed in..."

The spare parts on the lowest shelf are dusty, difficult to recognise, and the radiators are mostly at the back. Step forward further.

"Weekend motorists expecting..."

To reach into the lowest shelf the dusty floor must be knelt on. Step forward then, and kneel.

"I have known instances..." the Supervisor says, and then stops talking and looks down. "Can I help you Madam?"

The splinters on his office floor pierce through fine new tights. "That radiator at the back. That radiator at the back would fit my car."

"Spare parts on the bottom shelf are all on special order," the Supervisor says.

It is just possible to reach to the back. The pieces here are hard to move, but push to one side a gearbox and to the other side a battery. "This radiator has no name."

"Spare parts on the bottom shelf are all on special order," repeats the Supervisor. But the Volkswagen man kneels too. "She's right you know. It's got no label, and it's for a Mini at a guess."

The queue stands back as the Supervisor gets down from his high stool and walks round his desk. "Correct it is for an Austin Mini. Correct it has no label. But that radiator, Madam, is destined for some else's car."

"Then whose?"

He stands above. "I will consult my records. When I have dealt with other clients."

"Consult them now."

He stands by the "Queue Here" notice, holding his ledger

195

to the light. Inside, other people wait, leaning on the spare part shelves, or against his desk. Outside not much light at half past four in late October, but the rain belt still blows in.

"It's not a recent order."

"Then I can have it."

The Volkswagen man says he'll go home by coach and come back on Monday. His wife will be fed up not having the car for Saturday. The Supervisor closes his ledger and pushes past to put it on his desk.

"You could order another radiator for whoever wanted that one and put that one in my car."

When he got down from his stool the Supervisor was shorter than you would have expected when he was sitting behind his desk. She handed him the radiator which he seemed to find heavier than he had expected.

"I suggest you do that. Thank you."

The variable afternoon sun strikes on the motorway sign which says "A52 Nottingham-Derby". Check fuel, speed and mileage, but ignore the temperature gauge which said normal even when the engine boiled. Take the speed to sixty miles an hour and signal that you are turning left off the motorway. Then cross back over it and head for Derby, which you will circle on a ring road and follow the signs which say Burton-on-Trent. The rain belt has gone ahead and in the Trent Valley the sun strikes low over wooded hills on the right, flickering so that it is wise to move the sun-visor to that side.

The Trent Valley road is wide and flat with thick grass between two carriageways, and bypasses on the left the city of Lichfield. Lichfield, Harry says, is very small for a City, like St David's in Pembrokeshire which is only the size of some villages, and Burton-on-Trent which is much bigger is only called a town. The sun behind the woods throws streaks of light on the wet road and sprays of water spurt up as the Mini skims on the shiny surface. The grass between the carriageways is still thick, unmown, ungrazed and dark green.

The mechanic at the Services said it was a Friday last spring that a man came in with a Mini boiling dry and they'd sent over to Derby for a new radiator, taken the old cracked one out and pushed the car outside by the petrol pumps to wait. But when the radiator arrived from Derby they could not find either the car or the driver. That was on Saturday morning but no one remembered seeing him go and the petrol pumps are open all the night. On the Friday, when this man came, he'd said he was on his way to Oxford, but he could not have got there with no radiator the mechanic said.

"Friday is a good day for some people," said the man with the Volkswagen as she drove away.

For some people radiators turn up somehow in the end, just as the telephone always rings in the end and the post woman nearly always comes on the day in question. A good day Friday. What good cards, they say. What rotten cars. "What a lovely baby," said the nurse one Friday in the spare-room. "Well anyway he walks like Steve McQueen," said Alex. Some people can even drive to Oxford with no radiator in their car. "Is that what you think?" Alberta said. "I find you very positive, Edwina," said Lawrence the American.

"It's only three hours on the coach to Newcastle," said the man with the Volkswagen.

The motel foyer stretches into a distant and dark confusion of doors. Pools of light fall just inside the glass swinging entrance doors from low hanging lamps on to the receptionist's desk. Facing the desk there is an alcove lined with long sofas covered with peat-brown linen, and behind the sofas, curtains of the same colour are drawn at six o'clock.

Edwina sits alone in the alcove on the expanse of dark upholstery dotted with cream-coloured cushions. Her rabbit fur coat is open, her legs, which look their thinnest in the tight new boots, are crossed. Her fawn flared tweed skirt is knee length and her soft oatmeal sweater is unspectacular. The skirt length suggests a compromise between mini and maxi, or perhaps resignation, and the sweater is collar-less and could be worn with pearls. Excluding the boots, her mother could, and did, in the case of the rabbit fur, in some photographs look the same. Edwina's hair has grown just above her shoulders with an inch or so only of bleached streaked ends, and is kept out of her eyes with a kirby-grip.

As the swing doors of the foyer open, as people arrive, air gusts through; it by-passes the alcove and slightly opens the doors at the far end. There are low voices at the reception desk and round the corner at the bar counter. People who arrive put their suitcases down soundlessly on the carpet as they sign the register under the lamplight. At the bar, bottles and glasses chink and echo on a harder surface. An arriving couple look across at Edwina in the window alcove; the wife looks across and around the dark spaces while the husband signs the register; then both go through the far doors where the bedrooms must be.

Before sitting here she bought a single whisky and soda which is on the low polished table in front of her. She put the glass carefully on the table and sat down. Before buying the drink and sitting down she asked at the desk if a Mr Douglas had rung up at all and left a message for anyone. The receptionist whose blonde hair is piled on top of her head sits in the centre of a pool of light. She looked up and said there were no messages for anyone. Edwina then sat not facing the swing doors but so that she could see them only by turning her head over her right shoulder. Waiting for people you must never sit facing the way they will come. In the Rochdales she parked the Mini so that she saw him coming in the driving mirror. In the station she stood in the doorway and let Harry see the train come in. In the kitchen at home when Meredith comes in she stands facing the cooker.

At home in the kitchen now the sausages will be frying and the potatoes being mashed. Harry will have finished watching television. Diana at the Dower House will be finishing Maria's white dress and making salmon mousse for the party. Somewhere in London, Meredith will be in a taxi going from business conference to hotel or drinking sherry.

The telephone buzzes a low musical note on the receptionist's desk. She lifts it, speaks into it while looking across at Edwina and puts it down again. A young couple come through the swing doors to register. Edwina re-crosses her legs and takes another sip of the whisky. The young man signs the register eagerly and the girl with him stands beside their matching suitcases and looks over at the window alcove. Edwina opens her shoulder bag and takes out a new packet of Gauloises and a box of matches. She opens the cigarettes, puts one in her mouth and lights it. The young man by the reception desk picks up both suitcases and hurries towards the far dark doors followed by the girl. He walks like Harry rides his bicycle, head down, and pushes the doors open with his shoulder. Edwina stares at the way they went, smokes her cigarette, takes another sip of whisky and soda and hears the wind and feels the draught from the glass swing doors behind her again. But it will not be Stuart this time nor the next time, although there will be no doubt by the way the doors swing open when he does arrive.

He will have left home this morning, done a day's work, got into his new red Ford, the new car they or he bought in September (the old yellow one he gave to Christine), and, driving in the new one, having set off from the College at four, he will be very nearly here.

Or he will not have managed to get away and any minute the receptionist will lift the telephone and look, as she always does, at Edwina across the foyer, but this time hold out the telephone and say, "Are you the lady who is waiting for a message from a Mr Douglas?"

The bedroom, like the foyer, is muffled dark brown and cream with mushroom-coloured curtains and bedspreads. Above the padded headboard is a switchboard of knobs and dials to control the heat, the television, radio and lighting. The bedside lamps throw circles of light on the pillows. Stuart's suitcase glows red beside Edwina's blue on the long shelf beside the television, and he is beside her on the bedspread, cream-coloured cotton shirt beside oatmeal sweater, brown corduroy trousers beside long black boots.

At home at seven o'clock they will have eaten the sausages and mash and will perhaps be doing homework, depending upon whether Mal is there or not.

Walking from the reception desk through the doors and corridors they have both said "How are you?" several times, asked after Christine, Meredith and the children. They have enquired after journeys which took Edwina longer to tell than Stuart, they have unpacked half a bottle of Bell's whisky from each suitcase, taken off their coats and turned on the colour television which neither of them has at home. They have established that they are both very glad that they have arrived in the first fifteen minutes of the possible fifteen hours they have together.

They have also discussed, facing the television which they keep switching from channel to channel with remote control from the bedhead knob, whether they should eat a meal now at the motel restaurant, or undress and make love now and later go and buy fish and chips and eat it in the bedroom. They drink whisky from polished glass tumblers they found in the bathroom next door and mixed with water from the tap. They switch the television from channel to channel and turn to face each other from time to time, touching each other all the time.

Their two suitcases beside each other were packed in two bedrooms at points roughly equidistant from this room, two toothbrushes in the bathroom which have not been juxtaposed before, two people who have never watched television together before, two cars parked near each other in the floodlit courtyard which have not passed even in the street before.

The bedroom is a box containing bodies on a bed. It has four walls, a wall-to-wall carpet, a shelf with television and suitcases on it, a bathroom with a shower, a cupboard with no clothes in it.

At home it is difficult now to guess what they are doing because the time of the evening is uncertain, and it was a long time back you left and took this journey first in rain and then in the brighter and more changeable weather which arrived during the late afternoon, slowing down when it said reduce speed before roundabouts, accelerating on dual carriageways, reading the signs to go in that direction, keep in this lane, follow that arrow. Finding that it is getting dark and wondering where you are. Lichfield is small for a city, the Trent Valley is wide and flat, the Supervisor was not as tall as he looked on his stool, the man went to Oxford without a radiator in his Mini. All parts on the lowest shelf are special orders, but this one has no name on it. Conferences set you up wonderfully. I thought you'd make the Quiche Lorraine on Friday, said Diana. Meredith took ten pounds out of his wallet, and in case he was not back on Saturday, another twenty pounds later, it may have been. Mal held the dipstick in the air and said you were not forced to put more oil in there. The gauge always says normal regardless of the temperature of the engine. Hem, hem, said Alex, but the zip won't work, and Harry chose the best hotel in Leicester. Where are you, said the girl at the end of the blue telephone. I think I must be here. No that is you and this is me. Caller please state your position at once. No that is yours and this is mine, or is this mine and that yours? Come here and look, try and see, make sure. I want to show you. I've always wanted to know. It is very dark and I wonder if it could be lighting-up time. Will they be all right at home? We've been out a long time haven't we? Let's go this way for a change. I seem to have forgotten where I am and who you are and am wondering what the time is again. And after all the light is on.

One bottle of Bell's is empty and the evening programmes in colour still go on. The bathroom with shower is white, wet and slippery. The meal in the restaurant was tasteless. People sat at tables lit by individual lamps.

Back in the bedroom Stuart said, "Why don't we do this every half-term, every Christmas, every Easter?"

"Why not?"

"And at Whitsun at a pinch? Or is that playing games?"

"The nicest sort of games."

This time he hung his suit in the cupboard next to her skirt and her coat. He put the shirt he's going to wear tomorrow in a drawer. "Do I ask too much of you?" he asked.

"You couldn't."

"What about Meredith?"

"He doesn't ask much."

"Where is he?"

"Somewhere over there. It doesn't matter. Somewhere else."

"In some corner of a foreign field?"

"No in London actually."

Along at the end of the shelf which holds the television and the suitcases is an electric kettle, two cups, two coffee-bags, two tea-bags and some biscuits.

"I suppose if I did ask too much, you wouldn't tell me?"

"Probably not."

They sat propped on pillows with the sheets to their waists drinking coffee, not hearing what the news-reader on television was saying.

"Do *I* ask too much of *you*?" this time.

"Never."

"If I did would you tell me?"

"It isn't like that."

When they turned the television off at midnight she asked him. "Does Christine ask too much?"

"Only for what she needs."

202

"And gets it?"
"While she needs it."

The room is at body temperature with a minimal light from the motel forecourt now that the curtains are drawn back a few inches. People like Stuart sleep easily and on any availably near soft thing, and are worth watching asleep, even if it is only at half-term, Christmas, Easter and Whitsun at a pinch. In no circumstances to be missed. A new bit of being in the world no doubt, and a piece of education Miss Rogers would allow pupils to discover for themselves. A new way of crying too, for the first time not out of pique or disappointment. More like end-of-feature-film tears, mother-at-wedding tears, which cool on the face outside the cinema or church. But at the blood temperature of a motel bedroom the tears stay warm and the giant floodlights in the forecourt illuminate their cause.

Eyelashes on a man are unremarkable when he is awake. Asleep you find he has a narrow dark line of them. He has his right arm folded across his chest, and his left arm lying away on the sheet. The folded right arm shows dark hairs between wrist and elbow. On the left upturned arm the space between wrist and elbow is white, and beyond that the noted narrow wrist and piano-player's hand.

These warm tears could be as effectively binding as the few that fell in the spare-room, not recently, but seven-and-three-quarters, coming up to eight, years ago. These and those warm tears are bound to bind for life and doubtless are for re-weeping on all half-term or full-term greetings and goodbyes.

Stuart has the sheets covering him below the waist. Beyond him, at the end of his upturned arm and half-curled hand lie his cigarettes and lighter. On the floor beside him is his briefcase. He is thirty-six and a lecturer at a College of Education. He knows what he thinks life should be like, but he also knows how to go on if it isn't like that. He knows how to make effective love to one woman while putting double-glazing in for another and

203

looking up the skirts of a third. He likes preparing, measuring and planning and usually finishes what he has begun. He heard recently that he was awarded a distinction for his thesis on the development of the cognitive processes in reference to Mather's study of the disadvantaged pupil, which he said was nice to know at the time but does not make much difference in the long run.

He mucked up his O-levels because his mother was having an abortion and a nervous breakdown at the time. So he left school and went to work at the garage where his uncle was Chief Tester. When he was twenty he was screwing this woman whose car was under repair and she told him that it was always possible to go back to school whatever your age. So he got O-levels and A-levels (and even one S-level) while still working at the garage, and then a grant for what was then called a Teacher Training College where he met Christine.

Before he went to sleep he said something about all that.
He opens his eyes. "Stuart. What were you saying...?"
"What?"
"You said it was something important..."
"Did I?"
Stuart always wanted to go to University, but when he was taking his O-levels he was involved with this girl, really obsessed with her, he sometimes says. He probably minded quite a bit about his mother, the abortion and the nervous breakdown as well, but he wonders if his failure didn't add to her worries, so he has always wanted to make it up to his mother by succeeding.

Once he said he might not have afforded to go to University if he and Christine had had children. It was also something to do with their marriage being bad and empty; something had to change so they tried Yorkshire and career improvement. He is sorry, for Christine's sake, that it may finally have only changed things for the worse between them.

"Stuart. You can say anything you like. I can take it..."
"What did I say?"

"You murmured something..."

"Weren't we talking about deferred gratification...?"

Meredith went to public school because that is what you go to preparatory school for. His mother had insisted on a prep school, although it was a struggle on a pre-war small dental practice. She chose the prep school where his cousin who became a brain surgeon had been. She chose the minor public school because another cousin of hers had been there who had inherited a tin mine in the Sudan. It was in keeping with old boys from his minor public school that Meredith went into business. He had always wanted to go into business, but when you got there you found people who had been to major public schools.

Meredith always says he wanted to stay in the army but could not afford to do that and keep Edwina in the manner to which she seemed to be accustomed. He thought Lady Havergal preferred businessmen to dentists, although Lady Havergal always swore that she was equally nice to both.

Edwina used to say as a little girl she would never marry. She said this right up to the day she married Meredith. It was hearing him sing the bass line of Praise my Soul the King of Heaven loud and strong and clear beside her at the altar that made her realise she was married, she always says.

Edwina always wanted to be a chorus girl or a concert pianist but having got home to Havergal after years at boarding school it was terrible to think of going away again to train to be something else. There was quite a lot to be said at the time for being a child bride, for a time.

The light from the forecourt floodlights shines through the misted window, whitening Stuart's forehead and nose and leaving his hair black in the shadow. His hair in daylight is dull brown, but once was blond he says. When he goes bald it will start with a patch on his crown, but not for ten or twenty years will he be without a fringe.

He will get in his car in the morning and drive back to Christine's mother's house, although now that Christine drives the old car, Stuart may drive straight home and she will join him there when she wants to. Edwina will drive home, remember to stop somewhere, perhaps Derby, to get the zip for Alex's black velvet trousers and a present for Harry. She will drive fast, because of all the things still to be done before visitors arrive for the party.

When Meredith came into the kitchen to say he was going to London he gave her the ten pounds towards the party. Then he stopped in the doorway and took another ten pounds out of his wallet, or was it five or twenty? He said he would try to be back for the party, but his plans were a little vague. Well, not really vague. He might have been about to say something else.

"If God is omnipotent," the vicar said, "he cannot be Benevolent because a Benevolent God who was omnipotent as well would make a good world, and it isn't, is it?"

"God is Benevolent, there's no if about it," said Diana, who prays each night. But thank Benevolent God for Diana if there is an emergency anywhere tonight and remember her in your meditations.

Half-way home Edwina may decide after all to turn back and drive towards the M5 very fast after Stuart. She will decide that coming down the ramp in a multi-storey car park after buying Alex's zip and Harry's present in Derby.

Meredith sings the bass-line loud and clear in church, not only at weddings. He learnt that at his minor public school, but says that Harry, if all goes well, will learn more than that and be able to choose his career unbound by so many prevailing circumstances.

The vicar crossed his legs showing white hairless shins and said the whole thing was only an example he'd once heard at Theological College of a logical dilemma, and he did not know why he'd chosen the topic for the Young Wives on Tuesdays in the first place. And the knees of the Service Station Supervisor buckled as he carried the radiator of the Mini.

Stuart says Christine has stopped making rag-rugs since they bought a new fitted carpet; she drives very well now

206

and goes out in the evenings, sometimes playing badminton with another teacher at her school; and she has lost
weight since she was ill.

Edwina will clutch the steering wheel, turn on the radio
and head north between pantechnicons, believing every
approaching truck is aimed at her, but always ready to
take avoiding action if this truck, that lorry, that articu-
lated car-transporter shoots out of lane or jack-knifes
diagonally with its sharp edge towards her. "I find you
very positive," said the American. "There are better, much
better places," wrote Edwina diagonally across Meredith's
report. And when Stuart signed the register at the motel
he wrote Stuart and Christine Douglas and then laughed
because he said he'd never stayed at a hotel with Christine
in his life, not even on their honeymoon, so it could not
have been a Freudian slip, could it really?

Chapter 12

ALEX IS DANCING opposite Mal, arching her back, throwing
her arms up and behind her head, then flinging her body
forwards head-down so that her hair follows over the top
like a waterfall cascading. The drawing-room is un-
recognisable with the carpet rolled back and with Robert's
cousin's son's discotheque's flashing ultra violet which
turns bodies black and white so that people are patches of
light and dark, elegant and tribal. Susan dances with her
back to Alex and Mal like a giant gyrating goddess. Beside
her someone who might be a child of Victoria Rochdale,
lamp-post thin with pointed breasts, moves in a world of
her own.

Edwina walks through the noise between the dancers,
tacking to avoid them. She passes figures standing against
the curtains with folded arms and girls dancing non-
chalantly swinging their arms and their floor-length skirts.
The sound and light fulfil and blind all senses and the
rhythm is felt through the soles of the feet. There are no
human voices except the high hollow solo soprano on the
record, and between that and the drummed floor-carried
rhythm there is the whole spectrum of broad brass and
strings; impossible at this volume to distinguish one from
the others. But, as it were, in the distance, as you walk
in the dark, now weaving between upright figures and
dodging arms thrown out by arched ones, there is the echo
behind the disharmony, of tubular bells.

She walks out of the source of all the noise and into the
study where three girls in short sleeves and with goose-
pimples on their arms sit on the chaise-longue and four
boys on the floor by the window. A single joss-stick stuck

in a vase burns on the marble mantelpiece.

Then she goes out into the hall and across it up the stairs to take up the watch-dog position, designated by Diana, at the top of the first flight under the round-arched window, to look down at the boys as they process to their lavatory, and to move her long purple velvet skirt to one side as the girls trot up past her to theirs and to the spare-room where their coats and hairbrushes are.

"Well I think it is all going terribly well," said Diana before dashing home in the car for five minutes to see how Robert was and to tell him how terribly well it was all going.

Edwina, on the top tread of the first flight, smokes the last of the Gauloises packet she shared with Stuart last night and drops ash down the stair-well where boys with white ruffled shirts and pink faces stare up.

"Actually," said Diana, "it's early in the evening yet to expect any trouble, but if we establish a presence on the stairs right from the start, then later we can rest on our laurels and relax."

Above the stairs pale green balloons bob in the draught in a cluster anchored by string to the top banisters. At the end of the evening everyone will emerge from the dancing room and the sitting-out room and reach up for the balloons which will be released and shower down on them.

"After all," said Diana, "one must not forget they are still only children when all is said and done."

Where Edwina is sitting the stairs carry the vibrations of the music which buzzes in the woodwork and oscillates the brass stair rods.

"I think we should congratulate ourselves Edwina. Two women managing all this; but rather alone than with reluctant husbands don't you think?"

Edwina looks up at the dusty glass chandelier swinging from the ceiling over the stairs, at the balloons bumping together on the strings like thunder-clouds.

"I shall almost feel like dancing myself by the end of

the evening," said Diana. "It was unfair of me to say that about our husbands. Robert has been an absolute brick with all the excitement and guests at home."

In the kitchen Diana's team of Mrs Thwaite, the au pair girl and Mrs Thwaite's daughter work in pink nylon overalls moving plates and glasses and carrying trays to the dining-room hatch.

"Don't you feel that this is yet another way in which we enjoy ourselves now Edwina—through our children?"

Edwina stares at the boys who come from the dancing-room and lean against the wall by their lavatory. They look up and she looks down at them. Some, smoking cigarettes, tread them out on the stone flags.

"It is going so terribly well, Edwina. I've bought us a bottle of Bell's by the way to quaff at the end in triumph."

Mal stands by the lavatory, leaning on the wall. "Hi," he says, looking up briefly. "What you doing there then?"

She comes down the stairs where she has sat for the stipulated ten minutes, she dusts her skirt and turns along the stone hall and goes back into the dancing-room where the same people are dancing to the same sound, and through the dancers to the study where the same three girls are sitting together opposite the same four boys. She sniffs the stipulated sniff for pot which Diana says she has heard smells like tomcat, or sweet dung, or a sort of Indian smell, but only smells the thin trail of smoke from the red tip of the joss stick which burns under the photograph of Grandmother Havergal. She throws another log on the fire.

Then up the stairs again to the spare-room where the four-poster is piled high with coats, cloaks and handbags; she kneels on the floor in front of the electric fire, stretches her hands towards it and hears the sash windows rattling in the cold wind outside. The girls who come up flushed in the face from dancing brush their hair in front of the long mirror, let their hair swing on their shoulders, lean into the mirror to study their mascara and eyeshadow. They say what a lovely party it is and go away again.

Maria comes up in her broderie anglaise empire line dress with pink sash and turns round, swirling her skirt, in front of the mirror. She says it is a really marvellous party and she has never enjoyed herself so much. Maria's face is unflushed from dancing; she has the sort of white creamy skin which will never flush but only tan in the sun and return to unblemished white in the winter. Diana said Robert nearly cried with emotion when he saw Maria in her dress this evening.

"It's such fun down there," says Maria. "Are you all right, Mrs Measures-Smith?" and goes away again.

Alex puts her head round the door and says that the new zip is only just holding, that the party seems O.K. so far, but everyone is getting a bit hungry and thirsty so when is the buffet supper and all that?"

"When Mrs Golding gets back."

"Aren't you meant to be on the stairs then?"

"It's bloody cold on the stairs I can tell you."

"Oh sod Mrs Golding and her rules then. Why don't you dance then?"

"Alex! Do you mind?"

Alex says, "Still—the party's all right as these things go," and goes away again down the stairs two at a time. The rhythm keeps beating up through the spare-room floor, bouncing the electric fire on its burnished steel legs in the grate.

Sometimes Edwina goes back to the top of the first flight of the stairs and sits there, sometimes she is walking through the dancing-room in the flashing lights and sometimes looking at the same people sitting in the study watching the joss-stick burn.

She drove into the drive in the early afternoon against winds as strong as the day the pantechnicon blew over at the bottom of the field in March. The house, when she came here, was open from front door to back door; the leaves from the drive had blown up the pediment steps and scattered themselves in the hall and in the kitchen, where the boiler had gone out.

Diana was in the drive unloading plates, glasses and dishes of salmon mousse. "Wherever have you been, Edwina?"

"Is Harry all right?" Edwina asked.

"As far as I know. He's with Alex somewhere. They said you'd been away for the night."

They carried plates and food through the hall where, among dead leaves, Robert's cousin's son had stacked his boxes and cables for the discotheque.

"I must say, I had no idea you were going away, Edwina."

"It was a bit complicated," said Edwina. "Where is everyone?"

Susan was in the kitchen with a long broom sweeping leaves into a dustpan.

"It certainly is complicated now," said Diana. "You know I would have had the children to stay the night. You had only to ask."

Edwina ran upstairs. Alex and Harry were, with Kevin, Nigel and Mal, in Harry's room behind the shut door, blowing up balloons. Diana called, "Edwina? Where do you want me to put the salmon mousse?"

"It's all right," Edwina called from the top of the stairs. "I've found Harry."

She walks through the room where Robert's cousin's son stands by the discotheque. He moves with the music and Maria moves opposite him, a startling white figure, then a black figure with dead white hair in the next flickering quarter-second of the strobe light.

"Your mother," she shouts to Maria above the music, "wants you to tell everyone to come into supper. It is all in the dining-room."

With the gilt chairs piled behind them, Alex and Maria ladle the punch, let cucumber slices and cherries drop off the round ladles and into glasses and hand them to their guests across the table.

"Did I tell you," Diana whispers, "that Robert nearly cried when he saw Maria's dress?"

Diana brought the thick white tablecloth which covers the dining-room table; she suggested a blanket underneath it to protect Meredith's precious polish. She arranged the salmon mousse, the salad and the Quiche Lorraine which Mrs Thwaite and the others had put on the hatch.

"Mind you, Edwina, I think all the girls look simply ravishing. The fashions now have a tremendous air of innocence don't you think?"

Maria's white dress has puffed sleeves; its high waist fits neatly under her size 32 bust. She wears a coral necklace round her neck and her hair is pulled back and tied with a ribbon on the crown of her head and falls to the nape of her neck just touching the top vertebrae of her spine.

"Quite honestly, Edwina, don't you sometimes look forward to the girls' weddings? I told Robert today that we may have to enlarge the lawn for a marquee one of these days."

Beside and a little behind Maria stands her cousin who is running the discotheque, soft-featured with a down-turning moustache and deep-set eyes. Diana has decided that he is a good boy after all and, in his own way, works very hard. He has been very sweet to Maria all the day, considering how much older he is than her, and told her a lot of very interesting things about sociology and University. She wishes she had let him bring his sleeping-bag to the Dower House after all.

"But I expect you will have the first wedding, Edwina. Alex will settle down early I feel sure, and you will be able to tell me all about how to run big weddings."

Diana has tasted the punch and her cheeks glow. She is so relieved that they did not have beer. Only a few boys have asked for it and have been very understanding when she explained to them that there was none. Young people these days are very sympathetic, she believes. There may be a new kind of Christianity on the march; she holds up her glass to Maria and Robert's cousin and says to Edwina there is far too much talk about sex these days. "Trifle, anyone?" she calls.

After the buffet supper there will be two more hours until parents arrive to collect their children. With everything going so terribly well, Diana says, perhaps the watch on the stairs can be relaxed. What they will do now is that she will take Mrs Thwaite and the other helpers home the moment everything is cleared, and then the two women can sit in the kitchen and drink the Bell's whisky and chat: "I am dying to know what you were doing away last night; wicked woman that you are. More trifle, anyone?"

Alex and Mal stand back to back, leaning against each other and holding their bowls of trifle. Susan leans against the dining-room wall by the hatch not talking to a small boy in a dinner jacket who is standing beside her. The biggest group in the room surrounds the thin Rochdale daughter who goes to school in Switzerland. Maria gazes in wonder and delight into the deep eyes of her second cousin.

"Now that is the end of all the eats," says Diana. "Why don't you all go back and enjoy yourselves?"

The bunch of balloons bobbing over the stair-well were only half of those blown up by Mal and the others in Harry's room this afternoon. The others were left, blown up, tied at their ends but not together, bumping on the floor of Harry's room. When Diana went to drive Mrs Thwaite and the helpers home in the Range Rover she reminded Edwina about these. "Don't forget the other balloons in Harry's room," she said.

Harry went to bed with balloons moving in the heat of his convector fire. Mal had rubbed the sides of some of them, creating static electricity which held them magically on the walls. Some of them slipped down and some of them have burst on sharp corners of toy cars and tractors. Harry breathes easily, dosed with cold-cure medicine and decongestants; the room smells of the camphorated oil Edwina rubbed on his chest. In this room the sash windows do not rattle as they do in the spare-room because each winter she seals them shut with putty.

Harry's door must be kept shut to keep out the sound of the discotheque, although the rhythm beats up from the drawing-room below. In the dark she reaches down to the floor to feel, with her right hand, the outline of each balloon, follows each shape and grasps each string. She steps carefully into each corner of the room so that her high heels do not catch or burst a straying balloon. Her feet come down on a piece of railway track, which she moves with the toe of her shoe, plastic bricks and soldiers, which she picks up and puts out of the way for safety, model aeroplanes and bits of jig-saw puzzles. Under her hands as she kneels on the floor she feels small round cones of the game of Risk which Harry was playing with Kevin and Nigel while Mal and Alex blew up balloons this afternoon.

You have to creep carefully to avoid paint pots and water. At first the balloons were only shapes to feel with your hand, but as your eyes become accustomed to the dim light from the window you see them, but grey and not pale green.

Outside in the drive a car starts: Diana's Range Rover on its way to take the helpers home. The beam of its headlights swerves and illuminates the statue plinth; it rattles over the cattle grid and accelerates away down the avenue. In the window of Harry's room that temporary light showed three more balloons on the metal-bound trunk in the window. To reach them you have to lean across the trunk avoiding the model house Harry has built of plastic bricks, find the strings one by one, find them with the right hand and transfer them to form a bunch in the left hand. First you find yourself kneeling to do this and see that Harry's model outlined against the window is a model of Hodsworth Hall itself, finished, as far as can be seen, except for the pediment. It stands on a plastic notched plinth which rests on the white writing painted on the trunk top—"Meredith Measures-Smith"—still unfaded after nearly forty years.

Under your knees the rhythm goes on beating. Outside the room voices can just be heard and doors are banging. Outside in the drive another engine starts up, more head-lights circle the drive and another car crosses the cattle grid. Someone, perhaps, has been collected from the party early and left without saying goodbye.

Harry's model, lit up for a moment, is of red, white and blue plastic bricks. The sides of the house are red, the ridged roof is red and the front, where he has put in transparent bricks for windows, is white. The pediment he has constructed separately in a triangular block which will exactly fit on to the front of the ridged roof, but he has not yet prepared the pillars on which it will rest. He has collected a pile of round bricks with which to make them; they will be round, red and shiny pillars and they will be plugged at each base on to the notched plastic plinth upon which the building stands.

Edwina takes a handful of bricks to start on the first pillar. With the bunch of balloons still in her left hand she plugs one round brick into another, and, having thus created a pre-fabricated pillar, she sticks it on to the first notch in the front of the tray.

Outside the real house another car engine starts. A few older boys drove themselves here in their fathers' cars. Perhaps they are bored. Perhaps they know another, better party somewhere.

There are four pillars to be built, three equal spaces between the pillars to be allowed for, and the tray is twelve notches across. The pillars will take up four notches, leaving eight notches for the three spaces; therefore the spaces between the pillars cannot be equal.

Headlights in the drive again; Diana has returned, some-one has come late, or the boys who left early have changed their mind and driven back.

The thing to do is to divide the spaces between pillars not as they are in real life. This could be done by leaving a space of two notches between the first and second pillar and between the third and fourth. And then to make the space between the second and third pillars, the central space which leads to the front door, four notches wide.

Downstairs the telephone rings; someone will answer it; but Edwina still with round bricks in one hand and a bunch of balloons in the other creeps across the room and leans over the banisters where nothing can be heard but music. Then Alex appears, looking up, face blurred, hair falling everywhere. "That was Mrs Golding! In a call-box. She says the Range Rover's broken down outside Mrs Thwaite's. She says Mr Thwaite is putting it right or, if he can't, will bring her home. She says you are not to go and fetch her because she thinks someone ought to stay here. She'll be back as soon as she can."

"Well I suppose I'd better come down and see how everything is going."

"Don't fuss. It's all fine down here."

They have turned off the ultra violet and the flashing strobe in the drawing-room now and someone has put a pink bulb in a wall bracket. The only brilliance is Susan's red crêpe smock and skirt. She jogs her body from one foot to another and holds the hand of the small boy in a dinner jacket. The Rochdale girl still gyrates but not on her own. Another boy stands by the discotheque instead of Robert's cousin's son, who is standing in the alcove by the fireplace tapping his foot, flamenco fashion, while Maria twirls and skips around him, white skirt, pink sash and hair ribbon flying. There is no sign now of Alex, nor of Mal, even though it is possible to recognise Alex's favourite Pink Floyd record playing on the discotheque.

Edwina crosses the room again towards the study door, stopping as before to sniff. The presence of the joss-stick is still evident. Sniff again. Still no sweet dung, tomcat or Indian sort of smell. But there is an extra smell in the room, reminiscent of pubs and of lunchtimes and of Stuart. Beer no doubt.

The study lights are still on and reveal a couple

entwined on the chaise-longue unidentifiably. Another couple occupy the chair from which Meredith usually watches television; the floor is occupied by boys sitting, knees up, beer cans between their legs, Long Life from the Bay Leaf fetched by those with cars no doubt, drunk straight from the can after prising off the metal disc, poured down the throat. A can, or perhaps two cans for everyone in the room, and more beside them on the floor and on the television top and on the telephone table.

No one looks up. Nor is it possible to walk into the room and cross to the hall as in some of the earlier patrols. All there is to do is to turn and go back through the dancers in the pink-lit drawing-room, noticing, in passing, that Alex has come back and is dancing slowly hip-to-hip with Mal, her arms round his neck and hidden by his hair. Notice also that Robert's cousin's son has now left the dancing-room; nor is Maria there with twirling skirt in the alcove any more.

Edwina waits in the empty kitchen, sidened by Mrs Thwaite, her daughter and Diana's au pair girl; cleaned and polished plates and glasses take up most of the table now, and Diana has left, thoughtfully, the promised bottle of Bell's.

Then she goes upstairs again, and, picking up the bunch of balloons she collected in Harry's room, ties them with the others to the banisters. Then into Harry's room where he still breathes lightly and regularly, and downstairs again carrying carefully in two hands the model on the plastic plinth, and all the round bricks she needs to finish it in the pocket of her long skirt.

Under the kitchen strip-light the model shines, reflecting red and blue plastic on the white table and in the glass of whisky she has poured. It is easy in this light to plug the bricks firmly together and stand each pillar in turn on the front notches of the tray. There is something under an hour to go before the end of the party and Diana will be back soon to drink with. Then they will let down the balloons.

The first pillar of red round bricks stays in place. Count two notches for the space between and start the second pillar on the fourth notch. Model-making requires a clear head and, contrary to traditional thinking, the skill is much improved by drink. For the second pillar choose all yellow bricks, plug them together as you did the first, ten bricks high, and place them on the fourth notch. Shut the kitchen door, keep the heat in from the boiler, lean on the table keeping the model at eye level and the noise of Pink Floyd at a distance. This requires skilled fingers and absolute quiet. So that when the kitchen door opens and Maria, flushed in the face for the first time ever, stands there, you hardly look up, but go on putting one yellow brick on top of another and say: "What is it then, Maria?"

"Mrs Measures-Smith, could you tell me where I could find a cushion please?"

"A cushion Maria? Whatever do you want a cushion for?"

"Well all the sitting-out room is full and the floor everywhere else is hard."

"Look everywhere Maria. There are cushions everywhere."

"Oh thank you, Mrs Measures-Smith. Can I look anywhere?"

"Yes anywhere, but shut the kitchen door will you. And don't go into Harry's room."

Maria has gone out of the room, some time ago maybe. Diana has not yet come back. It must be only half an hour before the end of the party and the last pillar is in place. Diana will not help with the pillars when she returns; she loves her husband but does not make models for her children; she takes them riding, buys them ponies, makes them broderie-anglaise dresses and plans their weddings. Never would Diana at nearly midnight lean so lovingly over a toy on the kitchen table.

Harry has constructed the pediment to stretch the

width of the house, twelve bricks wide at its base, narrowing at the ridge to one. It is neatly capped with sloping blue bricks to fit against the roof of the main block already constructed. To lift it without breaking it from the table it will be necessary to slide a piece of cardboard under it. Then it must be raised with its back to fit on to the ledge one-brick wide Harry has prepared to hold it. Then the front of it will be placed to rest on the pillars just constructed here under the kitchen strip-light.

To find cardboard open the drawer on the table. Pull the drawer handle, and when it sticks feel inside with fingers to loosen whatever is holding it shut. Something thin and folded comes to hand, covered with thick blue writing; the numbered instruction list of yesterday's absence. But the drawer still sticks. Feel inside again and tear it again a bit harder. Shred the fragments which come away and scatter them on the purple velvet of your skirt and the tiles of the floor. Pull again and watch the Bell's bottle slide an inch on the table, and then another inch towards the pillars of the model. Watch one fall. Tear more paper with your left hand and hold the model still on the table with your right to shield it from the sliding bottle. The table hardly moves as your fingers grope in the drawer, but strangely the whisky bottle goes on sliding and bumps against the south wall of the house Harry built, dislodging a few roof bricks. Move the left hand, push the bottle back where it came from, but sweep, in this swift movement, the glass towards the house where it tips whisky on to the bricks and knocks more out of the blue ridge tiles.

The model of Hodsworth was constructed without attics or floors in between. When the roof bricks fall they land on the tray which is the foundation. To repair the damage a giant hand has to come down through the gaping roof hole and feel blindly with fumbling fingers. As the hand turns and the fingers grope, more bricks fall. The hand removes itself, pulls itself up and out of the building, carrying with it more of the roof which is levered up and over and falls both on the table and into the glass of whisky.

One hour later she was mending it again.

Fathers came soon after midnight and stood in the hall wearing great-coats and checking lists of their children and their children's friends who needed lifts home. Diana, still in her mink coat and having only just returned in the repaired Range Rover, said she would like to offer drinks to the fathers, but there seemed to be nothing in the house to offer.

When most people had gone Diana mustered the guests who were staying the night at the Dower House. They stood in a row waiting to shake hands and file into the Range Rover. Maria, it seemed, was not among them. Someone said she was being sick in the boys' lavatory.

"It must be migraine," said Diana. "I'm afraid she will have to stay here, Edwina."

Now Maria is upstairs, white faced in the four-poster with a plastic bucket on the floor and her dress spread at the foot end of the bed, less pristine white than hours ago. Her sash and hair ribbon are on the bedside table. Half an hour ago Edwina took her a hot water bottle. "This isn't your bed, is it, Mrs Measures-Smith? I'm awfully sorry being such a nuisance. I expect it was the beer." Edwina said she hoped Maria would be better in the morning.

"Don't tell Mummy about the beer, will you? Or about the cushion. She wouldn't understand and it might turn her against Jonathan."

"Jonathan?"

"My cousin. Is he here still?"

"Yes downstairs with Alex and the others."

"Where is he sleeping?"

"In the attic with the other boys."

Downstairs there was still soft music and lamplight in the study. Edwina went down and along the hall calling, "Alex!"

Alex came out of the study. "Yes?"

"All right?"

"Yes. Fine."

"Party O.K.?"

"Yes. Great."

"What about the others?"

"Who? Oh yeah. They all think so too."

"I mean. Are they all right ... in there?"

"Yeah. Fine."

"Susan?"

"She's in there. Asleep I think."

"The others ... the others who are staying? Do they all know where they are sleeping?"

"Sure. I'll see that they do anyway."

She went back towards the kitchen. Then remembered that Mal was not seen to have gone home with anyone. She called "Alex" again rather faintly. A noise from upstairs might be Maria, or might be Harry coughing. She stood in the well of the stairs listening and heard nothing more. She went back to lean over the kitchen table again and to peer into the roofless model and reach down for blue bricks inside it.

Under this roof tonight there will be, think hard and count: Maria in the spare-room, three boys and Jonathan in the attic, three girls plus Susan and Alex herself in Alex's room, and Harry in his own room. Eleven. Plus oneself. Twelve. And Mal, if he is still here, will perhaps make do with the chaise-longue in the study. There is also the front bedroom where the bed is made up for Meredith's return. He rang this morning, Alex reported, and said that he would leave London in the early evening, but that fog might prevent him being there in time for the party. He hoped it would go splendidly, Alex said, and she added that he did not ask where Edwina was "or anything like that".

It would be possible to go to the front bedroom and lie on the far side by the window as she used to. Or, since there are still two lots of bedclothes in that room, one set could be carried down and put in the study, if, that is, Mal has gone. The thing will be to wait for everyone to leave the study and then carry the bedclothes to the chaise-longue. Or take them to the spare-room and lie like a guard dog on the floor between the electric fire and Maria on the bed. When everyone has gone to their rooms, that is.

The roof bricks replace easily, especially if you lick the Bell's whisky off them before pegging them in position. In ten minutes, when she has finished the model she will go to the study and tell them all to go to where they are sleeping. If Mal is there, well, if Mal is there, then she could always say that perhaps it would be a good idea if he went home now. But that would mean him walking. So the chaise-longue could be made available. Then she will go upstairs and carry bedclothes to the spare-room floor. If there is roaming in the night it will not be to the spare-room.

Diana will ring as usual in the morning and come to finish clearing up, and by the time she comes the study will be clean of Long Life cans and the chaise-longue Hoovered.

There will be twelve for breakfast. If Meredith is there, there will be thirteen. If Mal is there, there will be fourteen. That is the only calculation it is possible to make. That is the only hypothetical prediction anyone could ever make.

Except that Harry will be the first to find the finished model on the kitchen table. He wakes up early before the post woman comes. Barefoot in pyjamas he goes down to the kitchen, gets the cereal packet and bowl out of the cupboard, looks in the refrigerator for milk and, if there is none, he goes out of the kitchen and across the stone hall. Then he drags the oak Havergal chair over the stone flags and reaches up to the brass bolt at the top of the double doors. The milk is left on the right of the door under the pediment. Harry carries the three, sometimes four, milk bottles back into the hall, puts them down on the stone flags, shuts the front door and drags the chair back across the floor. Then he carries the milk bottles towards the kitchen. Once when he was about four he dropped one bottle in the hall; jagged chunks of glass bounced around and splinters were being swept up for days. Harry's footprints in milk were seen all the way to the kitchen, but no blood.